DEATH OF A
TROPHY WIFE

Books by Laura Levine

THIS PEN FOR HIRE

LAST WRITES

KILLER BLONDE

SHOES TO DIE FOR

THE PMS MURDER

DEATH BY PANTYHOSE

KILLING BRIDEZILLA

KILLER CRUISE

DEATH OF A TROPHY WIFE

Published by Kensington Publishing Corporation

A Jaine Austen Mystery

DEATH OF A TROPHY WIFE

LAURA LEVINE

KENSINGTON BOOKS

KENSINGTON BOOKS are published by

Kensington Publishing Corp.
119 West 40th Street
New York, NY 10018

ISBN-13: 978-0-7582-3845-0

Printed in the United States of America

For Ben, again

ACKNOWLEDGMENTS

As always, I am enormously grateful to my editor John Scognamiglio for his unwavering faith in Jaine, and to my agent Evan Marshall for his valued guidance and support. Thanks to Hiro Kimura and Lou Malcangi, whose covers never fail to make a terrific first impression. And to "Vegas" Bob Kastner, my unofficial proofreader.

Special thanks to Joanne Fluke, who takes time out from writing her own bestselling Hannah Swensen mysteries to grace me with her insights and her brownies—not to mention a blurb to die for. And to John Fluke, product placement guru and all-around great guy.

Thanks to Mark Baker, who was there from the beginning. And to my wonderful readers who've taken the time to write me. Your e-mails truly brighten my day.

Finally, a loving thanks to my friends and family for hanging in with me all these years. And to my most loyal fan and sounding board, my husband Mark. I couldn't do it without you.

Chapter 1

It was Sunday morning and all across Los Angeles, the sun was shining, palm trees were swaying, and birds were tweeting their little hearts out. Yes, it was a picture perfect day in L.A. Except for one tiny part of town where storm clouds had descended and showed no signs of dissipating:

My apartment.

Here at Casa Austen, it was definitely monsoon season.

If, as my good buddy Siggy Freud once said, the two most important things in life were work and love, I was in deep doo doo. It had been weeks since my last freelance writing assignment. And the only men in my life were my longtime companions, Ben & Jerry, who were, in fact, keeping me company that very moment as I soaked in the tub.

With a sigh, I reached for a towel to wipe the fog from my sunglasses.

Why, you ask, was I wearing sunglasses in the tub? It's a long, ghastly story (one you can read all about in *Killer Cruise*, now available wherever fine paperbacks are sold), but thanks to a recent visit from my parents, my walls were painted a hideous shade of Tropical Orange.

Oranges are an excellent source of vitamin C, but trust me, you don't want them on your walls. And in the confines of my tiny bathroom, they were particularly blinding. I yearned to hire a painter to get rid of the mess, but no way was that going to happen, not with my checkbook on life support.

I gazed up at my cat, Prozac, who was sprawled out on the toilet tank.

"Oh, Pro," I moaned. "Life stinks."

"Cheer up, kiddo."

These comforting words did not come from Prozac, who was engrossed in a thorough examination of her privates, but from my next door neighbor Lance. Lance and I share a 1940s duplex, a modest little place with antique plumbing and walls the consistency of Kleenex. Due to these flimsy walls—and the fact that Lance can hear toilets flushing in San Diego—Lance is practically my roommate.

"Get out of that tub, lazybones!" he shouted. "I'm taking you to brunch."

"But, Lance," I said, eyeing the remains of my Chunky Monkey breakfast, "I just ate."

"That never stopped you before."

"Forget it. I am not about to stuff myself right after breakfast."

"I'll pick you up in five minutes."

"Make it ten," I sighed, unable to resist the lure of free calories.

I dragged myself out of the tub and threw on some elastic-waist jeans and a T-shirt. An outfit that failed to impress when Lance showed up at my apartment.

"My god, Jaine!" he gasped. "I've seen homeless people in nicer clothes."

Of course he has. Lance works as a shoe salesman at Neiman Marcus in the heart of Beverly Hills, where even the homeless wear designer labels.

"Thanks," I snapped. "You look lovely, too."

And in fact, he did look rather spiffy in perfectly creased chinos and a country club sports jacket, his tight blond curls gleaming with expensive goop.

"Sweetie," he chided, "you can't wear that outfit to The Four Seasons."

"The Four Seasons? But that place is nosebleed expensive."

"Not to worry, hon. My treat. I've been racking up sales like crazy lately. Neiman's is even talking about making me a buyer."

"Congratulations!" I said, happy that at least one of us was doing well.

"C'mon." He marched me to my bedroom. "Let's find you something decent to wear. You can't be seen in public in that outfit. Or in private, for that matter."

For some insane reason, Lance is convinced I am fashion-challenged, insisting that moths come to my closet to commit suicide.

"Gaaack!" he cried, holding up a perfectly serviceable polka dot polyester dress. "I may go blind!"

Ignoring my dagger glares, he rifled through my hangers and handed me a pair of simple gray slacks.

"But, Lance, they don't have an elastic waist."

"So?"

"I can't wear a set-in waist to brunch. How am I supposed to go back for seconds?"

"You're not. Put 'em on. And this blouse, too."

I stomped off to the bathroom, where I donned my Lance-approved outfit.

"Much better," he said when I presented myself for inspection.

"Thank you, your grace."

"Of course your hair's a mess," he said, eyeing my mop of curls swept up in a scrunchy, "but I don't have the energy to deal with that now."

Thank heavens for small favors.

"Let's go," he said, leading the way to the living room.

"Bye, honey," I called to Prozac, who had resumed her perusal of her privates on the sofa. "We're off to brunch."

She looked up at me in that loving way of hers that could mean only one thing:

Bring back crab cakes.

Then I grabbed my purse and headed out the door on that glorious Sunday morning, little dreaming that my personal storm cloud was headed straight for Lance.

Chapter 2

Brunch at The Four Seasons is like the Garden of Eden with mimosas.

Tucked away in a lushly landscaped courtyard, the restaurant is cut off from most mere mortals by a carefully tended jungle of tropical vines and gaspworthy prices.

Lance and I had been seated at a cozy table for two and were now sipping mimosas in the dappled sun, breathing in the heady aroma of gardenias.

Maybe life wasn't so bad after all.

"Ready to hit the buffet table?" Lance grinned.

When it comes to buffet tables, I'm always ready.

We got up from our seats and headed inside, where a lavish feast was laid out. Lord, what a spread. It was probably a good thing Lance made me leave my elastic-waist pants at home. I really couldn't afford to pig out. I'd just take some fruit and a blueberry muffin. And a smidgeon of lobster frittata. And maybe a tad of ham. And a dab of hash. And gosh, those omelettes looked good—

You can see where this is going, can't you?

When I was all done, I practically needed a forklift to carry my plate.

Needless to say, Mr. Goody Two Shoes had just an omelette and a few shards of fruit. Which, if you ask me, was a ridiculous waste of money. I mean, why pay a small fortune for an all-you-can-eat brunch when you're hardly going to eat anything?

"Hey, look," he said as we headed back outside with our plates. "There's one of my customers."

"Where?"

"Over there. The gal at the corner table." He nodded to a primo table, where a striking redhead was engrossed in conversation with a tubby bald guy. Something about the guy looked familiar, but I couldn't quite place him.

"That's Bunny and Marvin Cooper," Lance said as we took our seats. "They're swimming in money. He owns a chain of mattress stores."

"Wait a minute," I said, squinting at the guy. "Isn't he Marvelous Marv, the Mattress King?"

"None other."

No wonder he looked familiar. I'd seen him in dozens of tacky late-night commercials, wearing a crown and hawking his line of mattresses "fit for a king."

"He and Bunny got married last year. It was the Go To wedding on the Beverly Hills party circuit."

"Isn't she a little young for him?" I asked.

Indeed, Marvin had to be pushing sixty, while Bunny couldn't have been more than thirty. Tops.

"Trophy wives usually are," Lance said, checking out his reflection in a shiny Four Seasons silver knife. "It's a classic Rags to Bitches story. Struggling actress auditions for cheesy mattress commercial. Mattress mogul falls head over heels in love and dumps his wife of thirty years to marry her. Struggling actress now performing nightly on Mattress King mattress."

Men are such idiots, *n'est-ce pas?* I'd bet dollars to donuts Marvin Cooper had left a perfectly lovely woman, all for a pair of perky Double D's.

"Bunny and I met about a month ago," Lance said, spearing a piece of honeydew, "when she came to Neiman's to buy a pair of shoes. We bonded over a pair of Manolos, and now she's my best customer. We've even gone shopping together a couple of times. Her taste is a bit Frederick's of Hollywood for me, but it's fun tooling around in her Maserati. Anyhow, she's the reason my sales are going through the roof."

"Here's to Bunny," I said, lifting my glass in a toast. "Long may she buy."

"To Bunny," Lance said, clinking my glass.

"Oh, look, she sees you."

Indeed Bunny had spotted Lance and was now jumping up from her seat and heading in our direction.

Showgirl tall with a hubba-hubba bod, she was poured into designer jeans and a tank top so tight I could practically read the washing instructions on her bra. Her flaming red hair tumbled down past her shoulders in a cascade of carefully tousled extensions. Every eye on the patio was on her as she sashayed toward us on her seven hundred dollar Manolos.

Lance got up to greet her.

"Bunny, sweetheart!" he cooed, giving her an air kiss.

"Lance, darling! How's my favorite shoe guru? How much fun to run into each other like this! You look fab, as usual."

"You too, doll."

"Really? You don't think the bracelet's too much?" she asked, waving a mineful of diamonds on her wrist.

"On you, anything looks good."

"You shameless flatterer! That's why I love you, darling."

For the first time, she turned to look at me, hitting me with a blast of designer perfume.

"Who's your friend?"

"Bunny, this is my next door neighbor Jaine."

"She sure does eat a lot, doesn't she?"

Okay, so she didn't really say that, but I could tell that's what she was thinking by the way she was eyeing my plate.

"Jaine's a writer."

"Really?" Her eyes lit up, impressed. Most people are impressed when they learn I'm a writer.

"Yes, she wrote *In a Rush to Flush? Call Toiletmasters!*"

That's usually when people stop being impressed.

But Bunny didn't seem to mind that my creative muse came from a commode.

"I've seen that in the Yellow Pages. It's very cute."

I smiled modestly.

"It just so happens my husband is looking for someone new to write his commercials. You think you'd be interested?"

"Absolutely."

"Why don't you two drop by the house this afternoon, and I'll introduce you."

"That's awfully nice of you."

"It is, isn't it?" she said, with a toss of her fabulous mane. "Well, must dash. You know the address, Lance, honey. Oh, and don't forget to bring your bathing suits. We'll be hanging out at the pool."

Bathing suits? My fork froze en route to my mouth. If there are two things in this world I don't do, it's rice cakes and bathing suits.

"Sure thing, Bunny," Lance cried, as she skipped off.

"Forget it, Lance," I said the minute she was gone. "I'm not going. No way are me and my thighs appearing in public in a bathing suit."

"Okay, just tell her you forgot to bring one. But you've got to go. You can't afford to pass up the Mattress King account."

He was right, of course. At this point, I couldn't afford to pass up anything with a paycheck at the end of the rainbow.

We finished the rest of our meal in the sun-dappled splendor of the patio, chatting about this and that. Frankly, I can't remember much of what we said; I was too busy inhaling my mushroom and cheese omelette. In the end, though, I couldn't plow my way through everything on my plate and wound up taking my food home in a doggie bag.

And Lance's, too, if you must know.

Still feeling the glow from our heavenly brunch, Lance and I headed back to our duplex to get ready for Bunny's pool party.

The minute I walked into my apartment, Prozac leaped up from where she'd been napping on my computer keyboard and raced to my side.

"Miss me, honey?"

As if. Where's my crab cake?

I know how much she likes them, so I'd nabbed her one and now crumbled the fishy treasure into her bowl.

She sniffed at it disdainfully.

What—no tartar sauce?

"Oh, stop being such a darn fussbudget and eat it."

Which she proceeded to do with impressive speed, sucking it up like a Hoover on overdrive.

Free at last from Lance's critical gaze, I changed into a pair of comfy thigh-hiding shorts and my "good" T-shirt, an Eileen Fisher number, reduced from an exorbitant seventy-five dollars to an overpriced thirty-nine.

"Those shorts better not have an elastic waist," Lance said when he picked me up a few minutes later.

"Of course not."

And with that lie firmly planted on my lips, I set off with Lance for our poolside adventure.

Chapter 3

"Welcome to Casa Extravaganza," Lance said as we drove up the circular driveway to Marvin and Bunny's Beverly Hills estate.

It was extravagant all right, very Vegas Versailles, with so many wings, I almost expected to see a bellboy out front.

"She's a beauty, isn't she?" Lance said as we got out of his Mini Cooper.

"I guess. If you like living in Caesar's Palace."

"I wasn't talking about the house. I was talking about *that*." He pointed to a bright red Maserati parked in the driveway.

"Isn't she fantastic?" he asked, running his fingers along its high-gloss paint job. "This baby is worth at least a hundred and fifty grand."

"What an outrageous waste of money."

"Bunny's good at that."

After ushering me past a pair of massive stone pillars, he rang the doorbell and set off a volley of cathedral-esque chimes.

A diminutive Hispanic maid answered the door, dressed in a black uniform and a stiffly starched white apron. In her hand she held a feather duster.

"Hi, Lupe." Lance greeted her with a grin.

"*Buenos días,* Senor Lance." She smiled timidly. "Ms. Bunny and Mr. Marvin are out back at the pool. Follow me."

"I know the way, sweetheart. Don't bother."

The maid scurried off to resume her dusting, and Lance led me down a hallway past a series of ornately furnished rooms. A little too Marie Antoinette–ish for my tastes, but hey, I still have bookshelves made from cinder blocks, so what do I know?

"You've been here before?" I asked as we trotted along.

"A couple of times. Bunny just finished redecorating, and she loves to show it off. She claims she used the same decorator as Gloria Vanderbilt."

"Oh, really?"

I very much doubted that Gloria had a sofa cushion embroidered with the words *Kiss Me. I'm Easy.*

At last we'd trekked the marathon distance to the back of the house and stepped outside onto a flagstone patio. Now, in my neck of the woods, patio furniture is a couple of lawn chairs and a hibachi. But here at Casa Extravaganza, patio furniture meant matching sofas, dining table, full bar, stainless steel sink with tile backsplash, and a six-burner Viking stove.

"Yikes," I said, looking around. "They've got a whole other house back here."

"Neat, isn't it?"

"But what if it rains?"

"It never rains on the rich. And if it does, they just buy new furniture."

Beyond the patio and down a flight of steps was the pool, a huge turquoise gem glittering in the sun—surrounded by lounge chairs, patio tables, and colorful striped cabanas. All set against a mini-Sherwood Forest of trees.

"Wow," I said, gazing at the vista in awe, "I never realized there was so much money in mattresses."

Bunny was floating on a raft in the pool, scantily clad in a hot pink micro bikini. Marvin sat at one of the tables, chewing on a cigar and going over spreadsheets with a skinny guy in a Mattress King baseball cap.

And hunkered down on one of the lounge chairs was a chubby young woman, her nose buried in a magazine.

"The gal with the magazine is Sarah," Lance said. "Marvin's daughter. She's some sort of chemistry professor."

"That's his *daughter?* But she's Bunny's age."

"Occupational hazard of marrying someone thirty years younger than you."

"What about the guy in the baseball cap?"

"That's Sarah's husband, Owen Kendall. Started out as a lowly salesman, then married the boss's daughter, and now he's second in command. Classic case of The Son-in-Law Also Rises.

"Well," he said, squaring his shoulders, "time to make our grand entrance."

"Hello, everybody!" he called out.

Bunny looked up and grinned.

"If it isn't my favorite shoe salesman! C'mon down!"

My gut firmly tucked in my elastic-waist shorts, I followed Lance down the steps. Bunny scampered out of the pool in her bikini. Talk about itsy bitsy. I'd seen more latex in a Band-Aid. Then she slipped into a pair of sequined flip-flops and came trotting over to us, her Double-D's leading the way.

Once again, my nostrils were assaulted by her perfume, a distinctive bouquet of tea roses and Raid.

After air kissing Lance, she introduced me to the gang. Marvin greeted me with a vague hello, Owen barely glanced in my direction, and Sarah looked up from her copy of *Chemistry Today* just long enough to grunt a curt "hi."

I waited for Bunny to tell Marvin I was a would-be writer of mattress commercials, but I waited in vain.

Instead she said, "Why don't you two head for a cabana and change into your swimsuits?"

Time for my fashion fib.

"Um. Actually, I forgot to bring one."

"No problem. We have tons of suits! We may even," she added, eyeing my hips, "have one in your size."

Correct me if I'm wrong, but that was a zinger, *n'est-ce pas?*

"That's okay," I said. "I think I'll just enjoy the sun in my civvies."

As Lance trotted off to a cabana to change, I plopped resolutely down on the chaise next to Sarah. Up close I could see she'd had the misfortune to inherit Marvin's squinchy eyes and slightly bulbous nose.

Like me, she had opted out of a bathing suit and was clad in modest Bermuda shorts and a sleeveless shirt.

"Oh, you two," Bunny said, wagging her finger at us. "Such spoilsports. Now I'm the only gal here in a bathing suit."

With that, she sashayed over to Marvin, showing off her flawless figure with every step. And it occurred to me that she liked being the only gal in a bathing suit, that she reveled in her starring role as the beauty with the body that wouldn't quit.

"Marvin, sweetie," she cooed, wrapping her arms around his neck and covering him with chlorine kisses, "forget about business and come play in the pool."

"Later, hon," Marvin said with an indulgent smile.

"Well, don't take too long," she replied, doing her finger-wagging shtick. "Bunny misses her Marvy Man."

Next to me, Sarah rolled her eyes in disgust. Something told me there was no love lost between her and her recently acquired stepmother.

"I know!" Bunny said. "Let's all have gin and tonics!"

"Lupe!" She shouted into an intercom on one of the tables. "Gin and tonics for everyone!"

Oh, no. Not for me. The last thing I needed after that mimosa at lunch was a gin and tonic.

"Thanks, Bunny," I said, "but I don't think I want one."

"Sure you do!"

Sarah looked up from her issue of *Chemistry Today*.

"If Bunny says you want one," she muttered, "you want one. House Rules."

I don't know whether Sarah meant for Bunny to hear her, but clearly she had. She sauntered over to us and plastered on a smile as phony as her Double-D's.

"Sarah's so cute when she's sarcastic. It's part of her charm."

Then she kicked off her flip-flops and jumped in the pool, setting off a tidal wave of a splash and soaking both of us.

"She did that on purpose," Sarah snarled, shaking water from her arms.

At this happy juncture, Lance emerged from the cabana in his Speedo, giving Bunny a run for her money in the Hot Bod department.

"Come on in!" Bunny squealed. "The water's divine!"

"Are you sure you don't want to put on a suit, Jaine?" he asked. "It'll be fun."

"I'm sure, Lance," I said, shooting him a filthy look.

"Well, okay," he said with a shrug.

Then he dove into the pool, where he and Bunny splashed around, playing some kind of pool tag, Bunny shrieking like a five-year-old. With every shriek, Sarah winced. And I could see Owen was looking none too happy with the constant racket, either. Only Marvin seemed oblivious to the noise.

Now Bunny began tackling Lance in the water, throwing herself all over him. If he were straight, I'd think she was coming on to him.

"Your friend better enjoy it while it lasts," Sarah said, following my gaze. "He's her flavor of the month. Sooner or later she'll dump him."

No great loss, I thought. Bunny wasn't exactly BFF material. Clearly she'd forgotten about her offer to pitch me as a potential employee.

I was sitting there wishing I'd stayed home with my brunch leftovers when the maid came tottering down the flagstone steps with a tray of highball glasses.

"It's about time, Lupe," Bunny called from the pool. "Give one to Jaine."

She was determined to make me drink that damn gin and tonic, wasn't she?

Lupe held out the tray, her hands trembling. Poor thing was terrified.

"Better take it," Sarah whispered. "Her majesty will make a stink if you don't. And whatever you do, don't take her Marilyn Monroe glass."

Sarah pointed to a fancy crystal highball glass with the letters *MM* etched in the center.

"She bought a set of them at an auction. Supposedly they once belonged to Marilyn Monroe. Nobody's allowed to drink out of them except her royal highness."

And indeed, all the other glasses on the tray were no-frills plastic pool glasses.

"*Gracias,*" I said to Lupe, taking one of the peasant drinks.

"Just pretend to drink it," Sarah advised. "Bunny'll forget all about it. She has the attention span of a gnat."

After serving Owen and Marvin, Lupe headed over to the pool where Bunny and Lance were waiting for their drinks.

And then tragedy struck. Lupe stumbled over Bunny's flip-flops. I looked on in alarm as the two remaining glasses tumbled, spilling gin and tonic onto the tray. Luckily Lupe was able to catch the Marilyn Monroe glass before it fell.

"For crying out loud!" Bunny screeched. "Can't you watch where you're going? You've got to be the clumsiest creature on earth."

Lupe just stood there staring at the ground.

"Now go fix us some new drinks. I swear, Lupe, one of these days, I'm going to report you to *La Migra.*"

At the mention of the immigration authorities, Lupe looked up, her eyes wide with fear, then scurried up the steps.

"You shouldn't threaten Lupe like that, sweetheart," Marvin chided. "She doesn't realize you're kidding."

"Who's kidding?" Bunny said, stomping out of the pool. "If she breaks my Marilyn Monroe glasses, I'm turning her in. I paid a fortune for those things."

Then she plopped down on a chaise at the other side of the pool, about as far away from me and Sarah as she could get. I guess she figured our cellulite was contagious.

"Lance, honey," she said, patting the chaise next to her, "come sit next to me."

Lance joined her on the skinny side of the pool. And with a put-upon sigh, Bunny launched into a dissertation on the Difficulty of Finding Decent Help—the highlights of which included what a klutz Lupe was, how the pool man didn't clean out the filter properly, and how the gardener kept forgetting to put away his supplies.

"Just look," she said, pointing to a bottle on the flagstone steps. "He's left his damn weed killer out again. Honestly, Marv, we ought to fire the lot of them."

"Calm down, honey," Marvin said, holding out his drink. "Here. Have some of my gin and tonic."

"You know I don't drink from plastic," she pouted.

Several uncomfortable minutes later, Lupe came back down the steps with fresh drinks. And this time, she wasn't alone. Following her was a willowy gal with spiky white-blond hair, dressed to the nines in a flowing two-piece pants set.

"Bunny, darling!" the woman cried, floating down the steps in a cloud of chiffon and air kisses. "I had no idea you were having a party! So sorry to interrupt, but I just had to stop by and show you these fabulous outfits!"

And indeed draped over her arm were a bunch of garment bags.

"Wait till you try them on, sweetie! They're to die for."

"Not now, Fiona," Bunny snapped, still in a snit about the servant situation.

"Of course, darling," the willowy gal said smoothly. "I certainly didn't mean to interrupt your fun."

Trust me, if there was one thing she wasn't interrupting, it was fun.

"Take the clothes inside, Lupe," Bunny said. "And bring Fiona a drink."

"Yes, Ms. Bunny," Lupe said, hurrying back up the steps, eager to make her escape.

The newcomer stood there for an awkward beat until Bunny finally remembered her duties as a hostess.

"Fiona, you've met Lance before, haven't you?" she said.

"Of course." Fiona smiled warmly.

"And that's his friend, Jaine," Bunny said, with a bored wave in my direction.

"Hello, there!" Fiona said, trotting over and extending a perfectly manicured hand. "Lovely to meet you. I'm Bunny's personal stylist." She handed me her business card, which read:

FIONA WILLIAMS, CELEBRITY FASHION CONSULTANT.

Good news for Bunny. Apparently she'd just been upgraded from Bimbo to Celebrity.

"Not that Bunny needs my help," Fiona hastened to add. "She's got a fabulous sense of style."

This gal certainly knew where her croissant was buttered.

"C'mon over here and keep us company," Bunny called to her.

She'd glugged down her drink in record speed and seemed to be back in festive spirits.

Fiona joined Bunny and Lance on the other side of the

pool and the three of them started doing fashion chat, yakking about Giorgio and Calvin and the rest of the gang.

Here on the cellulite side of the pool, Sarah had her nose buried in *Chemistry Today*, reading it as avidly as I read the menu at The Cheesecake Factory. And over in the Business Section, Marvin and Owen were still talking profits and losses.

All of which left me sitting there like a lump.

"So," I said, turning to Sarah, "Lance tells me you teach chemistry."

Somehow she managed to tear herself away from her magazine long enough to say, "Yes, I'm a professor at UCLA."

"Wow. What's that like? Very interesting, I'll bet."

How wrong I was.

Sparking to her subject, Sarah started telling me about one of her lab courses, rambling on about compounds and ions, mole fractions and sigma bonds, electromagnetic spectrums and heaven knows what else. I, of course, understood not a syllable of what she was saying. But I nodded and smiled as if she was actually making sense.

Eternities passed as she explained the difference between a proton and a photon.

Finally she wound down. It's a good thing. I was *thisclose* to getting whiplash from all that nodding.

"Gee," she said, "it's been fun chatting with you."

"Yes, I learned so much."

Which was true. I learned never to ask a chemistry professor about her job.

By then, I was desperate to make my escape from Casa Extravaganza. I'd long since given up hope of pitching myself to Marvin. I just wanted to go home and dig into my brunch leftovers.

I tried to make eye contact with Lance, currently engrossed in a lively discussion about the wacky world of hemlines. After a while I managed to catch his attention and shot him a desperate look.

Thank heavens, he got the message.

"Gosh," he said, "look at the time. It's been a hoot, Bunny, but Jaine and I have to make tracks."

"So soon?" she pouted. "Can't you stay a little while longer?"

No! I wanted to shout. *Not one more nanosecond.*

"Well," Lance hesitated, "maybe just a few more minutes."

Over my bored-to-death body.

"But, Lance," I said, getting up and trotting to his side, "if we don't leave right now, I'll be late for my dinner date."

"Your dinner date?" Lance shot me a blank look.

"*You've* got a date?" Bunny asked, as shocked as if I'd said I was about to climb Mount Everest in my pajamas.

"Oh, right," Lance said, finally catching on. "Your date! Yes, you mustn't be late for your date. I'll just go change."

And as he headed off to the cabana, a wonderful thing happened. Bunny finally remembered why I was there.

"Marvin, honey," she said, hooking her arm through mine and leading me over to her husband. "I almost forgot to tell you. Jaine here is a writer. She wrote the most adorable toilet bowl ads!"

"Is that so?" Marvin looked up at me, as if noticing me for the first time.

"Yes, I've been handling the Toiletmasters account for several years now. Also Ackerman's Awnings. And Fiedler on the Roof roofers."

"I think she'd be perfect for the Mattress King account!" Bunny gushed.

Way to go, Bunny! I shot her a grateful smile.

Marvin looked me over for a beat, no doubt wondering if he could trust me with his account.

I plastered on my most capable bizgal expression, glad I hadn't opted to wear my *Cuckoo for Cocoa Puffs* T-shirt.

I must have met with his approval, because the next thing he said was, "Why don't you drop by my Beverly Hills showroom tomorrow morning, and show me your writing samples?"

"Great!"

And so it was with infinitely boosted spirits that I headed back up to Casa Extravaganza.

How do you like that? Bunny came through for me after all. Maybe I'd misjudged her. Maybe she wasn't as big a bitch as she seemed at first glance. Maybe underneath that brittle exterior beat a heart of gold.

Yeah, right. And maybe hot fudge sundaes weren't fattening.

Chapter 4

It wasn't till I got home to my bright orange walls that I realized I'd left my sunglasses at Casa Extravaganza. Oh, well. No biggie. I'd just pop by tomorrow and pick them up.

In the meanwhile, feeling slightly sweaty from my poolside adventure, I decided to hop in the tub for my second bath of the day. Soon I was up to my neck in strawberry-scented bubbles, lost in daydreams of landing the Mattress King account.

Just think of all the things I could do with the money. First, I'd get rid of these damn orange walls. Then I'd write a check to the friendly folks at MasterCard, who of late had not been so very friendly. Maybe I'd treat myself to a new cashmere sweater. Or a flat-screen TV. Or, better yet, membership in the Fudge of the Month Club.

Finally, when I'd run out of daydreams, I hauled myself out of the tub.

Then I slipped into my jammies and coffee-stained chenille bathrobe and toddled off to the kitchen for my long-awaited reunion with my brunch leftovers.

I opened my doggie bag (and Lance's) and instantly began salivating at the cornucopia of baked ham, roast beef, smoked trout, lobster frittata, and blueberry muffins I'd managed to stuff inside the boxes.

At first I was just going to eat it à la Austen, which is to say straight from the Styrofoam boxes, but then I figured what

the heck? Why not do a Martha Stewart and use actual din-
nerware for a change? So I arranged it all on a pretty plate
and set it out on the living room coffee table. Then I plopped
down on the sofa with a wee smidgeon of chardonnay and
my Sunday *Times* crossword puzzle.

Was this heaven, or what?

Unfortunately, I never did get to eat the trout. Prozac took
one look at it, forgot all about the Hearty Halibut Guts I'd
sloshed in her bowl, and swooped down on my plate.

Gone in sixty seconds.

But no matter. I still had the ham, the roast beef, and the
muffins. Not to mention that yummy frittata.

Just as I was about to bite into it, there was a knock on my
door.

Oh, rats. Why is someone always at the door when you're
about to chow down on a lobster frittata?

With a sigh I got up to answer it.

"Who is it?" I called out.

"Jaine, my beloved! It is I! Your own true love, Vladimir
Ivan Trotsky!"

Oh, crud! I groaned in dismay.

Vladimir Ivan Trotsky is a guy my mom met on a Universal
Studios tour when he was here in the States on a visit from
Uzbekistan. Always on the hunt for my future ex-husband,
Mom proceeded to give him my e-mail address.

Forget that the guy lived eight zillion miles away in a
country without Ben & Jerry's. Forget that I was not exactly
eager to tie the knot after my horrendous first marriage, a
rollicking four-year affair that made Dante's Inferno look
like an episode of *Leave It to Beaver.* Or that I was still licking my wounds from my last relationship with a water sports
enthusiast named Robbie, who quickly flew the coop when I
finally confessed the only water sport I truly enjoyed was
soaking in the tub.

Forget all logic. My mom dreams of the day when I will

once more trot down the aisle with a man at my side—any man, as long as he's breathing, and sometimes I'm not even sure if that's a requirement.

Anyhow, Vladimir checked out my picture on the Internet—a very flattering shot, I must admit, of me winning the Golden Plunger Award from the L.A. Plumbers Association—and had been bombarding me with marriage proposals ever since. Needless to say, I'd turned them all down, secure in the knowledge that he was eight zillion miles away in Uzbekistan.

Who'd ever think he'd show up on my doorstep?

Quel nightmare!

Reluctantly I opened the door to my would-be Romeo.

Oh, heavens. In person, he was even goofier than the photo he'd sent me, and that had been pretty darn goofy.

A short, skinny guy with a headful of tight black curls, he had a gap-toothed smile that made Alfred E. Newman look like a Rhodes scholar.

Now his slightly crossed eyes lit up at the sight of me.

"Jaine! My beloved!"

I shut my eyes for a second, hoping against hope he was a figment of my imagination brought on by an overdose of strawberry-scented bath bubbles. But alas, he was still there when I opened them again, grinning his Alfred E. Newman grin.

Somehow I managed to recover my powers of speech.

"Vladimir," I croaked. "What are you doing here?"

"I come to propose marriage to you, of course."

"But you've already proposed, Vladimir. At least seven times. And I've turned you down all seven times."

"Yes, but this time I propose in person! Like my mama told me, 'Once she sees you in person, Vladdie, how can she resist?'"

Oh, lord. Why are the nutcases always attracted to me?

"How on earth did you find my address?"

"Whitepages.com." He nodded proudly. "They give me your phone number, too."

I made a mental note to write a very nasty letter to those blabbermouths at whitepages.com.

"For you, my beloved," he said, thrusting a bouquet of wilted daisies into my hand.

"Thank you." I faked a smile as several dying petals fluttered to the floor.

"May I come in?" he asked, peering over my shoulder, "and see your charming home?"

Oh, foo. The last thing I wanted was to invite him in, but I couldn't send him away, not after he'd traveled halfway around the world to see me.

And for those of you clucking at the notion of me inviting a stranger into my apartment, let me assure you there was nothing to worry about. The guy weighed as much as my right thigh. I could take him down blindfolded.

"Yes, sure," I said halfheartedly.

As he trotted inside, toting a tattered shopping bag, I headed for the kitchen to put my dying daisies in water. Once again, I indulged in the foolish fantasy that somehow he'd be gone when I returned to the living room.

But nope, he was still there.

"What a beautiful abode!" he said upon my return, gazing in admiration at my orange walls. "A perfect setting for my princess! And what a cute kitty cat. Do you always let kitty eat human food?"

Prozac looked up, irritated, from where she'd been busy sucking up some roast beef.

Hey, mind your own beeswax, willya?

"Prozac, cut that out!" I whisked her off the sofa. "That's supposed to be my dinner."

"A thousand pardons!" Vladimir cried. "I interrupt your meal."

"Oh, that's okay," I lied.

"It looks delicious," he said, practically drooling onto my plate.

"Would you care to join me?" I forced myself to ask.

"Maybe just a tiny bite."

With that, he parked himself down on the sofa and began plowing through my chow like a John Deere at harvest time.

Prozac stared at him, wide-eyed. At last she'd met her match in the speed-eating department.

I quickly sat down next to him and tried to grab something before it all disappeared, but all I managed to nab was half a muffin and a square of frittata.

All the rest, down Vladimir's gullet.

Prozac hissed as he popped the last of the ham into his mouth.

Hey, wait a minute! I was going to eat that.

"Delicious!" Vladimir exclaimed when there was nothing left on the plate except his reflection. "Never have I eaten such wonderful food! What a wonderful cook you are, my beloved Jaine."

"Actually, I didn't cook any of this."

"Oh, but I can tell you are magnificent cook."

At that, Prozac practically rolled her eyes.

Are you kidding? She needs Mapquest to find the oven.

"You know what would taste wonderful right now?" He patted his nonexistent tummy.

The rest of that frittata, I felt like saying. *But you already ate it.*

"A nice glass of tea."

Ten minutes later, we were side by side on the sofa, sipping our teas, mine generously laced with Tylenol.

Vladimir had taken out a small photo album from his shopping bag and was showing me pictures of his family. I smiled gamely at photos of his babushka-ed mother and rifle-toting father. Between the two of them, they possessed a grand total of five teeth.

"And here is my beloved Svetlana!"

Svetlana was not, as you might have imagined, a local Uzbek lass, but his pet mountain goat.

"Svetlana is my very best friend in the whole world."

No surprise there.

"I told her all about you, Jaine. She can't wait to meet you."

As if that is ever going to happen.

At last, we were through looking at the Trotsky clan.

"Gosh, that was fun, Vladimir."

"Please, call me Vladdie."

"Right, um, Vladdie. It's been great catching up. But I've got a busy day ahead, and I've really got to turn in now."

"But wait! I must read love poem!"

He took out a piece of none-too-clean paper from his pocket and unfolded it with a flourish. Then he cleared his throat and read:

Ode to My Beloved Jaine

I love your eyes of baby blue
To you I will be always true
Your lips are red as bowl of borscht
Marry Vladdie and you never get divorced!

Prozac looked up from where she had been examining her privates.

Whew. That stinks worse than my litter box.

"How sweet." I smiled weakly. "But actually, my eyes aren't blue. They're hazel."

"Yes, but blue so much easier to rhyme—Wait, I know! Listen to this!"

Another phlegm-filled clearing of his throat, after which he proclaimed:

I love your eyes of sparkling hazel
So big and round like onion bagel

"How very touching," I managed to say.

"I knew you would love it. So how about it, Jaine? You marry with me?"

He looked up at me, practically panting with eagerness.

"I've already told you, Vladdie, I can't possibly marry you."

"But why?"

I figured telling him that on a scale of one to ten he was a minus forty-seven wasn't the way to go.

"For one thing, I don't even know you."

"Of course!" He smacked his hand against his head. "Vladimir idiot to think you fall in love with me so soon. It takes time. At least until Thursday. In the meanwhile, you come meet my family here in the United States. My Aunt Minna and my cousins Sofi and Boris. Aunt Minna cook dinner for you tomorrow."

No way was I about to meet his family. Absolutely not. I had to end this thing here and now. And I was just about to turn him down in no uncertain terms when he threw a curveball at me.

"I almost forgot!" he said. "I'm so busy staring at your beautiful hazel eyes, I didn't give you your gift!"

Once more he reached into his shopping bag.

"For you, Jaine," he said, handing me a beautiful white cable-knit sweater.

"This is lovely, Vladimir. You shouldn't have."

"Mama and Natasha made it for you."

"Natasha?"

"Our pet lamb. That's her wool. So what do you say, Jaine? You come meet my family?"

He looked up at me pleadingly with his slightly crossed eyes.

Oh, lord. I couldn't turn him down now, not after his mother knitted me a sweater from their pet lamb. I'd go meet his Aunt Minna, have dinner, and that'd be that. Finito. End of romance. Before I knew it, he'd be back in Uzbekistan and I'd never have to see him again.

And so I said three little words that would live to haunt me for years to come:

"Okay, I'll go."

YOU'VE GOT MAIL!

To: Jausten
From: Shoptillyoudrop
Subject: Exciting New Hobby!

Guess what, sweetheart? I've taken up the most exciting new hobby. Something I've wanted to learn for ages, along with origami and how to set the clock on the microwave.

I've joined a bridge club! You remember Lydia Pinkus, don't you? The librarian here at Tampa Vistas? She's teaching a bunch of us gals the rules of the game. And it's so much fun! A lot more challenging than Go Fish, I must admit. I've been trying to get Daddy to play, but he's not interested. Which is all for the best, I suppose. You know how he sulks when he loses.

Next week is my turn to host the gals for lunch. I can't wait. I'm going to make either quiche or chicken salad in tomato cups. Doesn't that sound lovely? And I'm going to serve it on my new luncheon china from the shopping channel. The show host said it was the exact same china Queen Elizabeth uses. Or maybe it was Queen Latifah. I forget who. All I know is, it's gorgeous, and service for four was just $69.95, plus shipping and handling.

Oh, dear. Must run. The UPS man is at the door and Daddy's making a fuss about something.

More later,

Mom

To: Jausten
From: DaddyO
Subject: It's Here!

Great news, lambchop! It's here at last! My Turbomaster 3000 convection oven! I saw it on an infomercial the other night when I was having trouble sleeping. The minute I saw it in action, I knew I had to have it. Would you believe this brilliant piece of culinary engineering can cook pork chops in five minutes? A rack of lamb in ten? And a turkey in just twenty-five minutes?!! Just think of all the money Mom and I will save on our energy bills!

And get this: Because I was one of the first five hundred callers, they threw in a free jar of their Turbomaster Secret Spice! A special blend of fifteen exotic spices. Guaranteed to make any dish come alive with flavor!

What a lucky break I couldn't sleep the other night, huh? Otherwise I might've missed out on one of the greatest inventions of the 21st century.

I can't wait to get started cooking!

Love and kisses from,

Daddy

To: Jausten
From: Shoptillyoudrop
Subject: Glorified Toaster Oven

Oh, for heaven's sake. Your father's gone and done it again. He's fallen under the spell of yet another infomercial and bought some ridiculous contraption that he claims will cook a turkey in twenty-five minutes. If you ask me, his silly Turbomaster is nothing more than a glorified toaster oven.

I can't believe he was crazy enough to spend $200 on that hunk of junk!

You know what's going to happen, don't you? In three days he'll lose interest in it, just like he lost interest in the slice 'n' dicer, the yogurt maker, the brisket brisker, the Magic Juicer, and the Mr. Waffle waffle maker gathering dust in the garage. I swear, honey, with all the junk we've got sitting out there, we could open our own museum of unused cooking appliances.

Your disgusted,

Mom

To: Jausten
From: DaddyO
Subject: She Can Scoff All She Wants

Your mom is a very sweet woman, lambchop, and I love her dearly, but she sure knows how to rain on a fella's parade. She hasn't said it in so many words, but it's clear she thinks my Turbomaster is a piece of junk. And she has the nerve to make fun of me because I ordered it from an infomercial! Look who's talking—the woman who's practically attached to the shopping channel by an umbilical cord.

Mom can scoff all she wants, but she can't dampen my excitement. No, sir. Tonight I'm going to break in the Turbomaster with some magnificent five-minute pork chops. I'm headed out to the market right now to go shopping.

Bon appetit!

From your loving,

Daddy

To: Jausten
From: Shoptillyoudrop
Subject: Im Possible!

I've got two words for your father: Im Possible! He went to the market to pick up a couple of pork chops and a carton of milk and just walked in the door with four bags of groceries. Filled with ridiculous food items we'll never use. Garlic-stuffed olives. Anchovies in truffle oil. Pickled artichoke hearts. And a five-pound bag of unpopped popcorn. I ask you, what on earth are we going to do with five pounds of unpopped popcorn, other than open our own concession stand at the movies? Would you believe he spent $127 on all that junk when all he needed was two measly pork chops??!

And PS. He forgot the milk!

Chapter 5

I spent a restless night tossing and turning. When I finally managed to drift off to sleep, I dreamed I was standing at the altar, exchanging wedding vows with Vladimir, his goat Svetlana my maid of honor.

For once I was actually grateful when Prozac clawed me awake for her breakfast.

After fixing her some Hearty Halibut Guts and nuking myself a cup of Folgers Crystals, I hunkered down at the computer and checked my parents' e-mails. Which is never a great way to start the day.

Don't get me wrong. My parents are very sweet people, and I love them to pieces, but their e-mails should come with a warning from the Surgeon General: *The News You Are About to Receive May Be Hazardous to Your Mental Health.*

Daddy is the main culprit, of course. The man has caused more ulcers than garlic and jalapeno peppers combined. I knew he'd drive poor Mom nuts with his Turbomaster contraption. And that she, in turn, would drive me nuts, in a daisy chain of unending aggravation.

But I couldn't sit around fretting about my parents. In less than an hour, I'd be meeting with Marvin Cooper to show him my writing samples.

So I dusted off my sample book, praying Marvin would be wowed by my colorful array of toilet bowl brochures. Then I dug out my one and only Prada pantsuit from the back of my closet and proceeded to get dressed, accessorizing with a tasteful gold bangle and a pair of black slingbacks I'd bought on sale at Nordstrom.

When I'd spritzed my final spritz of perfume and wrestled my curls into submission, I checked myself out in the mirror. Not bad. Not bad at all. Just goes to show what you can do when you choose your wardrobe wisely and stand really far away from the mirror.

"Wish me luck," I called to Prozac.

She looked up from where she was napping on my computer keyboard and gave me an encouraging yawn.

Minutes later, I was tooling over to Mattress King.

Marvin's Beverly Hills showroom was not in Beverly Hills, but in an area euphemistically called Beverly Hills Adjacent, by people who live there and wish they didn't. Lots of successful business are located there, however, and Marvin's was one of them.

A huge barn of a building, Mattress King's floor-to-ceiling plate-glass windows displayed a sea of thick, tufted mattresses. A sign in the window revealed that they were in the midst of a gala "Sleep-tacular."

I bypassed the parking lot in the rear and took a spot down the street. I was, after all, trying to make a good impression, and an ancient Corolla with an *I Brake for Chocolate* bumper sticker does not exactly scream *Hire Me*.

Gathering my sample book and my courage, I trotted over to the store, took a deep breath, and headed inside.

The place was practically deserted. Which was not all that surprising at 10:30 on a Monday morning.

A portly guy in a blue blazer jumped up from where he was doing a crossword puzzle and hurried over to greet me.

"Hello, there!" he said, buttoning his blazer over his substantial gut. "I'm Lenny."

And indeed his name tag informed me that he was "Sleep Specialist Lenny."

"How may I help you get a good night's rest?" he asked, running a hand over his comb-over.

He could start by getting Prozac to stop sleeping with her tail in my mouth, but I doubt that was what he had in mind.

"Actually, I'm here for a meeting with Marvin Cooper."

"Through the door over there," he sighed, kissing his sale good-bye. Then, noticing my sample book, he added, "Good luck."

He smiled a sad-eyed smile, as if luck was something he'd run out of long ago.

I made my way through a door at the back of the show-room to a no-frills office area, with rental-quality furniture, metal file cabinets, and a coffee machine in a corner. A pale young receptionist was clacking away on her computer key-board, peering at the monitor through a fringe of limp brown bangs.

When I told her I was there to see Marvin, she quickly ush-ered me into his inner sanctum. Unlike the reception area, Marvin's office was decorated to the hilt, crammed with or-nate antique furniture and froufrou vases, a riff on the Vegas Versailles theme I'd seen at Casa Extravaganza.

Marvin jumped up from where he was seated, his roly-poly body dwarfed behind a monster of a desk. "How nice to see you, Jaine!"

"What a lovely office," I managed to say.

"Would you believe Bunny decorated it all by herself?"

I'd believe it, all right. No decorator in her right mind would take credit for this mess.

"It's not really my style," he shrugged, "but she got a big kick out of doing it."

I could easily imagine Bunny decorating an office with ab-solutely no regard for the person who'd be using it.

"Please," Marvin said. "Sit down, make yourself comfy."

Me? Comfy? In Antique Alley? Not bloody likely.

I perched my fanny on a fussy little armchair across from his desk, hoping it wouldn't give way beneath me.

"So," he said, getting down to business, "let's see your stuff."

Discreetly wiping the sweat from my palms, I handed him my sample book.

I sat, fingers crossed, as he turned the pages, praying he'd like my ads. And indeed, he did seem to be smiling.

"Very cute," he said when he got to my ad for Ackerman's Awnings. "*Just a Shade Better.*"

He continued leafing through the book, that faint smile still on his lips. I just hoped he wasn't faking it. He seemed like the kind of guy who might want to spare my feelings.

At last he slapped the book shut, and his faint smile grew into a full-fledged grin.

"I like it."

Hallelujah!

"And I'd be happy to hear any ideas you want to pitch. Are you familiar with my commercials?"

"Of course."

Anybody who'd ever turned on a TV in the middle of the night in L.A. was familiar with Marvin's commercials. They were all the same: Marvin sitting on a throne in a cheesy ermine-trimmed robe and crown, waving a scepter and yapping about how his mattresses were fit for a king.

"I'm tired of that old slogan, *Fit for a King.* I want something new. Something with more oomph! You think you can do oomph?"

"Absolutely," I assured him, having no idea what he was talking about.

"Great! Now let's go look at some mattresses!" he said, jumping up. "To light your creative fire."

With happy heart, I followed him out to the office reception area, where I noticed a pudgy woman in a jog suit standing at the coffee machine.

"Oh, Marvin!" she called out. "Aren't you going to introduce me to your friend?"

Marvin looked distinctly uncomfortable.

"Of course," he replied.

Reluctantly he led me over to the coffee table where the woman was now reaching into a box of the most heavenly looking Krispy Kremes.

"This is Jaine," Marvin said. "She's going to work on ideas for a new slogan."

"How wonderful!" The woman shot me a warm smile. "The best of luck to you, dear."

With her round apple cheeks, bright blue eyes, and graying Dutch bob, she looked like she'd just stepped out of a Norman Rockwell painting.

Why on earth did Marvin seem so uncomfortable around her?

"Care for a donut?" she asked, holding out the box.

My eyes zeroed in on a chocolate-glazed beauty.

It was torture, but I managed to say, "No, thanks."

"Since Marvin obviously isn't going to introduce me," she said, "I'm Ellen Cooper."

"Cooper?" I asked. "Are you two related?"

Marvin's eyes shifted nervously.

"Ellen and I used to be married."

"That's right," Ellen said, still smiling her cherubic smile. "I'm a charter member of the First Wives Club."

I remembered what Lance told me about Marvin dumping his longtime spouse for Bunny. So this was Wife Number One.

"Marvin and I were married for thirty years until Ms. Bunny came along."

Uh-oh. I was beginning to sense some tension in the air. Ellen Cooper may have been smiling on the outside, but there was a definite edge to her voice.

"Aren't you going to tell Jaine what I do here at Mattress King?" she asked Marvin.

"Ellen is our bookkeeper," he snapped in reply.

"Correction, dear. Chief Financial Officer." Then she confided to me, "Marvin was kind enough to let me retain part ownership of the business, thanks to his generous nature and some serious threats from my barracuda divorce attorney."

By then Marvin was openly glaring at his ex.

"Let's go check out those mattresses," he said, yanking me away.

"Watch out for him, sweetheart!" Ellen called out. "He likes 'em young."

Marvin hustled me out of there so fast, I barely had time to grab a donut hole.

Out in the showroom, business had picked up, and Lenny was now showing an elderly couple one of his "sleep-tacular" mattresses.

"One of my best salesmen," Marvin said, nodding in Lenny's direction. "He's been with me since Day One."

Guiding me by the elbow, he took me on a tour of the place, yapping about inner springs and coil count and memory-foam pillow tops. Surrounded by his beloved mattresses, his anger at his ex-wife quickly dissipated.

"Go on," he said, pointing to a model called the Comfort Cloud. "Lie down and try it out."

I gulped in dismay.

"You want me to lie down?"

Oh, dear. The last time I parked myself on a bed in front of a man (some time during the Lincoln administration) there was foreplay involved.

"Sure!" Marvin said. "You'll never know how heavenly our mattresses are unless you take one for a test drive!"

Between the innerspring and the pillow top and lord knows how many layers of padding, this thing was The Incredible Hulk of mattresses. Awkwardly I climbed on board, my tush exposed for intimate inspection. Not quite the executive image I was hoping to impart.

When I stretched out on the tufted pillow top, my thighs expanded exponentially, as they always do in a reclining position. I cursed myself for not wearing industrial-strength pantyhose.

"Isn't she a honey?" Marvin beamed, his tiny eyes glowing with enthusiasm. "Just like a cloud, huh?"

"Yes," I echoed weakly. "Just like a cloud."

And I have to admit, if I hadn't felt so damn awkward, lying there with my thighs spreading like butter on a hotcake, it would've been quite cloud-like.

"So?" he asked. "Are you inspired yet?"

"I don't know about her," came a voice from behind Marvin, "but I sure am."

I recognized the voice right away. And the blast of pungent perfume that accompanied it.

It was Wife Number Two. Bunny Cooper. Poured into skintight jeans and midriff-baring T-shirt. Emblazoned in rhinestones across the mountainous terrain of her chest were the words *Wild Thing*.

Tossing back her flaming red hair extensions, Bunny slithered onto a nearby mattress and assumed a pose straight out of *Playboy*.

All that was missing were the staples in her navel.

"Just a preview of coming attractions," she cooed to her Marvy Man, puckering her lips in a kiss.

Marvin blushed.

"Bunny, please," he said. "The customers are watching."

And indeed, Lenny's elderly customers had lost all interest in mattresses and were staring at Bunny. Correction. Mr. Elderly was staring. So hard, I thought his eyeballs would bust through his bifocals. Mrs. Elderly, on the other hand, was harrumphing in disgust.

Lenny seemed to share her disgust, pursing his lips in disapproval.

But their reactions paled in comparison to what I saw next.

There, standing not far behind them, was Ellen Cooper. All traces of the Norman Rockwell dame with the sweet smile who'd offered me a Krispy Kreme had vanished into the ether. Now her jaw was clenched tight, her eyes burned with fury.

Clearly, Marvin wasn't the only one she was sore at.

If looks could kill, Bunny would be dead on a bed.

Chapter 6

I clambered down from the Comfort Cloud, eager to make my exit before Bunny ignited the mattress with her body heat.

"Guess I'd better be going," I said, grabbing my sample book.

"Take this." Marvin handed me one of those cutaway mattress samples, with the coils and padding exposed. "For added inspiration."

"Good luck, Jaine!" Bunny waved at me, still in centerfold mode.

I thanked the Wild Thing for her good wishes and scooted out the door, the elderly couple right behind me.

"I still don't see why we can't buy our mattress here," the man whined, casting a longing glance at Bunny.

"Forget it, Lester. We're going to Macy's."

The perpetual morning fog that hovers over L.A. had burned off by now, and I squinted into the bright midday sun. I really needed to stop by Casa Extravaganza and pick up my sunglasses. If I hurried right over, I could get them from the maid before Bunny got home.

The more I saw of Mrs. Marvin Cooper, the more I wanted to avoid her.

I was still reeling over her tacky performance on the mattress. She knew the first Mrs. Cooper was standing there watching her. I'd seen her gaze up at her with a triumphant smirk. *Eat your heart out, honey*, were her unspoken subtitles. *I won and you lost.*

What a piece of work, huh?

I made my way over to my Corolla and was just about to get in when my cell phone rang.

It was my best friend and constant dining companion, Kandi Tobolowski.

She did not waste any time on preliminaries.

"That damn cockroach is driving me crazy!"

No, Kandi did not have a pest problem. The cockroach to whom she referred was the lead character on the Saturday morning cartoon show, *Beanie & The Cockroach*, where Kandi is gainfully employed as a writer.

"That prima donna jerk keeps flubbing his lines," she sighed. "Anyhow, I need to get out of here. Meet me for lunch at Paco's Tacos. My treat."

Kandi makes scads more money than I do and is always offering to pick up the tab. I hardly ever let her, of course. Along with our noble brows and inability to carry a tune, we Austens have our pride, you know.

"Honey, I can't. I've got so much work to do, and the last things I need are the calories from a heavy Mexican meal."

"Meet you there in twenty minutes."

"Make it a half hour. Traffic looks heavy."

What can I say? When it comes to Mexican food, I simply can't say no. And Thai food. And Italian. And—well, it's quite a long list, and I've got a story to tell. So let's get on with it, shall we?

A half hour later I was sitting across from Kandi at Paco's Tacos, ordering the chimichanga combo plate from a most accommodating waiter.

Kandi, a pert little thing with a headful of enviably straight chestnut hair, perused the menu, trying to decide between the mahi mahi salad and the vegetarian tostada.

Unlike yours truly, Kandi has inherited the willpower gene, which is why she is able to maintain her Pert Little Thing status.

"I'll have the mahi mahi salad," she told the waiter. "And margaritas for both of us."

No way. No margaritas for me. I had to keep my head clear for thinking up brilliant mattress slogans.

"Kandi, I can't have a margarita in the middle of the day. I've got work to do."

"Salt or no salt?"

"Salt," I sighed.

"I've got the most fabulous news!" Kandi grinned, when the waiter had gone.

Kandi's idea of fabulous news is the opening of a new Pinkberry, so I remained somewhat skeptical.

"Oh, Jaine," she whispered, a dreamy look in her eyes. "I've finally met Mr. Right."

"Again?" I said, scooping up a hunk of salsa onto a chip.

"This time, it's the real thing! I swear! His name," she said, with the kind of reverence usually reserved for the pope, "is Denny. And you'll never guess how we met. He was in line behind me at Starbucks! Won't that be the cutest story to tell our grandkids?"

"Ranks right up there with Rick and Ilsa running into each other in *Casablanca*."

"I'll choose to ignore that," she said, arching an indignant brow. "Anyhow, he ordered a Venti Latte and I ordered a chai tea and we wound up sharing a lo-carb blueberry muffin!"

I managed to plow my way though half a basket of chips as she rambled on about the Divine Denny, who was, to her great delight, both a doctor and a Scrabble nut.

"I thought maybe we'd go on a Scrabble cruise for our honeymoon."

"Your honeymoon? Don't you think you're rushing things just a tad?"

"You're right, of course," she said, nibbling at a corner of a chip. "I haven't even planned the wedding yet!"

And she was off and running, lost in the pages of her own *True Romance* story. I remained on automatic pilot, nodding my head at periodic intervals as I daydreamed about my chimichanga plate.

"So what's new with you, cookie?" she asked, when she'd finally run out of steam. "Anybody interesting in your life?"

"Right now, just the waiter," I said, as he at last approached with our food.

Gosh, my chimichangas looked good, nestled on a bed of refried beans and rice, and topped with a luscious dollop of sour cream.

"Oh, foo," she pouted. "You're so boring."

"Boring, am I? Well, for your information, there *is* a man in my life."

"The pizza guy doesn't count."

"And it's not the pizza guy."

"Really?" Her eyes lit up with excitement. "Tell all! I want every last detail, in living color."

"Calm down. He's not Mr. Right. In fact, he's Mr. Couldn't Possibly Be Any More Wrong."

Wearily I told her about my visit from my would-be fiancé, Vladimir.

"I can't believe I actually agreed to go out with the guy."

Kandi looked up from a speck of mahi mahi on her fork and tsk tsked in disapproval. If it was sympathy I was after I was barking up the wrong girlfriend.

"That's your trouble, Jaine. You're way too fussy."

"Fussy? For crying out loud, Kandi. The guy has a picture of his goat in his wallet!"

"How charmingly ethnic!" she said with a carefree wave. "Don't be such a snob. It's time you let go of your shallow

Western values."

"This from a woman who once waited three hours to get her shoes autographed by Manolo Blahnik!"

"That's not the least bit shallow!" Kandi protested. "Manolo Blahnik shoes are considered works of art."

"And to think, some people waste their money on Picassos."

"Seriously, Jaine," she sighed, "you've got to start opening yourself up to new experiences."

"The only thing I want to open myself up to right now are these chimichangas."

And without any further ado, I dug right in.

It was after one by the time we tore ourselves away from Paco's.

"Give this Dimitri guy a chance," Kandi said as she hugged me good-bye. "He might be The One."

"His name is Vladimir, and the only thing he might be is certifiable."

"Oh, honey," she sighed. "No wonder you're still single."

I refrained from pointing out that I was not the only single person in our little duo.

Instead, I bid her a fond adieu and, several hours behind schedule, hurried over to Casa Extravaganza to get my sunglasses.

When I pulled up in the circular driveway, I groaned to see Bunny's Maserati parked on the gravel.

Phooey. She was home. Oh, well. With any luck she'd be lolling by the pool, and I could get my glasses from Lupe.

I was heading for the front door when it suddenly opened and out came Owen Kendall, his Mattress King baseball cap askew on his head.

What was he doing here at this time of day? And why was his shirt only half-tucked in his pants?

Enquiring minds wanted to know.

"Hi, Owen," I said, blocking his path. "What's up?"

He took one look at me and practically jumped out of his skin.

"Er . . . Jaine," he said, blushing furiously. "I was just picking up some papers for the office."

Oh, yeah? Then where were they? I sure didn't see any papers.

"Gotta run," he muttered, brushing past me.

And as he hurried by I got a whiff of perfume. Not just any perfume. I'd recognize that scent anywhere. It was Bunny's designer fragrance, the stuff she splashed between her cleavage with wild abandon. Owen positively reeked of it.

Now everybody let's take out our calculators and add two and two.

I don't know what you came up with, but I came up with dipsy doodle.

If I wasn't mistaken, The Trophy Wife was having an affair with The Nerdy Son-in-Law.

I watched Owen drive off in his car, a late model BMW with vanity plates that read *M KING II*. Not exactly a nerdmobile. Actually, now that I thought about it, Owen wasn't a bad looking guy. He was tall and thin and, beneath that Mattress King visor, his eyes were a most appealing blue.

Something told me he might look good without clothes on, and I suspected that's just how Bunny liked him.

I stood there, admiring the wisdom of that old you-can't-judge-a-book-by-its-cover gag, when I heard:

"Jaine, darling!"

I whirled around to see Bunny standing in the doorway, eyes narrowed into suspicious slits.

Now it was my turn to blush.

She knew that I'd seen Owen, and that I'd probably figured out what was going on.

"Hi, B-Bunny," I stammered. "I just stopped by to pick up my sunglasses. I left them here yesterday."

"Of course," she said, with an icy smile. "Lupe found them by the pool. Come on in and I'll get them."

I headed inside, feeling very much like Little Red Riding Hood popping in to the big bad wolf's place.

"Here they are," she said, plucking my sunglasses from a table in the foyer.

I reached out to take them, but she was not about to hand them over.

"I suppose you ran into Owen just now."

"Oh, right. Owen. Yes, I ran into him. Great guy, Owen. A real asset to the company. That's what Lance says. Actually, I'm sure everybody says that. Owen has 'asset' written all over him."

I tend to babble when I'm nervous, and the laser beam glint in her eyes definitely had me on edge.

"He was here dropping off some papers."

Owen said he was picking them up. Now he was dropping them off. Those two had better get their stories straight if they were going to keep an affair going.

"Right," I nodded. "Dropping off papers. Absolutely!"

Once more I held out my hand for my glasses, but she was not about to fork them over.

"I'm so happy you're trying out for the Mattress King account," she said, her smile dipping a few degrees below freezing. "It would be a shame if you said the wrong thing at your pitch meeting and didn't get the job."

Translation: *You breathe one word of what you just saw, and you're toast.*

"After all, you're such good friends with Lance, and he's such a dear. I'd hate for you to miss out on this opportunity. Almost as much," she added, after a meaningful pause, "as I'd hate to see anything happen to Lance's job."

Yikes. Was she threatening to get Lance fired, too?

I was tempted to tell her to take her threats and shove them up her wingwang. But then I remembered my ghastly orange walls and my near-death bank account. Not to mention Lance's job at Neiman's. So I kept my big yap shut.

"Don't worry, Bunny. I won't say a word."

"A word about what, dear?" she blinked, suddenly wide-eyed and innocent.

At which point, to my great relief, the doorbell chimed.

Bunny opened the door to Fiona.

"Sweetie!" Fiona said, breezing in with an armful of clothes. "Just wait till you see the amazing Versace I picked up for you—

"Oh, hello, Jaine," she said, catching sight of me. "I didn't realize you'd be here. Hope I'm not interrupting anything."

"Of course not," Bunny said. "Jaine was just leaving."

At last she handed me my sunglasses.

"C'mon," she said to Fiona, "let's go up to my room and try on clothes."

"So did that Dolce & Gabbana I brought the other day work out?" Fiona asked as the two of them tripped up the Tara-esque staircase.

I didn't stick around to find out whether her majesty gave her approval to Signors Dolce and Gabbana.

Not missing a beat, I hustled my own sweet gabbana the heck out of there.

Chapter 7

Poor Marvin, I thought, as I drove home, stuck with that cheating bitch of a trophy wife. Yes, I know he was no prizewinner himself, dumping Ellen the way he did, but he sure was paying his dues.

I did not have time, however, to worry about the lifestyles of the rich and deceitful. If I expected to inject some badly needed funds into my checking account, I had to drum up mattress slogans.

Back in my apartment, I hunkered down at my office desk, otherwise known as my dining room table, and opened a new file on my computer.

Prozac, sensing I was about to begin a work session, jumped down from the bookcase where she'd been napping and plopped herself on my keyboard.

She likes being part of the creative process.

After depositing her on the floor where she belonged, I spent several productive minutes scratching her belly with my big toe.

It's always tough getting started on a new project.

But I put my nose to the proverbial grindstone, and in no time my fingers were flying across the keyboard, pounding out mattress slogans.

Oh, who am I kidding?

In no time, I was standing in front of the refrigerator wishing I had something more interesting to eat than moldy Swiss cheese and martini olives.

With a sigh, I returned to the computer, where I proceeded to do some more intense space-staring.

Then I remembered the mattress sample Marvin had given me for "inspiration." I didn't really see how a bunch of exposed coils would inspire me, but it was worth a shot. So I brought it in from my car.

The minute I did, I smelled trouble.

Prozac looked up from her perch on my keyboard and gazed at it much like a lion gazes at an innocent gazelle.

Just what I wanted! A new scratching post!

That thing would be confetti in five minutes.

"Forget it, kiddo. Ain't gonna happen."

With that, I grabbed a legal pad and pencil and relocated to my Corolla, where I sat with the pad propped up against the steering wheel, gazing at the mattress sample I'd tossed on my passenger seat.

After a while I began writing. Sad to say, it was only a grocery list.

Clearly, inspiration wasn't striking.

Then I got a brainstorm. Why not lie down on my *own* mattress to get in mattress-selling mode? True, it was a tad lumpy, but I bet if I stretched out and felt a real mattress beneath me, the slogans would practically write themselves.

So I trotted back inside and stretched out on my bed, waiting for the mattress muse to show up.

Unfortunately, the only one who showed up was Mr. Sandman.

In no time, I was out like a light, only to be awakened several hours later by a loud pounding on my front door.

I hustled over to answer it and there on my doorstep was my would-be fiancé, Vladimir Ivan Trotsky, holding a bouquet of what looked suspiciously like my neighbor's tulips.

Oh, lord. I'd forgotten all about my date with him. Tonight

was the night I was supposed to have dinner at his Aunt Minna's.

"Good evening, my beloved Jaine!" he said, handing me the tulips. "How beautiful you look!"

"Er, thanks," I said, wiping the sleep from my eyes.

"Wonderful news!" He beamed.

The only wonderful news I wanted to hear was that our date was cancelled.

"I write you another poem."

With that, he whipped a piece of paper from his pocket and began reading me his latest opus:

> *To Jaine, whose lips are red as beet*
> *And also has such pretty feet*
> *I cannot wait to tie the knot*
> *Your Vladimir is hot to trot.*

At this point, I could hear the faint sounds of Elizabeth Barrett Browning rolling over in her grave.

"I already told you, Vladimir. There will be absolutely no knot-tying. You do understand that, don't you?"

"Of course, my beloved Jaine," he said, gazing at me with a lovestruck grin. Why did I get the feeling my message hadn't quite penetrated his skull?

"You ready to meet my family?" he asked.

"Can't wait," I lied. "Just let me change into something more presentable."

After putting the tulips in a vase, I scooted to my bedroom to throw on some slacks and a sweater. Then off to the bathroom for a quick splash of water on my face, a gargle of Listerine, and a hasty application of lipstick. I didn't bother with perfume. No sense getting the guy any more excited than he already was.

All the while, I could hear Vladimir crooning what sounded like an Uzbek lullaby to Prozac.

When I came out into the living room, I found the little hussy sprawled in his arms having her belly rubbed.

"Pretty kitty," Vladimir cooed. "You will love it in Uzbekistan. You and my goat Svetlana will be best friends."

She greeted that news with a cavernous yawn.

Whatever. Got any tuna?

"All set," I said, breaking up their little lovefest.

Vladimir leaped up at the sight of me, clutching his heart.

"Jaine, my beloved! You even more beautiful than before! In all my life I never see such beauty."

The guy obviously didn't get out much.

"Come, my beautiful future bride; it's time to meet my family."

"Look, Vladimir. How many times do I have to tell you? This bride thing is not going to happen. I'm just going to dinner. That's all. Get it?"

"Okey dokey! Vladimir understand. You still not in love with me. But don't worry. You will be."

On that ominous note, I headed off to meet the Trotsky clan.

Vladimir had borrowed his cousin Boris's car for the occasion, a rusty hunk of junk that looked like it had spent its formative years in a demolition derby. At one time it may have been red; now it had oxidized into a crusty orange.

The passenger door squealed in protest as he pried it open.

I was just about to climb in when I heard an angry "Hey!"

I looked up to see Mrs. Hurlbut, my neighbor from across the street, standing in front of her prized tulip bed.

"I saw you take those tulips!" she shrieked at Vladimir, marching over to us.

"So sorry, lady!" Vladimir graced her with his goofy grin. "I could not resist.

"Beautiful flowers, for my beautiful flower," he said, gesturing to me.

"Beautiful flower, my fanny!" she humphed.

"For you," he said, handing her a half-eaten roll of Life-savers.

"I don't want any crummy Lifesavers," she said, taking them anyway.

"I'm so sorry, Mrs. Hurlbut," I said. "I'll be happy to pay for some more bulbs."

"Okay," she said, somewhat mollified. "I got 'em from a catalog in Holland. Cost me forty-nine bucks."

For crying out loud, I could buy them at Home Depot for $4.99.

"I'll write you a check in the morning."

"Don't forget the ten dollars I paid for shipping and handling," were her cheery words of farewell.

With a sigh, I got into the rustmobile.

The less said about the drive over to Aunt Minna's place, the better. I waited for Vladimir to offer to pay for the tulips, but I waited in vain. Instead I spent the entire ride listening to him yak about his goat, Svetlana, and enjoying the view through a gaping hole in the floorboards.

But at last we arrived at our destination.

Lucerne Terrace was a run-down apartment building in the Mid-Wilshire area, devoid of any interesting architectural features, including terraces. It had definitely seen better days, I thought, as we made our way up the cracked cement pathway to the front door.

Vladimir pressed a grimy button on the intercom and seconds later we were buzzed in.

We rode up to Minna's apartment on a rickety elevator festooned with graffiti, one of which Vladimir pointed out as his own handiwork.

"Look!" he said. "I wrote that!"

There among the colorful compendium of four-letter words was:

Vladimir & Jaine & Svetlana
4 Ever!

Just what I always wanted. A ménage à trois with a goat.

Our creaky chariot screeched to a halt on the third floor. As we walked down the threadbare hallway, I smelled something delicious. Beef stew, maybe. Or London broil. Unfortunately, it was not coming from Aunt Minna's apartment. No, when we reached Aunt Minna's, a strange smell wafted out into the hallway. A heady aroma of cabbage and Clorox.

"Aunt Minna!" Vladimir called out, knocking on the door. "We're here!"

Seconds later the door was answered by a short, squat woman with beady eyes and a most disconcerting mustache. She stood planted in the doorway, her arms crossed over her chest, an old-fashioned bib apron covering her printed housedress. Her feet were clad in sneakers with holes cut out for her bunions, and her coarse gray hair, I was fascinated to see, had been hacked into a cut last seen on Moe of The Three Stooges.

Never again, I vowed, would I complain about my own bad hair days.

"Aunt Minna," Vladimir gushed, "this is my beloved Jaine."

I wished he'd stop calling me that.

"So nice to meet you," I said, managing a smile.

Her beady eyes raked me over.

Clearly she did not share Vladimir's enthusiasm for yours truly.

Then suddenly she grabbed me by the chin.

"Open wide," she instructed.

Incredulous, I opened my mouth and stood there like a horse on an auction block as she inspected my teeth.

"They all yours?"

"Yes," I managed to say.

"Good." She grunted, satisfied.

Having passed tooth inspection, I followed her and Vladimir into the living room, where I couldn't help but notice an enormous portrait of Stalin hanging over a fake fireplace.

A dark-haired, mustachioed fellow about Vladimir's age sat on a rumpsprung tweed sofa, eyes glued to a soccer game on TV. Wedged into a nearby armchair was a refrigerator of a gal, somewhere in her thirties, hard at work cracking walnuts in her fists.

"The American tootsie is here," Aunt Minna announced before shuffling off to the kitchen.

"Jaine, my beloved," Vladimir said, ushering me into the room. "Say hello to my cousins Boris and Sofi."

Boris barely glanced up from the game to grace me with a curt nod.

Sofi, on the other hand, eyed me with great intensity. She had her aunt's coarse hair, but unlike Minna's "Moe" do, Sofi's was caught up in a tight prison matron bun.

Lucky for Sofi, she had not inherited the family mustache. Unlucky for her, she *had* inherited a most forbidding unibrow. Which was now furrowed at the sight of me.

Following in the proud Trotsky family tradition, she greeted me with a grunt, simultaneously crushing a walnut in her beefy paw.

"I go help Aunt Minna in the kitchen," Vladimir said. "You stay here, Jaine, and make friends with the cousins."

With that, he dashed off, leaving me stranded with Boris and Sofi.

I sat down gingerly on an armchair littered with walnut shells and plastered on a stiff smile.

Making friends with these two wasn't going to be easy.

My break-the-ice gambit ("So how do you like living in America?") was met with a deafening silence, which continued for the next ten agonizing minutes, broken only by the occasional crunch of a walnut in Sofi's fist. Not one of which she offered to share, by the way.

At last Vladimir came bouncing back into the room.

For once, I was actually thrilled to see the guy.

"Food is ready!" he announced.

Sofi pried herself from her armchair, sending a small shower of walnut shells onto the floor. Boris reluctantly abandoned his soccer game but turned up the volume so he could keep track of the score.

We trooped through an archway into a dining area, where a white lace tablecloth was set with dented silverware and a colorful collection of paper napkins filched from various local eating establishments. Mine was from Polly's House of Pies.

Dinner Chez Trotsky turned out to be an eclectic affair.

First course was a watery cabbage soup featuring an Uzbek version of tortellini called *chuchvara*. Now I'm sure nine out of ten Uzbek housewives make a dynamite chuchvara. Sad to say, Aunt Minna was Housewife Number Ten. Hers were white doughy blobs the consistency of ping-pong balls.

"So," Aunt Minna asked as I tried to hack off a piece of my ping-pong ball, "how much money you got?"

"I beg your pardon?"

"Money! If you going to marry Vladimir, you got to pay dowry."

Sofi looked up from her soup, scowling.

"Who says she's going to marry Vladimir?"

"She will," Vladimir assured her, "just as soon as she falls in love with me. Any day now."

"Vladimir," I protested, "I already told you. There's not going to be any wedding—"

"Not for at least a week," Vladimir said, ever the optimist.

"Maybe two. So enough questions, everybody. Let my beloved Jaine eat her delicious cabbage soup in peace."

"You got any cattles?" Aunt Minna asked, not willing to let this dowry thing go. "Cattles okay if you don't got money."

"Please," Vladimir begged. "Not now, Aunt Minna. We're eating."

Well, not all of us. By now, I had given up on my ping-pong balls, and Boris had temporarily abandoned the table for his soccer game.

Eventually, the soup dishes were cleared away, and Aunt Minna waddled in with the main course—Domino's pizza topped off with big white blobs of what turned out to be an Uzbek yogurt called *katyk*.

A note to the culinary adventurous: I don't care how adventurous you are, do not under any circumstances try pepperoni pizza and katyk. You will, I guarantee, live to regret it.

Somehow I managed to swallow a few mouthfuls, washed down by Aunt Minna's homemade pomegranate wine, a piquant little vintage with the distinctive kick of nail polish remover.

This trip to culinary hell seemed to go on forever, with Vladimir blathering sweet nothings in my ear, Sofi and Minna shooting me dirty looks, and Boris periodically jumping up to check the soccer score.

On the plus side, in between shooting me dirty looks, Aunt Minna and Sofi kept muttering about how "skinny" I was.

The last time I'd been called skinny was, well, never. So frankly it felt rather nice. And indeed, compared to Minna and Sofi, I was a bit of a waif.

I was hoping the meal might perk up with dessert. Perhaps a little something from Polly's House of Pies. A banana cream pie sure would go a long way to erase the memory of that yogurt pizza.

But alas, for dessert, Minna trotted out lukewarm tea and cookies the consistency of hockey pucks.

"You like?" she asked as I took my first nibble.

"Dee-lish," I replied, trying not to chip a molar.

At last, the ghastly dinner ground to a halt, and I asked if I could help with the dishes.

"No," Minna grunted. "You too clumsy." She glared at a tiny stain on the tablecloth near my wine glass. "You spill wine."

I certainly did not spill any wine. That spot, I can assure you, was there when I sat down, along with several other colorful specimens. But I was not about to argue with the woman. After all, she had just fed me dinner. True, it was a spectacularly awful dinner. But it was dinner nonetheless.

Instead, I put on my most gracious smile and said, "I'm so terribly sorry."

"Not to worry. I'll send you cleaning bill."

Oh, for crying out loud. First Mrs. Hurlbut's tulips. Now a dry-cleaning bill. This date was costing me a fortune.

My smile slightly less gracious, I told her to go ahead and send me the bill.

"Such a wonderful meal, Aunt Minna!" Vladimir said, patting his flat tummy. Amazingly, he'd packed away quite a lot of pizza. "I go take Jaine home now for huggy kissy."

In your dreams, buster.

He dashed off to get the car keys, while Minna retreated to the kitchen to do the dishes. Boris had long since returned to his soccer game, which left me alone with Sofi. Who now got up from the table and, without any preamble, grabbed me by the collar of my sweater.

"Hey, wait a minute," I protested. "Go easy on the sweater, willya? It's fifty-five percent cashmere."

But Sofi didn't care about my sweater's cashmere content. With unibrow furrowed most menacingly, she muttered,

"You stay away from Vladimir. Otherwise I break your kneecaps with my bare hands."

And I knew she could do it, too. I'd seen the way she'd pulverized those walnuts.

"No need to resort to violence, Sofi," I said, trying to wriggle free from her grasp. "I have no designs on your cousin whatsoever."

"I love my Vladdie with all my heart." Her squinchy eyes glowed with what I assumed was a reasonable facsimile of affection. "And no skinny American tootsie is going to steal him away!"

"Not a problem," I assured her. "He's all yours."

"Good," she said, at last letting me go.

As she stomped off to the living room, no doubt to resume her walnut-cracking duties, I stared after her, boggled. To think there was a woman on this planet who actually found Vladimir attractive.

You could've knocked me over with a chuchvara.

Dinner Chez Minna having limped to a close, I climbed into the rustmobile gratefully.

The sound of its asthmatic engine coughing to life was music to my ears. Before long, I told myself, this hellish evening would be over and I would be cuddled in bed with Prozac and a comforting pint of Chunky Monkey.

Or not.

We weren't halfway home when the rustmobile sputtered to a halt.

"Not to worry, my beloved Jaine," Vladimir assured me. "This happens all the time. I just have to make sweet talk to her."

"Sweet talk?"

"Nice car," he said, patting Old Rusty on the dashboard. "Pretty car. Such pretty color. Such strong engine. And horn like the angels play. You start for Vladimir. Okey doke?"

This nauseating chatter went on for several minutes. Frankly, I was surprised he didn't write the darn thing a poem.

But the rustmobile, much like yours truly, was immune to Vladimir's charms. No matter how much Vladimir whispered sweet nothings, the car refused to start.

With a sigh, I took out my cell phone and called Triple A.

"Who you calling?" Vladimir asked.

"Someone to start the car."

Vladimir's eyes narrowed suspiciously.

"You know this guy? You make huggy kissy with him?"

"No, Vladimir. I don't know him and I haven't made huggy kissy with him."

"You sure?"

"Of course I'm sure."

"Well, okay," he grunted, not quite convinced.

The good news is the Triple A guy showed up in no time. Which meant my Alone Time with Vladimir was kept to a minimum.

But that's where the good news ended.

The Triple A guy, a very sweet fellow named Xavier, tried to jump-start the car, but the rustmobile's battery was beyond resuscitation. As was the alternator. And, according to Xavier, just about every part under the hood.

The entire time Xavier was working, Vladimir was giving him the evil eye, convinced he was my secret paramour.

"This thing isn't even worth towing," Xavier said, putting his jumper cables away.

"You tow!" Vladimir commanded, arms clamped across his chest à la Aunt Minna. I bet he didn't even know what the word *tow* meant, but because the Triple A guy said he didn't want to do it, Vladimir wanted it done.

"Okay," Xavier said, "but first you gotta sign this release form."

Vladimir signed the form with a flourish.

And that's when things got really painful.

Shaking his head skeptically, Xavier tried to hoist the car to his tow truck. But the minute he did, the front fender gave way and the car came crashing to the ground, scattering car parts everywhere. I groaned in dismay as the side view mirror clattered to my feet.

"See, Jaine?" Vladimir gloated. "He's not so smart. Don't worry. Boris and I come back tomorrow and fix."

Oh, please. Anyone with half a brain could see that Old Rusty had gone to that great Junk Yard in the Sky. Which left us stranded in the middle of nowhere. How the heck were we supposed to get home?

"Do you think you could give us a ride?" I asked Xavier.

"I'm sorry," he said, with an apologetic shrug. "I'd like to help, but I've got an emergency call out in Pasadena." Off my stricken look, he added, "Maybe you can take a bus."

A bus? At that hour of the night? For those of you unfamiliar with our local transit system, after-hours buses in L.A. run approximately every other Tuesday.

With sinking heart, I watched Xavier get into his tow truck and drive off.

Oh, well. There was no way out of it. I was going to have to spring for a cab.

And that's when lady luck really gave me the finger.

When I took out my cell phone, I discovered that—much like the rustmobile—it was dead as a doornail.

Fortunately, though, it was a mere twenty-seven blocks from my duplex, so with nary a bus in sight, we trudged the rest of the way home on foot, Vladimir regaling me with a fascinating tale of the time Svetlana ate his neighbor's wristwatch and the whole town stopped by to hear her stomach tick.

Quite a raconteur, that Vladimir. The minutes flew by like weeks.

At last we staggered up the front path to my apartment. By

now it was almost midnight. After informing Vladimir that there would be no huggy kissy of any kind, I used my landline to phone for a cab to take him home.

"I don't suppose you have any money to pay the fare?" I asked when the cab showed up.

"Of course! Vladimir has plenty money!"

He whipped out a wad of cash as big as my fist. Unfortunately, it turned out to be Uzbek currency, worth in total about six bucks. This would never cover the cost of his trip.

Racking up yet another charge to this fun-filled night, I forked over my credit card and paid for his ride home in advance.

With a jaunty wave, Vladimir climbed into the cab and disappeared into the night.

And if I had anything to say about it, out of my life forever.

YOU'VE GOT MAIL!

To: Jausten
From: Shoptillyoudrop
Subject: Chef Hank

Hi, darling—

Well, I thought for sure Daddy would have lost interest in that darn Turbomaster by now. How wrong I was. He's plastered to the kitchen like wallpaper, morning, noon and night, tinkering with that infernal machine.

Somehow he's convinced himself he's a world-class chef. You're not going to believe this, but he actually went to the cooking supply store and bought himself a professional chef's jacket. With "Chef Hank" embroidered on the pocket!

That's right. He now refers to himself as Chef Hank. And calls me his "sous chef." (Which means I get to clean up his messes.)

He insists on doing all the cooking, and everything he makes is "à la Hank." *Pork Chops à la Hank. Chicken à la Hank.* The man nukes some Tater Tots, and it's *Tater Tots à la Hank.* And he's constantly using his ridiculous Turbomaster "Secret Spice," which I swear is nothing but paprika. I'm lucky he doesn't put it on our oatmeal.

When he's not making a mess in the kitchen, he's glued to the Food Network, shouting at the *real* chefs, telling them what they're doing wrong!

Last night he used up some of that five-pound bag of popcorn and made roast chicken with popcorn stuffing.

Have you ever heard of anything so silly? He calls it his *Popalicious Chicken à la Hank*.

And don't even ask what it all tastes like. Ninety percent of the stuff that comes out of that dratted Turbomaster tastes like leather. (The other 10 percent tastes like rubber.) Even Edna Lindstrom's dog Buster won't eat Daddy's food, and Buster once ate a Frisbee. Usually I wind up tossing my meal into my napkin when he's not looking.

It's a good thing I've got my secret stash of Oreos in the broom closet.

Love from your frazzled,

Mom

To: Jausten
From: DaddyO
Subject: Discovering My Inner Chef

Has Mom told you about my exciting new life as a chef? Yes, it's true. I've taken over cooking duties and am preparing all our meals. It's about time I gave your poor mom a break in the kitchen. And although she hasn't come right out and said so, I can tell she's very grateful. You should see the way she gobbles up my food. Her plate is clean at the end of every meal.

Just between you and me, lambchop, I have to confess that my cooking is a lot better than hers. Not that your mom isn't a wonderful cook. She's just not on my advanced level. I never realized I had such an aptitude for the culinary arts. I'll always be grateful to the Turbomaster 3000 for helping me discover my Inner Chef.

Well, I think I'll mosey over to the clubhouse and see what's doing. Haven't been there in a dog's age.

Love & hugs from,

Chef Hank

(aka Daddy)

To: Jausten
From: Shoptillyoudrop
Subject: Encouraging News

Daddy just left to go to the clubhouse. It's the first time he's been out of the house in days. Maybe it means his interest in cooking has peaked. I'm keeping my fingers crossed that this ridiculous craze may soon be over.

XOXO,

Mom

To: Jausten
From: DaddyO
Subject: A Shoo-In to Win!

What a lucky thing I decided to go the clubhouse! I was just about to invite some of the guys over for some *Cheese Doodles à la Hank* when I happened to glance at the bulletin board. Imagine my delight when I saw a notice announcing the annual Tampa Vistas Cookathon. Isn't that exciting, lambchop? A cooking contest, right here in Tampa Vistas!

I'm a shoo-in to win, of course. I've decided to enter with a fabulous new recipe I've invented: popcorn-stuffed roast chicken. I call it my *Popalicious Chicken à la Hank.* Clever, huh?

Well, gotta run and tell Mom the exciting news!

Bon appetit from,

Chef Hank

(aka Daddy)

Chapter 8

I spent the next several days working on mattress ideas. Marvin had been kind of vague about what he wanted, so I tried lots of different approaches:

All-Purpose: *Sleep Like a King, with Mattress King*
Corny: *If You Can Find a Cheaper Mattress Anywhere,*
I'll Eat My Crown
Risqué: *We're Good in Bed*
Comedy: *Take My Mattress—Please*
Derivative: *Got Mattress?*

And following in Vladimir's poetic footsteps, I even tried haiku:

In the pale moonlight
My backache throbs—I should've shopped
At Marvelous Marv's

Clearly, my ideas needed work. So I hunkered down and pounded out some more. Finally, when I'd come up with a few I actually liked, I called Marvin and set up a meeting.

The day of my appointment, Prozac clawed me awake for a gourmet breakfast of Savory Shrimp 'n' Tuna Tidbits.

Her breakfast, of course. I had nothing more enticing in my fridge than cold pizza and those darn martini olives.

Today of all days, I wanted a decent breakfast. So I decided to treat myself to one of my all-time gourmet faves: a sausage and egg McMuffin, smothered with ketchup.

My meeting wasn't until 1 P.M., so I'd have plenty of time to shower and dress and go over my ideas when I got back.

I drove over to McDonald's, my mind abuzz with mattress slogans and, not incidentally, my parents' latest e-mails from Florida. I'd been foolish enough to read them before I left the house. So Daddy fancied himself a chef, huh? Not that I was surprised. Daddy goes through personas like I go through drugstore pantyhose. To the best of my recollection he's been an amateur attorney, plumber, painter, and archaeologist. (He once found a piece of a Coke bottle in our backyard that to this day he insists is a relic from King Tut's tomb). Mom's just lucky he hasn't taken up do-it-yourself neurosurgery.

But all thoughts of Daddy's culinary adventures quickly faded as I drove up to the Golden Arches.

The first thing to greet me when I opened the door was the heavenly aroma of sizzling sausage. Not quite so heavenly, however, was the aroma of the eccentric homeless guy singing *O Sole Mio* at the top of his lungs.

Needless to say, I ordered my McMuffin to go.

Too hungry to wait till I got home, I opened my culinary treasure in the car.

Now I just want to say before I proceed any further that there is a special place in hell for the guy who invented the ketchup packet. (It couldn't have been a woman; we're just not that sadistic.)

I don't know about you, but I can never open the darn things without a battle royale. At home I usually wind up using a pair of scissors. Unfortunately, I had no scissors in the car, so I struggled mightily, breaking a nail in the process.

After a string of colorful curses not often heard outside an HBO special, I finally managed to rip it open.

And that's when tragedy struck.

Before my horrified eyes, the ketchup spurted out of the packet with the force of a rocket and landed on my passenger seat.

Now under ordinary circumstances this would not be a tragedy. My passenger seat has its fair share of stains, chocolate being the primary offender.

But astute readers will recall that the last time I'd been in my car, I had something beside me on my passenger's seat.

Extra credit for those of you who remember what it was.

That's right. Marvelous Marv's mattress sample—whose snowy white pillow top was now sporting a big red ketchup blob.

Frantically I tried to blot it with a napkin, turning it into an even bigger red blob.

But I couldn't let myself panic. After all, I had plenty of time before my meeting. I'd simply go home and wash the stain out.

Bagging my uneaten McMuffin, I tore back home and spent the next hour scrubbing that damn mattress sample. I tried Wisk, Comet, even Head & Shoulders shampoo.

When I was all finished, I'm pleased to report that the mattress sample was dandruff free, but unfortunately still sported a faint red stain.

"Oh, Pro!" I wailed. "What on earth am I going to do now?"

She looked up from where she was sunning herself on my windowsill.

You could scratch my belly. That's always fun.

This is why there's no such thing as a Seeing-Eye Cat. They just don't care.

I, on the other hand, was beside myself with worry. I

couldn't possibly bring the sample back to Marvin this way. How could he depend on me to take care of his advertising if I couldn't take care of a silly mattress sample?

No, I had to prove to Marvin that I was reliable and responsible.

And there was only way to do this:

I had to drive over to another Mattress King and steal a replacement.

Now don't get all righteous on me. Once I landed the job—or even if I didn't—I'd explain to Marvin what happened and reimburse him. But right now I couldn't afford to make a bad impression.

So I googled the address of the Santa Monica Mattress King, and minutes later I was heading down Santa Monica Boulevard in my Corolla, trying to figure out a way to pull off my heist. The sample was way too big to slip into my purse. I'd just have to wait until the salespeople were distracted with other customers and try to sneak out with it then.

Unfortunately, when I got there, the place was deserted. Not a customer in sight. The lone salesman, a dapper black guy whose name tag read *Carlton*, jumped up from his desk, thrilled to see me.

"Hi, there," he said, flashing me a dazzling smile. "How can I help you get a Sleeptacular night's rest?"

"Actually, I'm just looking," I said, spotting the store's mattress sample, tossed casually atop a bed not three feet away from me.

So near and yet so far.

For an instant I considered grabbing it and running. But a quick glance at Carlton's muscles rippling under his crisp white shirt told me how futile that would be. He'd take me down in no time.

Playing it casual, I started wandering around, feeling the

different mattresses, praying that Carlton would leave me alone.

But Carlton was on me like glue, extolling the virtues of the various Mattress King models: the Sweet Dreamer, the Heavenly Rest, and—in Carlton's words—"the Mercedes of mattresses," the Comfort Cloud.

"Sleeping on this baby," Carlton crooned, running a loving hand across its plush surface, "is like sleeping in paradise."

Unlike the lugubrious Lenny, Carlton was one heck of a salesman. If I'd actually been in the market for a mattress, he undoubtedly would have hypnotized me into springing for the Comfort Cloud. Along with a matching ergonomic pillow.

But, as we all know, I was not in the market for a mattress. All I cared about was that dratted sample.

I casually strolled over and picked it up.

"Wow, this is fascinating," I said. "You can see the springs and everything."

"More coils to the inch," Carlton said, still standing over me like a hawk. "That's what we give you here at Mattress King."

He flashed me another dazzler smile.

By now I could tell I was never going to get rid of this guy.

There was no way out of it. I'd simply have to try my heist at another branch.

"Thanks so much for your help," I sighed. "I'll think it over."

"You leaving? So soon?" His eyes widened in surprise. I got the feeling very few customers, especially those of the female persuasion, were able to resist his charms. "Don't you want to at least try one out?"

"Some other time," I demurred.

"Take my card," he said, thrusting his business card into my hand. "Come back and see me if you change your mind."

"Will do," I said with a feeble smile, then scurried out the door.

Back in my Corolla, I got out my cell phone and was just about to call Information for the address of the nearest Mattress King when I got an idea. One that just might work.

I fished out Carlton's business card and punched in his number.

"Mattress King," he answered. "Where every customer is king."

"Hi," I said, doing my best to disguise my voice, "I was in your store last week and saw a mattress I really liked. The Comfort Cloud."

"Oh, yes, the Mercedes of mattresses."

"Anyhow, I've decided to buy it, and I'm wondering if I can order it over the phone with my credit card."

"Of course you can," he said, his voice brimming with excitement. "What size did you want?"

"California King."

"Wonderful!" he gushed. I could practically hear him calculating his commission. "Have you got your credit card number?"

"Yes, here it is. It's a MasterCard 5466—oh, darn."

"What's wrong?"

"The doorbell's ringing. Hold on just a sec while I get it, okay?"

"Of course," he said. "Take your time."

I did not take my time. Au contraire. I put the phone down on the car seat and hightailed it back into the store.

Carlton looked up, surprised to see me.

"You're back," he said, covering the mouthpiece.

"Yes, I changed my mind."

"I'll be right with you; I'm just writing up a sale."

"No problem," I said, trotting over to the mattress sample.

Then, bold as brass, I picked it up and trotted back to the front door.

"Hey!" Carlton shouted, jumping up. "Where are you going? You can't take that with you!"

Wanna bet?

I was out of there in a flash.

For a brief second it looked like he was going to chase me, but in the end, he did what I thought he'd do. He stood there, holding on to the phone, unwilling to let the commission on a Comfort Cloud slip through his fingers.

Chapter 9

Back home, I barely had enough time to shower, dress, and scarf down my now ice-cold Sausage & Egg McMuffin. Then I grabbed my car keys and raced out the door, praying I wouldn't be late for my meeting with Marvin.

But I needn't have rushed.

"Marvin isn't here," his mousy receptionist informed me when I showed up at the store. "Mattress emergency at the main warehouse." Waving toward a row of no-frills plastic chairs, she said, "Have a seat. He should be back soon. And help yourself to a donut while you're waiting."

I looked over and once more saw a box of Krispy Kremes nestled next to the Mr. Coffee machine. Marvin may have had lousy taste in trophy wives, but he sure knew what he was doing when it came to office snacks.

I was still a bit peckish after my hurried McMuffin. But I wasn't about to stuff my face with empty calories. No siree. Not moi. Instead I took out my briefcase and began fine-tuning my slogans.

You'll be happy to know I kept this up for a whole thirteen seconds.

After which I tossed aside my slogans and made a beeline for the donut box. I was just about to reach for a chocolate-glazed beauty when Ellen Cooper came out from her office.

"Hi, there," Marvin's ex-wife said, flashing me a friendly

smile. What a difference from the last time I saw her, when she was shooting death ray looks at Bunny.

But now she had returned to her apple-cheeked, Norman Rockwell persona.

"You here to present your ideas to Marvin?" she asked, pouring herself some coffee.

"Yes." I tried not to sound as nervous as I felt. "I hope he likes them."

"I'm sure he will." Then a wary look crept in her eyes. "You're Bunny's friend, aren't you?"

"Oh, no," I assured her. I didn't have to be a rocket scientist to figure out that any friend of Bunny's was an enemy of hers. "I just met her recently. Through my neighbor, Lance Venable. Bunny's one of his most loyal customers at Neiman Marcus."

"This month she is," she said with a bitter laugh. "Bunny's fickle."

In more ways than one, I thought, remembering Bunny's recent tryst with Owen at Casa Extravaganza.

"Poor Marvin," she chirped merrily, as if reading my thoughts. "Sooner or later, Bunny's bound to break his heart." Then she added with a wink, "And it couldn't happen to a more deserving fellow! Well, good luck with your ideas, sweetheart."

Then she trotted back to her office, no doubt to stick pins in her Marvin and Bunny voodoo dolls.

Alone at last with the Krispy Kremes, I plucked my chocolate-glazed beauty from the box. Then I took a seat opposite the receptionist, whose name, according to the nameplate on her desk, was Amy Flannagan. She sat hunched over her computer, her bony fingers tapping away at her keyboard. How she could work so close to all those donuts without grabbing one was a mystery to me.

A mystery I pondered as I gulped mine down in record

speed. The last thing I wanted was for Marvin to come back and find me sitting there with a mouthful of Krispy Kreme.

But as it turned out, Marvin didn't show up for another three hours. By the time he finally puffed in at around 4 P.M., I'd scarfed down two more donuts, checked my phone messages sixteen times, and read the latest issue of *Mattress Digest* from cover to cover.

"I'm so sorry I'm late, Jaine!" Marvin cried, catching sight of me.

"Oh, that's okay," I lied.

"Some idiot in the main warehouse set off the sprinkler system and I had to make sure all the mattresses were okay."

"I totally understand," I said, hoping I didn't have donut crumbs in the corners of my mouth.

"Come on in," he said, waving me into his office.

I trotted after him and took a seat in the froufrou antique chair across from his desk.

"So!" Marvin beamed. "Ready to pitch your ideas?"

"Absolutely!" I faked a confident smile. "But before I begin, I want to return this to you."

With great pride, I handed him my purloined mattress sample.

"Oh, you didn't have to return it," he said, tossing it aside. "We're getting a new shipment any day now."

For crying out loud. Can you beat that? I'd just run myself ragged for nothing!

"Okay," he said, getting down to business. "Whaddaya got?"

With sweaty palms, I reached for my slogans and was just about to begin my pitch when his intercom buzzed.

"Yes, Amy?" Marvin said, speaking into the box.

"Your wife is on line one, Mr. Cooper."

"Sorry, Jaine." He shrugged apologetically. "This won't take very long."

Oh, yes, it did.

I sat squirming in that damn excuse for a chair, my palms getting sweatier by the minute, as Marvin held the receiver to his ear, nodding his head, and periodically murmuring, "Yes, dear."

In the background, I could hear Bunny barking orders to him.

At last, he managed to hang up.

"I'm so sorry, Jaine, but Bunny needs me at the house. She's throwing a party tonight, and she wants me home early."

"That's okay," I said, forcing a smile. "I'll come back another time."

"I know! Why don't you stop by the party tonight, and you can pitch your ideas to me then?"

"Are you sure Bunny won't mind?" I asked, not exactly relishing the thought of running into her again.

"Of course Bunny won't mind," he assured me. "At our house, the door is always open."

If he only knew *how* open.

"So is it a date?" he asked.

"It's a date," I said, girding my loins for a fun-filled evening with Her Royal Bitchiness.

I stopped off at Lance's place on my way back to my apartment to see if he was going to Bunny's bash.

Indeed he was.

"How did you find out about it?" he asked, as his tiny fluffball of a dog, Mamie, covered my ankles with slobbery kisses.

Mamie, unlike a certain pampered feline I know, is one of the most affectionate pets on the planet. I knelt down to give her a love scratch.

"You are the cutest-wootest wittle thing in all the world."

"I know I am," Lance said, "but how did you find out about the party?"

"Marvin invited me."

"That's odd. Usually Bunny's the one who hands out the invites."

Then I told him about my endless afternoon at Mattress King.

"You went to pitch slogans looking like that?" he asked, eyeing my outfit with no small degree of disapproval.

"What on earth is wrong with what I'm wearing? This happens to be an Eileen Fisher blouse."

"Did you know your Eileen Fisher blouse happens to have a blob of chocolate on it?"

I looked down and saw the aforementioned chocolate blob.

Damn those Krispy Kremes.

"Honestly, Jaine. For your next birthday, I'm buying you a bib."

"And for your next birthday," I said, in my frostiest tone of voice, "I'm buying you absolutely nothing."

"Oh, don't get all pissy," he said, putting his arm around me. "I only nag you because I love you. And I'm thrilled you're coming to the party. We can hang out together and count facelifts."

"All right," I sniffed, somewhat mollified.

"By the way," he said as I started to go. "Some goofy-looking guy stopped by your apartment today. I heard him knocking on your door and calling out, 'Jaine, my beloved!' "

Oh, groan. Not Vladimir.

With a sigh, I trudged back to my apartment, only to find a bouquet of wilted flowers lying on my front steps. At least these hadn't been filched from Mrs. Hurlbut's yard. I could see the *Reduced for Clearance* price sticker on the cellophane wrapping.

When I picked them up, I noticed an envelope underneath. Inside was a poem from Vladimir:

TO MY BELOVED JAINE

I think you are a girl most fab
Here's fifty bucks to pay for cab

Sure enough, along with the poem, I found five ten-dollar bills to cover the cost of last night's cab fare.

In spite of myself, I was touched by the gesture.

Chapter 10

"Lance! Sweetie!"

Bunny stood at the front door of Casa Extravaganza, in another boob-and-fanny-baring outfit.

"How wonderful to see you, hon!" she called out as he headed up the front path. "Now the party can officially begin."

Then she caught sight of me trailing behind him.

"What the hell are you doing here?"

Okay, so what she really said was, "I didn't know you were coming, Jaine."

"Marvin invited me."

"Did he? How nice."

That was spoken with all the enthusiasm of a hostess discovering a cockroach in her centerpiece. After which she turned her spray-tanned back to me and directed all her charms on Lance.

"It's going to be such a wonderful party!" she gushed, leading him inside. "All the best people are here. I'm serving dirty martinis, and I've even hired a fortune-teller! I've got her reading palms in the den. What a hoot, huh? C'mon, honey. I'll introduce you to everyone."

With that, she linked her arm through his and whisked him away, leaving me alone on the doorstep.

Lance shot me an apologetic look and shrugged helplessly, trapped in her vise-like grip.

I followed them into Casa Extravaganza's cavernous living room and saw about a dozen of "the best people" milling around. The gals were anatomically correct Barbies, complete with surgically tightened faces, man-made boobs, and clothes so trendy they practically had expiration dates. Most of the men affected the Hip Hollywood Producer look: jeans and a T-shirt topped off with a blazer. Ponytail optional. Which works well for hip Hollywood producers, not so well for guys with paunches and hair plugs.

If these were the best people, somebody better alert the gang at Newport.

Joining in the festivities were Sarah and Owen, both fashion rebels in their L.L.Bean togs, Sarah scowling into her drink, and Owen still sporting his Mattress King baseball cap. I was beginning to wonder if it was welded to his scalp.

Much to my surprise I also spotted Ellen Cooper, chatting with a handsome, silver-haired guy near the patio.

And over by a fireplace big enough to park my Corolla in, Marvin was deep in conversation with one of the T-Shirt & Blazer guys. I would've liked nothing more than to pitch my ideas to him and make a quick escape, but I felt funny about interrupting his conversation. Instead I just stood in the midst of the chattering guests, the party's designated wallflower.

So much for me and Lance hanging out together and counting facelifts. By now he was cozily ensconced on a sofa, sandwiched between Bunny and Fiona, no doubt engaged in heavy-duty fashion chat.

And then I saw a sight that warmed my heart—Lupe circulating with a tray of hors d'oeuvres.

"Hey, Lupe!" I cried, weaving my way to her side. "How's it going?"

"Fine, Ms. Jaine," she replied, with a timid smile.

My eyes zeroed in on her tray and saw one lone rumaki, a plump bacon-wrapped beauty with my name on it.

Or so I thought.

Just as I was about to reach for it, one of the Barbies popped up out of nowhere and grabbed it. I told myself not to be bitter. It was probably her caloric intake for the week.

"I'll be right back with some more," Lupe said, scooting off.

Counting the minutes till her return, I made my way over to a bar on the far side of the room. I longed for the company of my friend Mr. Chardonnay, but I simply could not afford to get tootled before a presentation.

"I'll have a ginger ale," I said to the stunning actor manning the bar.

"I'm sorry, but all I'm serving are dirty martinis."

And indeed, the only bottles of booze on the makeshift bar were gin and vermouth.

"Don't you have anything else?"

"Afraid not."

"Haven't you heard, Jaine?" I turned to see Sarah at my side, waving a martini glass. "Dirty martinis are Bunny's favorite drink. This week, anyway. And whatever Bunny wants, *everybody* wants.

"So if you don't like dirty martinis," she said, polishing hers off with impressive speed, "you're out of luck. Although, actually, they're pretty good."

With that, she signaled the bartender for a refill.

"It's good to see you again, Sarah," I said, making a feeble stab at conversation.

"Wish I could say the same. Nothing personal, of course. It's just that these parties are so damn awful."

She glared at Bunny, who was now busy raking Lupe over the coals.

"I can't drink this!" Bunny screeched, holding out her martini in disgust. "It's not in my Marilyn Monroe glass!"

Lupe whipped the offending glass away.

"Go get me another one, in the right glass this time."

"Yes, Ms. Bunny."

"And don't forget the olive."

Next to me, Sarah made a gagging noise.

"The hostess with the mostest," she sneered. "She has to invite fifty people to her parties to get twenty to show up. The only reason I make an appearance at these things is because Owen insists."

Her gaze shifted to Owen, who had now taken Mr. T-Shirt & Blazer's place at the fireplace with Marvin.

"Sometimes I wish he'd never started working for my father. We were a lot happier when he was teaching."

"Owen used to be a teacher?" I blinked in surprise.

"Yes, he taught high school physics when I first met him. Now all he wants to do is talk mattresses and hang out with Dad."

Marvin wasn't the only in-law he wanted to hang out with, but I wasn't about to give her that newsflash.

"Does your mother always show up at these things, too?" I asked, eyeing Ellen as she chatted with her silver-haired companion.

"Yep. Bunny invites Mom so she can gloat about the divorce. And Mom shows up so she can gloat about her hunky new boyfriend."

He was a looker, all right. The kind of foxy AARPster you see drinking mai tais at sunset on cruise ship commercials. I couldn't help wondering what an uber-handsome guy like him was doing with the frankly frumpy Ellen. Something told me the answer involved her bank account.

"Meet the Coopers," Sarah sighed. "Just one big, happy, dysfunctional family."

She grabbed a fresh martini from the bartender and took a deep swig.

"Well, nice talking to you, Jaine. You should go to the den and try Bunny's fortune-teller."

"Is she any good?"

"Not really, but at least you get to leave the party for a while."

As she shuffled away on unsteady feet, I couldn't help but feel sorry for her. Maybe there was some truth, after all, in that old ditty about money not buying happiness.

But all clichéd musings flew from my brain at the sight of Lupe returning with a fresh tray of hors d'oeuvres.

I was at her side like a shot, thrilled to see a small army of succulent baby lamb chops lined up on her tray.

To hell with manners. I grabbed two.

"There's going to be a buffet dinner later," Lupe whispered. "They're setting it up in the dining room now."

Indeed, the tantalizing aroma of what I hoped was roast beef wafted my way. Maybe I could grab a bite after my pitch.

Which, at the rate things were going, wasn't about to take place any time soon. Marvin, alas, was still entrenched in conversation with Owen, who was busy making notes on a cocktail napkin. Lord knows how long they'd be at it.

With a sigh, I headed back to the bar and ordered a dirty martini. After all, I needed something to wash down my lamb chops. I promised myself I'd have only a few sips, just enough to deaden the awkwardness of this ghastly party.

Drink and lamb chops in hand, I wandered out the French doors onto the patio, where I heard one of the T-Shirt & Blazers saying, *God, I'd kill for a scotch.*

I took a seat on one of the patio chairs and scarfed down my three lamb chops. (Okay, so I took three.) My, they were good. By far, the highlight of the evening. After polishing them off, I sat there, staring out into the night, hoping to pass myself off as a soulful thinker rather than the social pariah I actually was.

The patio was bathed in moonlight, and in the distance the

pool glistened, bright as a Home Shopping zirconia. Breathing deeply, I could smell the heady aroma of night- blooming jasmine.

The only jarring note in this picture postcard scenario was a rusty rake and a container of weed killer propped up against the patio's stone balustrade. It looked like the gardener was still forgetting to put his supplies away. I only hoped Bunny wouldn't notice it, or there'd be hell to pay.

After a while, tired of my soulful thinker act, I went back inside, only to find Owen still glued to Marvin's side. Didn't those two ever get enough of each other?

Once more, I sought solace from Lupe, who was now passing out melted Brie in pastry puffs. I plucked one and took a bite. Divine.

Happily munching on my Brie ball, I decided to take Sarah's advice and pay a visit to the fortune-teller.

I found her ensconced behind a desk in the den, a striking brunette clad in a gypsy outfit straight out of a 1940s MGM musical: off-the-shoulder blouse, peasant skirt, and lace-up espadrilles—topped off with dangly hoop earrings and a colorful bandana headband.

"Come in," she said with an accent meant to be Exotic European, but sounding more like Count Chocula. "I am the fabulous Fortuna. I see all. I tell all."

I sat down across from her at what must have been Bunny's desk, an ornate little number painted with tiny pink rosebuds.

Up close I could see a sprinkling of distinctly non-gypsy freckles underneath the fabulous Fortuna's heavy make-up. If this woman was born in a Slavic nation, I was a full-blooded Cherokee.

"Let me see your palm," she commanded in her hammy accent.

Surreptitiously wiping the last remnants of Brie from my hand, I showed her my palm.

"You have a very interesting lifeline," Fortuna said, running her finger along a scar I've had since I was twelve.

"Actually, that's a scar."

"Really?" she said, flustered.

"I cut my hand trying to open a can of macadamia nuts."

"Gee, it looks just like a lifeline. Oh, here. Now I found it." She pointed to another spot on my palm. "It says you will live a long and healthy life."

Not if I kept eating those Brie balls, I wouldn't.

"Wait!" she suddenly cried, pressing her hands to her forehead. "I hear a noise coming from the spirit world."

"I hear it, too. I think it's just someone trying to get into the guest bathroom."

"No, no. It's a message for you. From someone dearly beloved who's gone to the other side. Someone whose name begins with a *B*. Do you have a departed loved one whose name begins with *B*?"

I ran through my list of deceased relatives, which was fortunately quite short, but the initial *B* did not make an appearance.

"Nope, afraid not."

"How about *G*?"

"No."

"*C*?"

"Gee, all I can think of is my grandma's dog Chester and we really weren't that close."

"How about *Z*?"

"Sorry," I shrugged. "I guess whoever's calling from the other side must have a wrong number."

And then she threw in the towel.

"Oh, what's the use?" she sighed, all traces of her accent gone. "I stink at this."

"You're not so bad. Maybe Chester really is trying to talk to me."

"No, he's not. It's all a big act. I'm not really a fortune-teller. I'm an actress."

And apparently, not a very good one.

"Everything I know about palm reading I learned from this stupid book," she said, taking a copy of *Palmistry for Dummies* out from where she'd stashed it in Bunny's desk drawer.

"See?" She pointed to a dog-eared page. "The book says right here that practically everyone knows someone dead whose name starts with a *B*.

"Dammit." She slammed the book shut in disgust. "I oughta get my money back."

"Hey, don't worry about it. Nobody takes these things seriously."

"Look, don't tell Mrs. Cooper how I've been screwing up, willya? If I know that bitch, she'll have me fired."

At last. An accurate prediction.

"I won't say a thing to Mrs. Cooper," I assured her, getting up to go.

"Thanks." She shot me a grateful smile. "I may stink at this stuff, but I hope good things are headed your way."

Not that night, they weren't. That's for darn sure.

Chapter 11

Back in the living room, I groaned to see Marvin and Owen still going at it hot and heavy. But by now I'd run out of patience. Enough was enough. I marched over to the fireplace, gathering my courage to interrupt them.

And I was just about to break up their little duo when Bunny beat me to it.

"What the hell is *he* doing here?" she hissed at Marvin.

She pointed to the doorway, where Lenny, the sad-eyed salesman, had just wandered in.

"It's no big deal," Marvin said, with a placating smile. "I asked him to stop by."

"No big deal?" Bunny fumed. "First that Austen creature. And now Lenny. What do you think this is? *My Life on the D List?*"

"Lenny happens to be my best friend," Marvin said, allowing a hint of irritation to creep into his voice.

"Not anymore, he's not," Bunny snapped. "Not if I have anything to do with it."

And with that she sashayed back to Lance.

"C'mon, sweetie," she said, grabbing her Marilyn Monroe glass and taking a healthy slug. "Let's get some fresh air."

Marvin watched unhappily as, martini in hand, Bunny steered Lance out onto the patio.

And I took advantage of the lull in the conversation to make my move.

"Excuse me, Mr. Cooper."

"Oh, Jaine," he said, turning to see me for the first time. "How long have you been standing here?"

Clearly he was worried I'd heard Bunny call me "that Austen creature."

"Not long at all," I lied. "I thought maybe I could pitch my slogans to you."

"Of course, of course. I'll be with you in a minute. Owen and I are just wrapping things up."

Forcing a smile, I left them alone and resumed my role as the Party Pariah. I spent the next twenty minutes standing around, inhaling hors d'oeuvres, ignored by one and all.

Finally Fiona took pity on me and came over to talk.

"Jaine," she cooed. "How lovely to see you!"

Quite the dramatic figure she was, just a scarf away from Isadora Duncan in wide palazzo pants and a flowy silk tunic.

"Don't mind Bunny," she said, with a sympathetic smile. "She's an equal opportunity insulter. She says the most atrocious things about everyone."

Great. How nice to know that the entire party heard her refer to me as "that Austen creature."

"By the way," she added, "adore your outfit. Old Navy puts out such clever fashions."

If I wasn't mistaken, that was a bit of a dig. But at this point, thanks to my dirty martini, I didn't much care. Yes, somewhere along the line, I'd lost track of my sips and polished off the whole darn drink.

It was with dismay that I now looked down into my martini glass and discovered that, aside from an olive skewer, it was totally empty. How could I have been stupid enough to get tootled right before a presentation?

And there was no doubt about it. I was a bit tootled. I realized this when I found myself giggling at Fiona's Old Navy crack.

I excused myself and hurried off to the guest bathroom to splash some cold water on my face. A charming little sanctuary straight out of a Beatrix Potter tale, the room was done up in a bunny theme, with faucets and guest soaps shaped like the furry critters.

Wasting no time, I started splashing. The cold water was bracing, and after a while, I felt the fuzz in my brain begin to dissipate.

Then I patted my face dry with one of Bunny's fine Irish linen guest towels, embroidered with yet more bunnies.

(Where was Elmer Fudd when you needed him?)

While I was there I figured I might as well do a final prep for my presentation, so I whipped out my slogans from my purse and went over them one last time.

With confidence fully restored, I checked out my reflection in the mirror and slapped on some lipstick.

And then I did something I would sorely live to regret. I snooped in the medicine cabinet. Yes, I confess. I am a confirmed medicine cabinet snooper. I've tried to quit many times, but the lure is always too great to resist.

Not that I expected to find anything juicy in the guest bathroom. I mean, all the serious stuff, like the Grecian Formula and Preparation H, would be upstairs in the master bath. But a snoop can dream, can't she?

All I found was a bottle of aspirin, a box of Q-tips, and a jar of hand cream. Nothing you'd read about in the *Enquirer*. The hand cream, however, wasn't your everyday Jergens. It was the zillion-dollar-an-ounce kind of stuff you see in the glossy pages of *Vogue*.

I opened it and took a sniff. Mmmm. Heavenly.

Now, if Bunny had wanted guests to use it, she would have put it out on her travertine marble counter along with her bunny guest soaps. This was obviously primo, Grade A hand cream, reserved for Her Royal Bitchiness.

Which meant, of course, that I had to try it. Still smarting over her earlier insults, I slathered it on with abandon.

And that was my second big mistake.

Lord knows what mysterious stuff that hand cream was made of. Probably the embryo of some hapless endangered species. Whatever it was, it was darn slippery. When I started to put it back in the medicine cabinet, my hands were so slick, the bottle slipped from my grasp and crashed onto the tile floor.

Oh, hell. I stared in dismay at the goo at my feet.

I searched under the sink for something to clean it up with. But there was nothing. The only thing at my disposal were the bunny guest towels. I couldn't possibly use those. So minutes later I was on my hands and knees scraping the stuff up with toilet paper.

Unwilling to leave behind any incriminating evidence, I dumped it all into my purse. Somehow I managed to cram the whole mess in. At last I finished, and, wiping the sweat from my brow, I unlocked the door and headed out into the hallway.

I hadn't gone very far when I realized I'd forgotten my slogans. I hurried back to the bathroom, and sure enough, they were right where I left them on the counter. So I dashed over to get them.

And that's when my luck went from bad to unthinkably bad.

As much as I'd tried to clean up the goo, I had apparently not gotten it all. The floor still had a few slick spots. One of which I proceeded to step in. *Oh, no!* Suddenly I felt myself about to take a tumble.

Frantically I grabbed the towel rack for support and gasped in horror as it came flying out of the wall.

Then, like a scene from my own personal disaster movie, I watched as the towel rack slammed into the medicine cabinet mirror with a godawful crash, and then—my seven years of bad luck off to a booming start—whacked one of the bunny faucets loose.

Glass scattered everywhere. And worse, infinitely worse, water gushed wildly from the space where the faucet used to be.

Quel nightmare!

I grabbed one of the bunny guest towels and desperately tried to staunch the flow of gushing water.

So busy was I that I did not hear the sound of approaching footsteps thundering down the hallway.

Suddenly the door burst open.

"What the hell is going on here?"

I looked up to see Bunny standing in the doorway, the other guests huddled behind her, taking in the show.

"Hey!" one of them shouted. "That's the woman who stole my mattress sample!"

Oh, crud. It was Carlton!

"Look, I can explain about that—"

"Who cares about a goddamn mattress sample," Bunny shrieked, "when my bathroom is flooded?"

"You!" She snapped her fingers at the actor/bartender, who'd abandoned his post to catch the action. "Shut off the water valve under the sink."

The water valve under the sink! Why hadn't I thought of that?

"And when you're finished, get a mop from the kitchen and clean up the mess."

"I'll help," I offered, hating to see the poor guy saddled with something I was responsible for.

"Don't you dare touch a thing!" Bunny screeched. "I want to save what little of my bathroom I have left."

With that, she stormed out to the living room, trailed by her wide-eyed guests, all eager to catch the next act of this exciting drama.

"Jaine, honey, are you okay?"

I turned to see Lance by my side.

"Oh, Lance," I wailed, as he put a comforting arm around my shoulder. "It was so awful. All I did was rub on a little hand cream and the next thing I knew the bathroom was in shambles."

A pathetic little tear, I'm ashamed to admit, made its way down my cheek.

Now Lance may give me a rough time when it comes to my fashion choices, but when it comes to being a friend, he's always there for me. Well, almost always. Okay, a lot of times, anyway. And this was one of those times.

"C'mon," he said. "Let's go home. I've had enough of Bunny and her stupid party. The more I see of that woman, the less I like her."

"Okay, but I'd better apologize first. After all, I did just destroy her bathroom."

I found Bunny in the living room, surrounded by a bevy of Barbies, tsk-tsking in sympathy.

"I know just what you're going through," one of them was commiserating. "Why, just the other day the speakers in our media room blew out. It was devastating, simply devastating."

Not surprisingly, this touching anecdote failed to comfort Bunny in her time of need.

"I need a drink," she announced. "Lupe! Get me my martini from the patio!"

Lupe, who'd been hovering at the edge of the crowd, jumped to attention and skittered out to the patio.

My cue to face the dragon lady. I took a deep breath and walked up to her.

"Are you still here?" she snapped.

I swear, if she'd had a flyswatter, she would've used it on me.

"I just want to tell you how very sorry I am, Bunny, and let you know I'll be happy to reimburse you for whatever damage I caused."

"Hah!" she snorted. "You couldn't afford to reimburse me for a guest towel."

She was right about that.

"There's no need to reimburse us, Jaine," Marvin piped up. "It was an accident; it could've happened to anyone."

"An accident?" Bunny shrieked. "Are you kidding? The woman is a walking catastrophe!"

"No," a bitter voice called from over by the fireplace. "You're the catastrophe, Bunny."

All eyes riveted to Sarah, who now came weaving over to Bunny, drink in hand.

Ellen looked over at her daughter in alarm.

"Sweetheart," she said, taking Sarah gently by the elbow, "I think maybe you've had a bit too much to drink."

"Of course I have, Mom. How else do you think I can stand to be in the same room with her?"

Then, brushing her mother aside, she resumed her critique of Bunny.

"You're a vain, venal, vicious bitch," she hissed. "And those are your *good* qualities. My god, Bunny, you make Lucrezia Borgia look like Mother Teresa."

Next to me, I heard one of the Barbies whisper, "Who's Lucrezia Borgia?"

"I'm not sure," her pal replied. "I think she's on *Desperate Housewives*."

Bunny, meanwhile, unused to having her character traits so accurately summed up, was fuming.

"Go to hell, Sarah!"

"After one of your parties, that can only be an improvement."

"Lupe!" Bunny screeched, now flushed with rage. "Where's my goddamn martini?"

At last Lupe came racing in from the patio with Bunny's prized Marilyn Monroe glass.

"It's about time," Bunny said, polishing off the drink in a single gulp. "What took you so long?"

But Lupe never got a chance to reply, because it was around about then that Bunny began keeling over in pain.

"Omigod!" Ellen cried. "She's having a heart attack! Somebody call 911!"

"It's not a heart attack," one of the Barbies called out. "It's food poisoning. Those Brie balls tasted funny to me."

"Me, too," seconded another. "It's a good thing I threw mine up."

"This can't be happening," Fiona gasped. "Not to Bunny."

I, too, blinked in disbelief as the seemingly indestructible Bunny crumpled to her knees.

"It's not my fault!" Lupe wailed.

"Bunny, darling," Marvin cried, kneeling at her side. "What's wrong?"

What was wrong, as it turned out, was the fatal dose of weed killer someone had slipped in Bunny's martini.

But we didn't know that then.

All we knew then was that she'd stopped breathing.

By the time the ambulance showed up, she was dead as last year's fashions.

Chapter 12

The media called it The Dirty Martini Murder.

Traces of cyanide had been found in both Bunny's stomach and her martini glass. The same kind of cyanide commonly found in weed killer.

Bunny's drink was fine before she left for the patio with Lance. I'd seen her drink from it. So the way I figured it, whoever did it must've slipped the poison in Bunny's martini while everyone was huddled around the guest bathroom gawking at me in The Great Guest Bathroom Fiasco.

It would have been easy enough to do. The weed killer was right there on the patio where the gardener had left it. Ready for the taking. And after that scene Bunny made with Lupe over her Marilyn Monroe glass, everyone at the party knew exactly which glass she'd been drinking from. How ironic. If only she hadn't been so insistent on drinking out of that damn glass, she might never have been killed. Not that night, anyway.

Naturally, I was overwhelmed with grief. Not over Bunny's death. I was sorry she was dead, of course, but it was hard to work up any real tears over such a dreadful woman.

No, the death I was mourning was the Mattress King account. Marvin would never hire me now, not after the havoc I'd wreaked in his guest bathroom.

It was back to toilet bowl ads for moi.

I was sitting on my sofa a few days later, eating peanut butter—one of nature's most comforting comfort foods—straight from the jar. Prozac was sprawled out beside me, staring fixedly at her genitals, enjoying a brief siesta between naps.

"Oh, Pro," I sighed. "It would've been so nice to get that account."

Tearing her gaze away from her privates, she looked up at me with big green eyes that seemed to say:

Can I try some of that peanut butter?

This tender moment was interrupted by a loud pounding at my front door.

I got up to answer it and found Lance, breathless with excitement.

"Big news!"

"What?"

But he was not about to tell me.

"What are you eating?" he asked, catching sight of my Skippy jar.

Uh-oh. I felt a lecture coming on.

"Peanut butter. Extra chunky."

"For breakfast?" A tsk of disapproval.

"Yes. I was all out of cold pizza."

"Very amusing. But don't come whining to me when you can't fit into anything except elastic-waist pants."

What did I tell you? A lecture.

"Lance, I happen to like my elastic-waist pants. You're the only one who whines about them. Now are we are going to stand around discussing my eating habits, or are you going to tell me your news?"

"Oh, right," he said, plopping down on my sofa. "I just heard it on the radio. The cops have someone they want to bring in for questioning in Bunny's murder."

"Who?"

"They didn't say. But my money's on Lupe. She probably did it when she went to get Bunny her drink."

My heart sank at the thought of poor little Lupe being hauled off to jail.

"I don't know, Lance. I just can't picture Lupe as a killer. The woman is afraid of her own shadow."

"Okay, then. What about Sarah? She detested Bunny. Remember that scene she made at the party? Frankly, I'm surprised she didn't strangle her right then and there."

It turned out it was neither Lupe nor Sarah. As we were about to discover not three seconds later when there was another knock on my door.

I opened it to find two guys in shiny suits standing on my doorstep.

"May I help you?" I smiled.

"Yes, ma'am," replied one of them, a hulking bear of a guy, his gut just a millimeter away from popping a suit button.

He whipped out a badge from his wallet and introduced himself.

"Detective Perlmutter, L.A.P.D."

Omigod! *I* was the one they were bringing in for questioning!

I was speechless. Part of it was the peanut butter stuck to the roof of my mouth, but most of it was sheer terror. The cops must've heard how I'd wrecked Bunny's bathroom. Maybe they thought that I'd done it on purpose, that I was her enemy, out to annihilate not only her bathroom fixtures, but Bunny herself!

"I swear I didn't do it!" I wailed, regaining my powers of speech. "I couldn't have! I was in the bathroom the entire time Bunny's drink was out on the patio! You can't possibly suspect *me*."

"Don't worry, Jaine." Lance hurried to my side. "I'll get

you the best attorney money can buy. I know a real bar-racuda, the guy who sued my chiropractor. We'll take this thing all the way to the Supreme Court, if need be."

"I'd hold that call to the Supreme Court if I were you," Detective Perlmutter advised. "We're not accusing you of anything, ma'am. Who are you, anyway?"

"You don't know?" I blinked, puzzled.

"I think her name is Jaine Austen, Frank."

Perlmutter's partner, an only marginally thinner version of Perlmutter, checked a list of names on a clipboard.

"She's on the guest list. The one who broke the bathroom sink."

"I did not break the sink! I broke the faucet. And the mir-ror. And a jar of hand cream. But that's all. And I swear, I didn't kill anyone!"

"Okay, okay. Calm down. We're looking for your neigh-bor. Lance Venable."

Next to me, Lance gasped.

"We just rang his bell, but he's not in. He hasn't left town, has he?"

I shook my head.

"Do you have any idea where he is?"

"I'm Lance Venable," Lance squeaked.

"We have a few questions we'd like to ask you."

"No problem, fellas," Lance said, pasting on a phony smile. "But right now I'm late for my Pilates class. Can we do this another time? Say next week? Why don't you give me your card and I'll give you a buzz."

"I'm afraid that's not possible, sir."

The two detectives stood shoulder to shoulder, like twin rottweilers, blocking any possible escape.

"We need you to come with us to headquarters now."

I stood there, speechless, as they carted him away.

* * *

Needless to say, I was beyond stunned. Why on earth were the cops interested in Lance? He had zero motive to kill Bunny. After all, she'd been one of his most valued customers at Neiman's.

I got my answer when he staggered back to my apartment later that morning.

"You're not going to believe this," he said, slouching in my armchair, his normally tight blond curls wilted under the morning's stress. "Bunny left me her Maserati in her will. Apparently it's worth a hundred and seventy-five thousand dollars."

Let's all pause for a moment of righteous indignation, shall we, at the thought of anyone spending a hundred and seventy-five thousand dollars on a car when certain people were starving in Africa and certain other people's orange walls needed desperately to be painted.

"The cops think I killed her to get my hands on the car."

"But you didn't even know she'd left it to you."

"That's what I told them," he sighed. "But I don't think they believed me."

"Surely she left money to other people in her will."

"Not really. She had no money of her own. It was all in Marvin's name. All she owned of value was that car. And I got it."

He slouched down farther in the chair.

"And it just gets worse. Apparently someone at the party saw me stay out on the patio after Bunny came inside."

I gulped in dismay.

"You were alone out on the balcony with her drink?"

"I needed some peace and quiet. A little bit of Bunny goes a long way. I only stayed outside a minute or two. And I swear, I didn't touch that drink."

"Of course you didn't."

"Oh, Jaine," he moaned, raking his fingers through his

hair. "They're going to arrest me. I can just feel it. I don't want to go to jail for a crime I didn't commit!

"I know!" he exclaimed, jumping up. "I'll grab a plane to Bora Bora and hide out in the jungle. Assuming they have jungles in Bora Bora. I can live off the fruit of the land. I've always wanted to live in the South Pacific. The weather's nice and hot. And so are the guys. So what if I'm ten thousand miles from the nearest Barney's? I'll adjust."

"Lance, don't you think you're overreacting just a tad?"

"You're right. I can't go running all the way to Bora Bora. That's crazy. I'll hide out closer to home. In the Amazon. Just me and the alligators. They'll never find me there!"

"Lance! Get a grip! Just because the police brought you in for questioning doesn't mean they're going to arrest you! I'm sure they're going to be questioning lots of people before this is all over."

"You think so?"

"I know so," I said, knowing no such thing. "In the meanwhile, why don't I snoop around and see if I can come up with any juicy suspects?"

For those of you who don't already know, snooping around and finding juicy suspects happens to be a hobby of mine. A dangerous one, to be sure, right up there with bungee jumping and bikini waxing. But it's something to keep me occupied between toilet bowl ads.

"Oh, Jaine," Lance said, a faint ray of hope shining in his eyes. "You are such a doll. I promise I will never lecture you about calories or clothing ever again."

Poor guy had such a rough morning, I pretended to believe him.

Chapter 13

First on my list of suspects was Sarah, the seething stepdaughter. Having watched Bunny slither her way into Marvin's life and destroy her family, had Sarah decided to get rid of her with a deadly martini? And yet, why make such a scene at the party and draw attention to herself if she'd just dropped a dose of cyanide in Bunny's drink? Maybe she was so full of rage, she just couldn't stop herself.

I tracked down her phone number at the UCLA chemistry department and left a message on her voice mail, telling her I needed to see her about an urgent matter.

She returned my call the next morning and said she could squeeze me in between chem labs early that afternoon.

And Sarah wasn't the only one who called. I'm happy to report I also heard from the gang at Toiletmasters, who gave me a much-appreciated assignment. I got started on it right away and spent the next few hours churning out a stirring opus called *You and Your Septic Tank*. Then, after a nutritious lunch of Cheerios and halibut guts (Cheerios for me, halibut guts for Prozac), I got ready to head over to UCLA.

I was just slapping on some lipstick when Lance shuffled over to my apartment in his bathrobe, blond stubble on his unshaven face, his hair a rat's nest of tangled curls. Not a good sign. This was a guy who usually mousses to answer the phone.

"My gosh, Lance. What's wrong?"

"Horrible news," he sighed, sinking down onto my sofa.

"Not the cops again?"

"No. Neiman's. They found out about my little visit to police headquarters and they've put me on a temporary leave of absence."

He looked up at me, misery oozing from every pore.

"Got any of that peanut butter?"

"Of course! You want some gherkins with that? They're really quite yummy together."

"I'm depressed, Jaine. Not pregnant. Just the peanut butter."

I went to the kitchen to get him the peanut butter, and when I got back I found Prozac curled in his lap, nuzzling her head in the crook of his arm.

"Oh, Pro, sweetie," Lance crooned. "You're such a comfort to your old Uncle Lance."

Why the heck couldn't she do this loving angel routine with me? When I've got a problem, she's about as comforting as an ingrown toenail.

"Here you go," I said, handing him the peanut butter.

I watched as he took a listless spoonful.

"Please don't worry, Lance. Everything's going to be fine. I've got my investigation under way. In fact, I'm about to go question Sarah Cooper."

"You are?" Suddenly he perked up. "Hey, I've got a great idea! Why don't I go with you?"

"Gee, I dunno—"

"We'll be partners. Like Spade and Archer! Nick and Nora! Charlie Chan and his Number One Son!"

"But you've got to know how to question people."

"Sweetie, I'm a people person. I deal with people all day long. Besides," he said, flashing me a pitiful puppy dog look, "I'm going out of my mind with boredom."

"Okay," I relented. "Why not?"

"Great!" He jumped up. "I'll go get dressed. What are you wearing?"

"This."

He eyed my elastic-waist jeans and L.L.Bean blazer ensemble with undisguised disdain.

"You're wearing *that* to an investigation? Nora Charles wouldn't be caught dead in that."

"What happened to never nagging me about my clothes again?"

"Oh, please, sweetheart, we both knew that was never going to happen. You really intend to wear that ghastly outfit?"

"Yes, I intend to wear this perfectly serviceable outfit. I'm the boss of this team and I'll wear what I want. And if you expect to tag along as my humble assistant, you'd better keep your lips zipped. Got it?"

"Okay, okay. You needn't be so snarky to your dear friend who might soon be going to jail."

He sure knew how to play the prison card, didn't he?

"Just go get ready," I said. "We don't want to be late."

Fifteen minutes later, he showed up at my apartment impeccably groomed and moussed to perfection, and the detective team of Austen & Venable started out on their very first case.

Stanley had an easier time finding Dr. Livingstone than most people have finding a parking spot at UCLA.

A helpful student at the information kiosk directed us to a lot somewhere between Sunset Boulevard and Outer Mongolia. And after forking over a hefty fee that in some schools would qualify as tuition, we found a spot deep in the bowels of the earth. From there we made the endless trek across campus to Sarah's lab and showed up just as Sarah's students were filing out.

As I gazed around the fluorescent-lit room, taking in the beakers and burners and cornucopia of chemicals, I realized how easy it would have been for Sarah to get her hands on a batch of deadly cyanide. Heck, I bet she could whip some up on her lunch hour.

She stood at the front of the room in a lab coat, talking with a lanky, dark-skinned guy in his late twenties. Seeing us standing in the doorway, she motioned us inside.

"Hi, guys!"

And for the first time since I'd met her, I saw a smile on her face. A big, bright, perky one. What a far cry from the angry woman who'd reamed into Bunny the night of the murder.

"This is Zubin, my teaching assistant," she said.

The guy in the lab coat nodded hello.

"Just give me a few minutes with these people, Zubin, and then we can set up for the next lab."

How comfortable and self-assured she seemed in this academic setting, away from the glitz and glitter of the party circuit.

"So what was this urgent matter you wanted to talk to me about?" she asked when Zubin had gone.

"Bunny's murder," I said.

"Yes, ma'am." Lance stepped forward, suddenly channeling Detective Perlmutter. "We have some questions we'd like to ask you."

He clamped his arms across his chest, much like Perlmutter had done before carting him off to police headquarters.

But if he expected to intimidate Sarah, he was sadly mistaken. She looked up from the test tubes she'd been lining up on a tray.

"What do you mean, you have questions? Who died and made you two the police?"

It looked like Angry Sarah was alive and well, after all.

"Actually, Sarah," I said, stepping in. "I do some private investigating on a part-time basis."

"You? The woman who can't even wash her hands without demolishing a bathroom?"

Okay, so she didn't say that part about me demolishing a bathroom, but I could read the subtitles.

"And I'm her invaluable right hand man," Lance preened.

Once more, she gawked in disbelief.

"But you're the one they brought in for questioning."

"That's why we're here," I piped up, subtly shoving Lance aside. "We're trying to clear Lance's name. We're wondering if you saw anyone loitering near Bunny's drink the night of the party."

"The only person I saw loitering near her drink was him," she said, pointing to Lance. "Like I told the cops, he was out on the patio, all alone, while everyone else was gathered in the hallway."

Lance's eyes narrowed into angry slits.

"So *you're* the one who ratted on me to the cops!"

"Yes, they asked me if I saw anyone out on the patio alone with Bunny's drink, and I did. I saw you."

"Well, how do we know *you* didn't slip outside after I came in?" he huffed.

"Because I didn't, that's why."

"Hearsay!" he cried, now channeling Perry Mason. "It'll never hold up in court."

"What are you talking about? That's not hearsay."

"She's right, Lance," I said. "It isn't hearsay. So let's just calm down and not make any rash accusations, shall we?"

But Lance was on a roll and was not about to stop.

"I submit that you saw me leave, and when the coast was clear, you crept outside and slipped the poison in Bunny's drink."

"I did not creep outside," Sarah said with clenched jaw. "I followed everybody else to see what the commotion in the bathroom was all about."

"I further submit that you've hated Bunny since the day she married your father, and that you took advantage of Jaine's unfortunate plumbing mishap to get rid of Bunny once and for all!"

"Yeah, well, I submit that you're a stark raving loony, and if you don't get out of here this instant I'm calling security."

Sarah slammed down her test tubes so hard, it's a miracle they didn't break.

"I'm so sorry, Sarah," I said, shoving Lance aside, this time not so gently. "We didn't mean to upset you. Lance just got a little carried away. He's been under a lot of stress."

"Yeah, well," she sniffed, "I don't like being accused of murder."

"Nobody's accusing you of murder, Sarah."

"Yes, I am!" Lance cried, springing back into action. "I'm accusing her of the cold-blooded murder of Bunny Cooper. And I rest my case!"

"That's it," Sarah snapped. "I'm calling security."

"I'd like to see you try," Lance sneered.

His wish was granted.

It's amazing how fast those security goons showed up.

The next thing we knew we were being forcibly escorted to our parking lot (at least this time we got to ride in a golf cart), with a warning to never darken the UCLA campus again.

Lance was puffed up with pride as we got in my Corolla.

"I sure put the fear of God in her, didn't I?" he said, fluffing his hair in the passenger visor.

Grinding my teeth to a fine pulp, I shoved the key in the ignition.

"So? Whaddaya say, Jaine? It went pretty well, huh?"

"I'd say there was room for improvement, Lance."

"I know. You were awfully quiet."

"Not *me*, Lance. *You!* What on earth got into you? We'll be lucky if she doesn't sue us."

I gunned the accelerator and took off in an angry burst of speed.

"From now on," I informed him, "I work alone."

"But what am I going to do all day?" He pouted.

"You'll think of something."

Oh, did he ever.

Chapter 14

"I still don't see why we can't work together," Lance said when I dropped him off at our duplex.

"Because if we do, I will probably wind up killing you and that would be most inconvenient for both of us."

Somehow I managed to convince him that our parting of the ways was for the best and set out to resume my investigation.

Next stop was Marvin Cooper. True, he'd seemed besotted with Bunny, but at this stage of the game, I couldn't rule anybody out. For all I knew, he and Bunny fought like cats and dogs when they were alone on their Comfort Cloud. When I called Mattress King to set up an appointment, his receptionist told me he was home, still in mourning.

So I tooled over to Casa Extravaganza to pay a visit to the grieving widower.

Lupe answered the door.

Like Sarah, she was a lot chirpier than the last time I'd seen her.

"Ms. Jaine!" she beamed, with no trace of her usual deer-in-the-headlights look. "I'm so glad you came. Mr. Marvin had visitors all morning, but he's alone now. It's no good for him to be alone. Not at a time like this. Alone is no good."

I'd never heard so many words come out of her mouth at

once. Compared to her usual "Yes, Ms. Bunny" and "No, Ms. Bunny," that was practically a Shakespearean soliloquy.

"Come in," she said, ushering me inside. "Mr. Marvin's outside on the patio. I just baked him some empanadas. Fresh from the oven."

She picked up a platter from a table in the foyer. On it, as advertised, was a batch of golden brown empanadas, gooey cheese bursting from the crimped pastry seams.

"They look delicious," I said, barely restraining myself from grabbing one.

"They are," she said with a refreshing lack of modesty. "You'll eat some with Mr. Marvin and keep him company."

No problemo there.

"Mr. Marvin loves my empanadas," she said, as we headed out to the patio. "But Ms. Bunny, she never let him eat them. I think they will cheer him up. Poor Mr. Marvin is so unhappy.

"I'm making him carne asada tonight," she added with a conspiratorial wink. "He loves my carne asada."

What a difference a death made. Without Bunny around to browbeat her, Lupe had morphed from a terrified mouse into a self-assured little dynamo. And suddenly I wondered if Lupe could be the killer after all. Bunny had threatened to have her deported. Had Lupe taken Bunny seriously? Seriously enough to shut her up forever with a cyanide martini?

Lupe was right about Marvin. He did look pretty miserable, slumped at one of the patio tables in Bermuda shorts and a rumpled T-shirt, his chubby cheeks sallow, his few remaining hairs uncombed.

"Mr. Marvin, I brought you empanadas!"

"Thanks, Lupe," he said as she set them down on the table. "That's very thoughtful."

"And look who's here to see you. Ms. Jaine!"

"Jaine." He managed a wan smile. "How nice of you to come and keep me company."

He thought I'd stopped by to pay my respects, and I didn't correct him.

"Eat the empanadas while they're nice and hot," Lupe instructed, before trotting back to the house.

"Poor Lupe's been worried about me," Marvin said, as I took a seat across from him. "For the first time in my life, I seem to have lost my appetite. But please, Jaine. Help yourself."

He gestured to the platter.

"Oh, I shouldn't." I felt a tad awkward about stuffing my face in his time of grief.

"Go ahead. They're really delicious."

"Well, maybe just one."

I swooped down on that thing like Prozac on a minced mackerel.

"Have another," Marvin offered, after I'd wolfed it down.

"I couldn't possibly."

Oh, yes I could. And I did. When I at last finished chomping, I remembered my manners.

"I'm so sorry about Bunny," I said, wiping flaky pastry crumbs from my lap. If I'd been alone, of course, I'd have eaten them.

"Thank you." His eyes misted over. "I was just looking at pictures from our honeymoon."

Indeed, there was an ornately tooled leather photo album on the table, with a place for a photo in the center. Marvin gazed down at the cover picture: a snapshot of him and Bunny holding hands in some tropical paradise, wearing leis and grinning into the camera.

"Bunny and I sure had some good times together," he sighed. "I still can't believe she's gone."

"I wonder who possibly could have done it," I said, casually launching the investigative portion of my visit.

"The police think it's your friend Lance."

"I can assure you, Mr. Cooper, Lance Venable did not kill your wife."

"He seems like a nice enough guy," Marvin conceded.

"I don't suppose you saw anyone go out to the patio after Bunny left her drink there?"

"No, I'm afraid that's when everyone was standing outside the guest bathroom, watching you."

I cringed at the memory of that ghastly moment.

"I think whoever did it must've slipped away from the crowd," I said, steering the conversation back where it belonged. "Do you remember anyone missing from the group?"

"No, all I remember is you, trying to staunch the flow of water with one of Bunny's guest towels."

"I'm so sorry about that, Mr. Cooper. As I told Bunny, I'd be happy to repay you for the damages. Naturally, it would have to be in installments."

Which I'd be paying off some time into the next millennium.

"Don't worry about it. Bunny would have redecorated it within the year anyway. She got such a kick out of doing things like that."

Once again his eyes misted over.

"I'm feeling a bit tired now, Jaine. I think I'll go stretch out on the chaise for a while."

"Of course. I understand."

It looked like my questions would have to wait.

"I almost forgot," he said, as I started to get up. "You never did get to pitch me your mattress slogans."

I stopped in my tracks. Was he actually still interested in hiring me?

"Why don't you drop off your ideas, and I'll look them over when I'm feeling better."

"Absolutely, Mr. Cooper," I said, thrilled to be getting this second chance. Not to mention a third empanada. Which he insisted I take.

"One for the road," he said.

What a sweet guy. And his grief over Bunny's death seemed pretty genuine. By now, I was having a tough time picturing him as a killer.

Then, just as I was mentally erasing him from my suspect list, I glanced down and saw a piece of paper poking out from under the photo album. A paper with some sort of grid on it.

As I headed for the house, I realized what it was: a business spreadsheet.

Very interesting. Marvin couldn't have been all that grief-stricken if he was going over his mattress sales. Back inside, I waited a minute or two, then peeked out to the patio.

And guess what? Marvin was not stretched out on a chaise. Au contraire, folks. He was still at the patio table, chomping down on an empanada, making notes on the spreadsheet.

And just like that, he was back on my suspect list.

Was it possible Marvin had known about Bunny's affair with Owen? After all, Bunny wasn't exactly a rocket scientist. Maybe she'd left clues all over the place. Had Marvin discovered her cheating ways and poisoned her drink in a moment of crazed jealousy?

More than anyone, Marvin knew about that weed killer out on the patio. He probably walked past it every day. He said he'd seen me starring in The Great Guest Bathroom Fiasco. But maybe he hadn't seen me at all. Maybe he'd just heard everybody talking about it. Maybe he'd been out on the patio the entire time.

I was trotting along the corridors of Casa Extravaganza, munching my empanada and trying to picture Marvin in handcuffs, when I passed the living room and saw Lupe gadding about with a feather duster. She hummed a jolly tune as she flicked the duster hither and yon. And once again, I was struck by what a happy camper she was.

Time for a little Q & A.

"Hey, Lupe," I said, strolling into the room. "Your empanadas are fantastic."

"*Gracias,* Ms. Jaine. I used Manchego cheese. Ms. Bunny never let me use Manchego. 'Too fattening,' she said. Made me use cheese from skim milk."

She wrinkled her nose in disgust.

"I bet she was pretty hard to work for, huh?"

"Ms. Bunny, she was a—" And then came a string of colorful Spanish words which I'm guessing did not mean "really swell gal."

"You must've been scared when she died."

A wary look crept into her eyes.

"*No comprende.* What do you mean?"

"After all, you were alone out on the patio with her drink. What if the police thought you poisoned it?"

Suddenly the frightened rabbit was back.

"The police don't suspect me!" she cried. "They told me so! One of Ms. Bunny's friends was watching me through the French doors the whole time I was outside and told the police I did nothing wrong."

So one of the Barbies had given her an alibi. Frankly, I was relieved. I didn't really want her to be the killer.

"I'm sorry, Lupe. I didn't mean to upset you. I'm sure you didn't do anything wrong. Actually, the police think Lance is the one who might have done it."

"It's so hard to believe," she said, shaking her head. "Mr. Lance is such a nice man."

"Yes, he's a very nice man. And I know he didn't kill Ms. Bunny. So I'm trying to find out who did. Did you see anyone, anyone at all, go out to the patio when Bunny's drink was out there?"

"No, Ms. Jaine. I was watching you in the bathroom."

Would I never live that down? Any minute now, I expected to see it on You Tube.

"Did you notice any of the guests missing from the crowd?"

And that's when I hit pay dirt.

"Yes," she nodded. "Mr. Lenny."

"Lenny? How can you be so sure?"

"Mr. Lenny doesn't like martinis. So he asked me to bring him a Coca-Cola from the kitchen. When I came back out to bring it to him, everyone was standing in the hallway outside the guest bathroom. But not Mr. Lenny. I couldn't see him anywhere."

So Lenny had been missing in action. Very interesting.

Clearly there'd been no love lost between him and Bunny.

I made a mental note to pay a little visit to the sad-eyed salesman first thing tomorrow.

Before tackling Lenny, however, I had the small matter of earning a living to attend to. So I hustled home to put the finishing touches on *You and Your Septic Tank*.

Heading up the path to my apartment, I spotted a box of chocolates on my doorstep.

Normally my heart would do handsprings at the sight of a box of chocolates. But not this time. That's because I had a pretty good idea who they were from.

The accompanying note confirmed my suspicions:

TO MY BELOVED JAINE

These chocolates I do give to you
I hope you don't mind,
I ate a few

Your devoted, Vladimir

You're not going to believe this, but when I opened the box, there was exactly one chocolate left. Slightly stale.

Clearly my Uzbek Romeo was still hot on my trail.

Shoving all thoughts of Vladimir to the dusty corner of my

brain reserved for toothaches and IRS audits, I spent the next couple of hours waxing euphoric about septic tanks.

When at last I finished, I faxed my opus to the gang at Toiletmasters. After which I grabbed my sunglasses and treated myself to a luxurious soak in the tub, up to my neck in strawberry-scented bubbles. Instead of using the time to mull over the murder like a good little detective, however, I whiled away the minutes trying to decide what color to paint my walls when and if I got the Mattress King account.

"What do you think, Pro?"

I gazed up at Prozac, who was stretched out on the toilet tank.

"How about a pale aqua for the bathroom, a whispery celadon for the bedroom, lemon yellow for the kitchen, and adobe beige for the living room and hallway? Or I could do adobe in the bedroom and celadon in the living room, with maybe an off-white kitchen with cherry red trim. Or I could go with off-white in the living room, lemon in the living room, and aqua in the bedroom."

Prozac opened one eye and glared at me balefully.

Or you could quit yapping and let me get some sleep.

What can I say? Some cats just aren't into decorating.

When I finally tired of flipping mental paint chips, I hauled myself from the tub and changed into my jammies. Then I poured myself a lovely glass of chardonnay and phoned for a pizza. Sausage and pepperoni.

Prozac swished her tail with great urgency as I placed the order.

Don't forget the anchovies!

In no time the pizza delivery guy was at my door.

"Here you go, Jaine," he said, handing me the steaming box.

"Thanks, Kiril."

Yes, it's true. I'm on a first name basis with my pizza guy. They send me a Christmas card every year. And Valentine's

Day. Frankly, I'm surprised they haven't offered me stock options.

After I tipped Kiril, I headed for the bedroom and settled in bed with my gooey pepperoni treasure.

Prozac, who not an hour earlier had inhaled every speck of her minced mackerel dinner, was now practically burrowing a hole through the box with her nose.

I opened it and breathed in the heavenly aroma.

"Pepperoni pizza." I sighed with pleasure. "Yum!"

"Can I have some, too?"

No, Prozac still hadn't mastered the art of actual speech.

It was Lance and his X-ray hearing.

"Can I come over, Jaine?" he called out from his apartment. "I'm bored."

Five minutes later, he was camped out on my bed. And he was not alone. He'd brought his adorable white fluffball, Mamie.

Prozac took one look at her canine neighbor and arched her back.

What the heck is Snow White doing here?

"Now, Prozac," I chided. "Be nice."

Not about to happen.

With a parting hiss, she stalked off to the living room, tail swishing every step of the way. Which left Mamie free to gallop across my bedspread and cover me with slobbery kisses.

Eventually I distracted her with a piece of sausage, which she thoughtfully began smearing across my pillow sham.

Meanwhile, Lance had curled up beside me and was busy eating the pepperonis off my pizza, leaving a trail of unsightly craters in his wake.

"Lance can't you just eat a piece of pizza like a normal person?"

"I don't want a whole slice. I just want the pepperonis," he said, plucking one off with surgical precision.

I watched with gritted teeth as he popped it into his mouth.

"So how did it go today?" he asked. "Did you find the killer yet?"

"No, I didn't find the killer yet. I've been on the case less than a day."

"Oh," he said, crestfallen.

"Hang in there, Lance. I'm detecting as fast as I can."

With a sigh, I turned on the TV. I'd been planning to watch one of my all-time favorite movies, *Rosemary's Baby*. It's hardly ever on, and I'd been thrilled to discover it on the Turner Classic Movies schedule.

Now I zapped to it eagerly.

"You don't really want to watch *this*, do you?" Lance said, grabbing the remote during the opening credits.

"Yes, Lance, I do. I love this movie."

"But there's a *Dynasty* marathon on TV Land!"

Absolutely not. I was not about to give up an all-time classic movie for endless hours of Joan Collins in shoulder pads.

"Forget it, Lance. We're watching *Rosemary's Baby*."

"They'll probably never let me watch *Dynasty* in prison."

This uttered with huge sad eyes.

Dammit. He was playing the prison card again. And like a fool, I fell for it.

"Okay," I grunted. "We'll watch *Dynasty*."

I spent the next several hours watching Joan Collins and Linda Evans engage in a vicious power struggle over men, money, and close-ups.

Not even a pint of Chunky Monkey managed to cheer me up. Mainly because Lance kept plucking out all the chocolate bits.

When I finally fell asleep around midnight, he was busy color coding my socks.

YOU'VE GOT MAIL!

To: Jausten
From: Shoptillyoudrop
Subject: Pork Chops and Cheese Doodles

Well, sweetheart, today's the big day! My turn to host the bridge club! The gals are coming over at noon, and I want everything to be just right.

I set the table with my Queen Elizabeth/Latifah plates, and if I do say so myself they look exquisite. Especially with my Duchess of Windsor silver (only $79.99 plus shipping and handling). And I finished it all off with a lovely centerpiece of roses from our garden.

The only fly in the ointment is Daddy. He wanted to "cater" the affair with *Pork Chops and Cheese Doodles à la Hank.* Of course I laid down the law, and banished him from the house for the afternoon. No way is he getting near my kitchen. I'm making salad and quiche and I'm cooking the quiche in an old-fashioned oven, thank you very much!

Frankly, I can't wait to get rid of him. You should see the mess he's been making in the kitchen, perfecting his *Popalicious Chicken à la Hank* for that darn cookathon. I've eaten so much chicken, I'm surprised I haven't sprouted feathers.

If Daddy thinks he has a snowball's chance in hell of beating Lydia Pinkus, who's won the cookathon with her Salmon Wellington for the past five years, he's sadly mistaken.

On the plus side, though, at least he's using up that popcorn!

Well, honey, must run and start my quiche.

Looking forward to a heavenly Daddy-free afternoon. . . ..

XXX

Mom

To: Jausten
From: DaddyO
Subject: Banished!

You're not going to believe this, lambchop, but I've been banished from my own house!

Your mother says she wants me out of her hair while she entertains her bridge club ladies. And she actually turned down my generous offer to wow her guests with my *Pork Chops and Cheese Doodles à la Hank.* Oh, well. It's all for the best. I didn't really want to do it anyway, not with that battleaxe Lydia Pinkus coming to the house.

You remember Lydia, don't you? The librarian who made such a fuss just because I was a wee bit late returning a library book? Apparently she's a member of the bridge club.

Your mother tells me Old Pruneface is entering the cookathon with her Salmon Wellington. Oh, please. Anyone can toss some salmon in a pastry crust, but only a true culinary genius can stuff a chicken with popcorn! Trust me, sweetheart. With Chef Hank in the race, Lydia's "Salmon Smellington" is headed straight for the losers' circle.

Well, I'm off to the cooking supply store to buy a chef's hat for the cookathon. I'm going to have *Popalicious Chicken à la Hank* embroidered on the headband. Pretty snazzy, huh? Just another creative culinary touch from—

Your loving daddy,

Chef Hank

To: Jausten
From: Shoptillyoudrop
Subject: Smash Success

Hi, sweetheart—

I'm happy to report that my bridge luncheon was a smash success. The ladies loved my quiche. When I think how Daddy wanted to serve them pork chops and cheese doodles, I could just die! Now he's back in the kitchen, fixing dinner, yet another "popalicious" roast chicken.

Oh, dear. He's hollering about something. I'd better go see what the ruckus is all about.

XOXO,

Mom

To: Jausten
From: DaddyO
Subject: Spice Thief!

Tragic news, lambchop! My Secret Spice is missing. And I know who took it. Old Pruneface herself, Lydia Pinkus. Clearly, she's heard about my prowess in the kitchen, and stole it to keep me from winning the cookathon. That cheating battleaxe would stoop at nothing to destroy me!

Your outraged,

Daddy

To: Jausten
From: Shoptillyoudrop
Subject: False Accusations

You're not going to believe this, darling, but for some insane reason Daddy thinks Lydia Pinkus stole his Secret Spice. He's always resented her ever since she very justifiably asked him to return an overdue library book. Which is a crying shame, because Lydia is such a lovely woman.

True, she did happen to go to the kitchen for a glass of water this afternoon, so I suppose it's possible she could have taken Daddy's Secret Spice, but why would she want to? Daddy insists she did it to damage his chances in the cookathon, but she doesn't need to steal spices to beat Daddy. Lydia Pinkus can cook rings around your father with one hand tied behind her apron.

He probably just misplaced it. The man can't find his own glasses when he's wearing them, for heaven's sake!

Love from,

Mom

PS. I'm just glad you're three thousand miles away from all this madness, and living such a carefree life in sunny Los Angeles.

Chapter 15

I was thrilled to find Lance gone when I woke up the next morning. What a joy to have my bed—and my remote—back to myself again.

Prozac was still in a bit of a snit about Mamie, but she cheered up enormously when I slopped some Hearty Lamb Innards in her breakfast bowl.

Yes, the two of us were happy indeed to be the sole inhabitants of our humble hovel. Some might even say ecstatic. But our happiness was short-lived. I'd not even finished nuking my Folgers Crystals when I heard Lance banging on my door.

For a minute I considered pretending I was still asleep.

"Hey, Jaine," he shouted. "I know you're up. I heard your toilet flushing."

With a sigh, I trudged to the front door and let him in.

"I come bearing breakfast," he said, holding out a bakery bag. "Muffins, fresh from the oven!"

I took one whiff of those beauties, and all thoughts of last night faded into the ether. So what if Lance had been a little overbearing? The poor guy was under a lot of stress. What sort of friend was I to get all pissy just because he hogged the remote and ate a few pepperonis?

"Lance, sweetie! Come in!"

Okay, so I'm a muffin whore.

Minutes later we were sitting at my dining room table, freshly nuked instant coffee and muffins before us.

"Aren't you going to have any?" I asked, eyeing his empty plate.

"Nah, I ate earlier. I've been up for hours. I'm feeling so much better today."

And indeed, he did look bright-eyed and bushy-tailed, his blond curls moussed, his eyes shining with enthusiasm.

"I found a terrific stress management site online, with all sorts of wonderful ways to handle crisis situations!"

"That's great, Lance," I said, cutting into one of the still-warm beauties.

"The main thing I learned is: It's not about what happens to you, but how you react to what happens that counts."

"Absolutely," I said, only half-listening.

It's hard to pay attention when faced with a plump, blueberry-studded muffin. I was just about to slather it with butter when Lance reached over to my plate.

"You touch one blueberry on this muffin," I said, whipping it away, "and you're a dead man."

"Okay, okay. Somebody sure got up on the wrong side of the muffin tin this morning."

He let me attend to my muffin in peace while he rattled on about the power of positive thinking and the importance of keeping busy.

I have to confess I missed most of it while trying to decide between grape jelly and strawberry jam. (Strawberry won.)

"Well, I'd better get going," he said when I'd scarfed down my blueberry beauty. "I've already intruded enough in your life."

"Don't be silly, Lance," I said, feeling like a world-class creep for having been annoyed with him. "That's what friends are for."

After he left, I spent the next hour or so paying bills and

vacuuming. (Okay, so I read my horoscope and did the cross-word puzzle. And had another muffin, if you must know.) Then I headed to the bedroom to get dressed for my meeting with Lenny at Mattress King. Not that Lenny knew I was coming. I wanted to catch him by surprise.

Normally I would've used the drive time to plot out what questions to ask Lenny. But right before leaving the house, I'd been foolish enough to check my parents' e-mails. One of these days, I've got to put a sign up on my computer that says, *Just Say No to DaddyO.* Now I couldn't stop thinking about Daddy and his missing Secret Spice. I didn't believe for one minute that Lydia Pinkus took it. But that's Daddy for you. For years he was convinced the mailman was stealing his prize money from Publishers Clearing House. Oh, well. I couldn't think about Daddy. Not now. Not when I had a hot murder suspect on my hands.

And as suspects went, Lenny was sizzling.

According to Lupe, he was missing from the crowd gathered around the guest bathroom the night of the murder. Perhaps because he was out on the patio slipping some weed killer into Bunny's martini.

Marvin said he and Lenny were best friends. But Bunny had clearly been doing her best to drive a wedge between them. Had Lenny poisoned her drink in a desperate attempt to save their friendship?

He was on the phone when I walked into the showroom, a half-eaten danish at his side. How spiffy he looked, clad in what appeared to be a brand new sport coat, his comb-over plastered at a rakish angle across his bald spot. Gone was the mopey look in his eyes. On the contrary, they sparkled with anticipation as he yakked on the phone.

"I'll pick you up tomorrow at noon," he was saying.

"We'll hit the links, play a few holes, then head for the club-house. It'll be like old times, Marv."

Aha. A golf date with Marvin. It looked like their friend-ship was back on the front burner.

"Hey, Jaine," he said when he hung up. "Great to see you, sweetheart!"

He beamed me a broad smile. Which would've been a lot more impressive if there hadn't been a bit of danish stuck be-tween his teeth.

"Good seeing you, too, Lenny."

"If you came to see Marv, he isn't here right now. In fact, I was just talking to him on the phone. We're playing golf to-gether tomorrow."

He grinned like a kid about to go to the circus.

"Actually, Lenny, I'm here to see you."

"In the market for a mattress?" He jumped up in full-tilt salesman mode. "We got a sleep-tacular deal on a Comfort Cloud. C'mere, lemme show ya!"

He put his arm around me, steering me over to the mile-high mattress.

Then, with a wink, he added, "But I'd better keep an eye on my mattress sample, huh? Hahaha! Carlton told me how you lifted his."

Damn that blabbermouth Carlton.

"I'm not here to buy a mattress, Lenny," I said, wiggling free from his grasp. "I want to talk to you about Bunny's murder."

And at that, his grin went bye-bye.

"What about it?"

"The police think my friend Lance did it, and I'm trying to help him clear his name."

"Good luck with that," he said, flicking a piece of imagi-nary lint from the Comfort Cloud.

"Lupe told me she was looking for you at the party, but couldn't find you."

"I see." Now he was busy fluffing a Mattress King Neck Support Pillow. "And you think I was out on the patio poisoning Bunny's drink?"

"Something along those lines."

At last he turned to face me.

"As much as I hated the bitch, I can assure you I didn't kill her."

"Then where were you when Lupe tried to find you?"

"In the media room, watching TV. I'd had it up to here with Bunny. I walked into that party, and from clear across the room I heard her trashing me. Like I was something the cat dragged in."

I remembered that feeling well.

He slumped down on the mattress, that sorrowful look back in his eyes.

"I faked a smile and tried to pretend it didn't matter, but it did. I didn't care about her stupid party, but I cared about Marvin. I always have. We were best friends for decades. When my wife died, he and Ellen saved my life. But then Bunny came along and ruined everything. She led poor Marvin around by the nose. He never complained, but it made me sick to see the way she treated him. That night at the party, I put up with it for as long as I could, and then when I couldn't take any more, I slipped away and watched the Lakers."

"But from what I hear," he added, getting up from the mattress, "I missed a much better show in the guest bathroom."

Touché, Lenny.

"Any other questions?" he asked.

"I don't suppose you know who really killed her?"

"Nope. Not a clue. But if you find out who it was, let me know. I want to buy 'em a drink."

* * *

Our tête à tête concluded, I made my way to the back offices. I figured while I was there, I might as well question Owen, the cheating son-in-law. And Ellen, the bitter ex-wife.

For once Marvin's receptionist did not have her fingers glued to the keyboard. In his absence, she was gazing down at a bunch of travel brochures splayed out in front of her.

"Hey, Amy!" I chirped. "Planning a trip?"

She looked up at me from under her limp bangs and smiled shyly.

"My boyfriend's taking me away for a romantic getaway weekend!"

"How nice."

I tried to contain my surprise that Little Miss Mousy not only had a boyfriend, but that she was actually headed off for a weekend of whoopsy doodle.

"Doesn't this one look nice?" she asked, handing me a glossy brochure for a B&B down in Laguna Beach. "It has a fireplace in the bedroom, and a view of the ocean. It's called the Romeo and Juliet Suite."

I made appropriate cooing noises at a photo of a chintz and ruffle-studded room with a canopy bed and a flotilla of heart-shaped throw pillows.

"Isn't that just the sweetest thing you ever saw?"

Any sweeter and I'd need an insulin shot.

I continued to ooh and aah through a series of B&B brochures—all of whose rooms had been highly influenced by the Rebecca of Sunnybrook Farm School of Decorating. All the while, I was trying to figure out how to steer the subject to Bunny's murder. Not that I expected Amy to be the source of any vital clues. But one never knows, does one? Out of the mouths of babes and receptionists, and all that.

"*Ye Olde Inn by the Sea*," I said, picking up one of the brochures. "Isn't that where Marvin took Bunny on their honeymoon?"

"Bunny?" she sniffed. "Are you kidding? She made him take her to Tahiti for a month."

"What a tragedy about her getting killed, huh?"

"Yeah, I guess," she said, tearing her eyes away from a brochure. "To be perfectly honest, she was never very nice to me. But poor Mr. Cooper was crazy about her. Frankly, I could never see why. She wore hair extensions, you know."

She lowered her voice to a whisper, as if about to impart a deep, dark secret.

"And I don't think her breasts were real, either."

I did my best to look shocked.

"Some men like that kind of woman, I guess. But thank heavens they aren't all like that. There are still some men who appreciate a woman for who she really is."

"How true," I said, neglecting to mention that 99 percent of those men are usually married to a guy named Duane.

Time to lob her a question or two.

"I wonder who could have done it."

"It's that shoe salesman from Neiman Marcus. That's what they said on the news."

"They only brought him in for questioning," I said, eager to nip this guilty-until-proven-innocent thing in the bud. "Doesn't mean he did it."

"So who did?" she asked, wide-eyed.

"I have no idea," I admitted, the truth of those words weighing heavily on me. "Can you think of anyone who might have wanted to?"

"Not really. Bunny once had Mr. Cooper fire the cleaning crew because she didn't like the way they were dusting the antiques in his office. But I don't think they cared. They've got clients all over town.

"Anyhow," she said, her eyes drifting back to her brochures, "Mr. Cooper isn't here, if you came to see him. He's still home, in mourning."

"I know. Actually I came to see Owen. And the first Mrs. Cooper."

"Ellen's not in today, and Owen's out in the stockroom."

"The stockroom?" I asked, looking around.

"Out the back door, across the alley from the parking lot."

"Thanks," I said, and left her gazing moonily at her brochures, no doubt dreaming of torrid nights in the Romeo & Juliet Suite.

Chapter 16

At first I thought Amy was wrong about Owen being in the stockroom.

When I stepped inside the squat, windowless building, the place was shrouded in darkness, the only illumination filtering in from the half-open garage door in front.

Stacks of mattresses were propped up against the walls, casting eerie shadows in the gloom.

"Owen?" I called out.

No answer.

"Owen?" I tried again.

Still no answer.

I was just about to leave when I heard a strange rattling noise coming from somewhere in back.

Following the sound, I made my way down the aisle between the stacked mattresses until I came to an alcove where a mattress had been laid out on the floor. I blinked in surprise to see Owen's lanky body sprawled on it, his baseball cap pulled down over his eyes, his mouth wide open, snoring to beat the band.

So, the number one son-in-law was asleep on the job. I thought for sure I'd find him clipboard in hand, taking inventory or some such industrious pursuit.

"Ahem," I said, clearing my throat.

As much as I hated to interrupt his beauty sleep, I had some questions to ask.

But he kept on snoring.

"Owen," I crooned. "Wake up."

No dice. The snoring just grew louder.

The sound of those rattlers reminded me of the hours I'd spent lying in bed listening to my ex-husband, The Blob, whose snores have been known to register on the Richter scale. (And those were just the snores.)

"Owen!" I said, shaking him vigorously by the shoulder. "Wake up!"

That did the trick.

"What the hell are you doing here?" he growled, bolting up.

"Nice to see you, too." I smiled genially. "Sorry to interrupt you when you're so hard at work."

"So I took a nap," he said, scrambling up from the mattress. "Big deal. Not that it's any business of yours, but I haven't been sleeping well lately."

Guilty conscience, perhaps?

He strode to the front of the room and flipped on the lights, flooding the place in a harsh fluorescent glare.

"I know why you're here," he said, marching back to me and grabbing his clipboard from where it lay on the mattress. "Sarah told me you're some kind of half-baked private eye. I know all about how you and your nutcase friend harassed her."

"I'm afraid Lance got a bit carried away," I admitted, "and I'm sorry about that. We just wanted to ask Sarah a few questions about Bunny's murder."

"If you expect me to answer your questions, forget it. You're not a cop. I don't have to talk to you."

With that, he started making notes on his clipboard, his charming way of telling me to get lost.

Time to play rough. Well, as rough as a P.I. with an *I ♥ My Cat* T-shirt can get.

"I think you do have to talk to me," I said, lobbing him my sternest look. "That is, if you don't want me telling Sarah about your affair with Bunny."

A brief flicker of panic shone in his eyes.

"What do you mean?" he asked, doing a very bad impersonation of someone who wasn't scared out of his wits. "What affair with Bunny?"

"Oh, please. We both know what was going on that day I ran into you outside the Coopers' house. You were reeking of Bunny's perfume. And if that wasn't a dead giveaway, the lipstick on your pocket protector was."

Tossing aside his clipboard, he crumpled down at the edge of the mattress.

"Okay," he sighed, "what do you want to know?"

"First of all," I said, squatting down next to him, "I want to know where you were when Bunny left her drink out on the patio."

"I was standing outside the guest bathroom watching you make a fool of yourself."

That said with a most irritating smirk.

"That's funny. Because I don't remember seeing you there."

Of course, I was in such a fog of humiliation at the time, I didn't remember seeing anyone, but I wasn't about to tell him that.

"I was there. I swear. And besides, why would I kill Bunny?"

"Who knows? From what I hear, she was a mighty fickle gal. She was cheating on Marvin with you. Maybe she was cheating on you with the pool man. Maybe you found out about it, and killed her in a fit of passion."

"I could never kill Bunny! I was crazy about her. Oh, God," he said, burying his face in his hands, "I never meant to fall in love with her, but I couldn't help myself. I'd never met anybody like Bunny before."

He looked up at me with earnest blue eyes.

"You can't imagine how exciting she was to a skinny science nerd from Downey."

Oh, I could imagine, all right. I'd seen her in action on the Comfort Cloud.

"She was my whole life. I begged her to leave Marvin and run off with me. I told her that we didn't need his money, that we could make it on our own. I almost had her convinced."

"Yeah, right. I can just picture Bunny shopping at Kmart."

"You don't understand. Bunny had faith in me. She knew someday I'd make it big. Why kill her when I was so close to having her forever?"

A lone tear trickled down his cheek. Embarrassed, he quickly wiped it away.

I had to admit, that tear was awfully convincing.

"You're not going to tell Sarah, are you?" he asked. "It'd break her heart."

"No, I won't tell Sarah. Not unless I find out you're lying."

Which, of course, was entirely possible.

If there's one thing I've learned in my years as a part-time, semi-professional private eye, it's to never trust a guy who snores like my ex-husband.

Next stop—Sarah.

Clearly she was steamed about our little visit yesterday, and I had to make amends. The last thing I needed was for her to go bad-mouthing me to Marvin.

Yes, I know I was warned never to darken the UCLA campus again, but I wasn't about to let a pesky little warning stop me.

After forking over a small ransom to park, I made the endless trek to Sarah's lab. Unfortunately, a class was in progress when I got there, so I sat down in the hallway to wait for it to end. About five minutes into my vigil, the door opened and a student in a lab coat came out, a diminutive brunette smelling faintly of sulfur.

When I asked what time the class would be over, she said one o'clock. It was now a little after noon. Which meant I had almost an hour to kill. And it had been a while since I'd scarfed down those muffins, so I was hungry. I remembered passing a university café on my way to the lab, a charming little cafeteria with an outdoor patio. If I scooted over right now, I'd have more than enough time to grab some lunch and be back by one.

So I proceeded to scoot. Unfortunately, when I showed up, the charming little cafeteria had a line snaking out the door.

I took my place at the end of the line and spent the next fifteen minutes tormented by the smells of the hot lunches cooking inside. When at last I reached the steam table, my eyes zeroed in on a fragrant vat of beef stew. My salivary glands sprang into action. As I ladled some into a bowl, I saw it was gloppy enough to caulk a bathtub. Just the way I like it.

Then I grabbed a roll and butter to sop up the glop, plus a Diet Coke and giant chocolate chip cookie, and settled my tab.

Now before you get your panties in an uproar about that cookie, let me assure you it was not for me, but rather a peace offering for Sarah. I figured I'd melt her heart with chocolate chips.

Quite a clever ploy, if I do say so myself.

I'd just settled down at a shady table out on the patio and was about to dig into my beef stew when I glanced up and gulped in dismay. There, waddling up the path to the cafeteria, were the two security goons who'd given me the boot yesterday. The two of them, side by side, practically took up the whole path.

Oh, for crying out loud. Of all places on campus for them to show up!

Desperate for camouflage, I looked around and spotted an abandoned newspaper at a nearby table. I quickly snatched it up and held it in front of my face, praying that the goons would walk on by and leave me in peace.

But my rotten luck was still hanging in there.

I groaned to see them heading into the cafeteria. There was no longer a line (there never is, after I've been served), which meant they'd be out with their food in no time. I couldn't risk having them see me.

So I shoveled a hurried forkful of beef stew in my mouth, grabbed my Diet Coke and my cookie, and ran.

Back in the chemistry building, I resumed my vigil outside Sarah's lab, sucking down my Diet Coke and yearning for my lost beef stew.

Finally the bell rang, and students began filing out of the lab.

When the last one had gone, I took a deep breath and stepped inside.

As expected, I was not exactly greeted with open arms.

"You again?" Sarah said, taking out her cell phone. "I'm calling security."

"Please don't, Sarah. I came to apologize. I'm so sorry we upset you yesterday. Lance's behavior was inexcusable. I know you didn't kill Bunny."

I knew no such thing, but I had to appease her somehow.

"Of course I didn't kill Bunny!" she huffed.

But I could see she was somewhat mollified.

"Apology accepted?" I put on my most repentant look.

She thought it over for a beat, then flipped her phone closed.

"Apology accepted."

"I brought you a peace offering," I said, holding up the chocolate chip cookie. "But unfortunately I ate half of it."

Okay, so I ate half the darn cookie while I was waiting in the hallway. After all, I never did get to eat my beef stew, and I was hungry.

"That's all right," she said, taking the cookie with a smile. "I'm not fussy."

Now that we were back on speaking terms, I figured I might as well ask for her help.

"Look," I said, "Lance may be impossible, but he's not a killer. So if you remember seeing anything the night of the murder that might help him out, please give me a call."

"Okay," she said, as I handed her my card, "but honestly, the only one I saw on the patio was Lance."

"Well, if something else should occur to you, please call me."

"Will do." She smiled wryly. "Anything for a chocolate chip cookie."

I bid her and my cookie a fond adieu and headed down the hallway to the ladies' room. That Diet Coke had raced through my system and I needed to make a pit stop.

A middle-aged woman in a lab coat came in at the same time as I did. Probably one of the professors. She was finished before me and was at the sink washing her hands when the ladies' room door opened and someone else walked in.

"Hi, Sarah."

My ears perked up. Was this *my* Sarah?

"Oh, hi, Belinda."

It sure sounded like her.

I peeked through that embarrassing space that always seems to exist between a stall door and its adjoining wall.

It was Sarah, all right. What a perfect opportunity to eavesdrop.

I watched through the crack as she headed for a stall just

two doors down from mine. I only hoped she wouldn't look over and recognize my shoes.

"So how are your labs going this semester?" the other woman asked.

"Same old same old. No major explosions so far."

They proceeded to engage in a little Chemistry Department chat, involving recalcitrant students and back orders of Bunsen burners, all quite boring. It wasn't until Sarah left her stall and went over to the sinks that things got interesting.

After washing her hands, she took some sort of tube from her purse. At first I couldn't tell what it was. But then she lifted up one of the legs of her slacks and started applying ointment to her shin.

"Wow, that's a nasty cut," the other woman said. "What happened?"

"Oh, it's nothing. I just tripped over a rake."

I didn't hear what they said after that. My mind was too busy buzzing with speculation. All you A+ students out there will no doubt remember that the night of the murder I'd trotted out to the patio and seen a jar of weed killer. But that wasn't all I'd seen. Extra credit to those of you who remember I'd also seen a rake.

What if the rake Sarah had tripped over had been the one on the Coopers' patio? That would mean she'd been lying when she said she hadn't been out there. It would also mean she might very well be the killer.

And with that, Sarah aced her dad off the Number One spot on my suspect list.

Chapter 17

Getting a lead on a juicy suspect is all very well and good, but there are more important things in life than solving murders, you know. Things like world peace and classic literature and beef stew thick enough to caulk a bathtub.

Still lusting over my lost culinary treasure, I stopped off at the outdoor café on my way back to the parking lot and gazed wistfully at my former table, hoping against hope that my beef stew would still be there. But it was long gone. All that remained on the table was a plastic fork and balled-up paper napkin.

I thought about dashing inside for another bowl, but I couldn't risk it. Just my luck those damn security goons would come strolling by again.

So I swung over to McDonald's, where I consoled myself with a Quarter Pounder and fries. Which, I have to confess, was a very tasty consolation prize. I was just popping the last fry into my mouth when my cell phone rang.

"Hey, Jaine. Nick here."

It was Nick Angelides, the proud owner of Toiletmasters Plumbers, serving the greater Los Angeles area since 1989.

"Great job on *You and Your Septic Tank*," he grunted in his raspy voice.

"Glad you liked it, Nick."

"Except one thing needs a little tweaking."

Uh-oh. In writer-speak that means: *Batten down the hatches. It's rewrite time.*

"That ⌐⌐tion on *The Dangers of Flushing Non-Biodegradaᵛles Down the Toilet.* Somehow it lacks drama."

The guy spent his days snaking glop out of drains, and suddenly he was a drama critic. But he spelled my name right on my paychecks and that's all that counted.

"Think you can punch it up?" he asked.

"Sure, Nick. No problem."

I promised I'd fax him the changes by the end of the day, and clicked my phone shut with a sigh. How nice it would be to write about mattresses for a change, instead of the dangers of flushing Q-tips down the toilet.

Then I headed back to my apartment to get the job started.

"Hi, sweetie, I'm back!" I called out to Prozac when I let myself in.

I looked around, but she wasn't in the living room. I figured she was probably in the bedroom, hard at work clawing my pantyhose to shreds. But when I went there to change into some sweats, she wasn't there either.

Nor was she was in the kitchen, where I'd hoped to find her grabbing her umpteenth snack of the day.

Now I was beginning to get concerned.

"Prozac, honey!" I called out, hurrying down the hallway to the bathroom. "Where are you?"

Not in the bathroom.

I searched her favorite hiding places: under my bed, on top of my closet, and behind the P. G. Wodehouse paperbacks on my bookshelf.

Still no sign of her.

And then a horrible thought occurred to me. What if, after countless years of trying, Prozac finally managed to claw open the refrigerator door—and then somehow locked herself in?

My poor, poor kitty! I thought, racing to the fridge. *What an awful way to go!*

I flung open the door, certain I would find her cold, dead body sprawled out on my crisper. But thank heavens, all I saw was the same moldy cheese and martini olives that were there the last time I looked.

I was leaning against the refrigerator, limp with relief, when I heard a key turning in my front door. Oh, God. Someone was breaking in! What if it was the killer? Maybe Sarah recognized my shoes in the ladies' room stall, after all. Maybe she knew I'd put two and two together about that rake and was here to shut me up forever. She probably discovered the emergency key I kept outside under my potted impatiens and let herself in earlier. Poor Prozac, sensing danger, had undoubtedly dashed out the front door.

And now Sarah had come back to kill me!

Well, I wasn't about to go down without a fight. I yanked open a drawer and grabbed my pizza cutter. I'd slash her face to ribbons if I had to.

My weapon clutched in my hot little hands, I was just about to launch my attack when I heard, "Honey, I'm home!"

Oh, for heaven's sakes. It was only Lance.

I hurried to the living room to find him with Mamie in one arm and my precious Prozac in the other.

"Sweetie!" I cried. "You're okay!"

"Well, actually," Lance yawned, "I'm a little tired."

"Not you," I said, snatching Prozac into my arms. "I was worried senseless when I came home and Prozac wasn't here. Where on earth have you been?"

"Sorry, hon. I should've left you a note. I let myself in with your emergency key and took the girls to The Pampered Pet."

"The Pampered Pet?"

"A pet spa and clothing boutique on Melrose."

Oh, lord. Only in L.A.

"We had so much fun, didn't we, girls? They had massages and perfumed bubble baths and hair styling, too. And how do you like their outfits?"

I'd been so consumed with worry, I hadn't even noticed that Mamie and Prozac were wearing matching pink angora sweaters. With fur trim at the legs. Mamie sported a pink bow in her hair, while Prozac was adorned with a pink rhinestone collar.

"Doesn't Pro look adorable?" Lance beamed with pride.

Prozac, however, did not share his enthusiasm.

If somebody doesn't get me out of this outfit soon, blood will flow.

"And look what else I bought her! It's called 'The Cat's Pajamas.' "

He held up what looked like a red and white striped baby layette.

"And it comes with a matching nightcap!" he said, waving a pointy cap with a tassel at the tip. "Let me put it on her!"

Prozac greeted this announcement with a rather frightening hiss.

Try it, buster, and you'll be singing soprano the rest of your life.

"Maybe later, Lance," I said, unsnapping her sweater. "In the meanwhile, I'll just get her out of this outfit."

I unloosened her rhinestone collar and she sprinted off to the top of the bookcase, where she proceeded to lick away the remains of her perfumed bubble bath.

"We'll put on her pajamas after dinner," Lance said. "Which reminds me. I almost forgot about the groceries. They're out in the car."

"What groceries?"

"Didn't I tell you? I'm cooking us dinner tonight."

"You are? That's very sweet of you, Lance."

My heart always melts at the thought of a hot meal that doesn't come on a plastic tray.

"I'll be right back and get started."

"Here? Why can't you cook at your place?"

"Aw, Jaine." He looked at me with big, sad eyes. "I don't want to be alone. I'll just start feeling depressed again. You'll keep me company while I cook."

"I can't keep you company. I've got work to do."

"You mean, like on the case?" His eyes lit up. "You're zeroing in on the killer, aren't you? Oh, Jaine! I knew you'd come through for me."

"Actually, I've got to wrap up a Toiletmasters brochure."

"Oh," he said, coming down off his bubble of hope.

"But I'm making lots of progress, really."

Okay, so technically that was a bit of a whopper, but I couldn't bear to tell him I didn't have anything even resembling a shred of evidence.

"You just have to give me a little more time. In the meanwhile, though, I've got to concentrate on my brochure. So maybe cooking dinner here isn't the best idea."

"I promise I'll be quiet as a mouse."

Yeah, right. I spent the next several hours trapped at my dining room table desk listening to Lance banging what seemed to be every pot I owned, whistling while he worked. I desperately tried to tune him out, but it was impossible.

And as it turned out, he didn't need me to talk to. He had Mamie, with whom he kept up a steady stream of nauseating baby talk.

Would oo like a taste of cawwot, sweetcakes? Isn't it yummy? Yes, it is! Yummy yum yumsters!

You think *you* want to upchuck? I had to listen to that glop all afternoon.

At first I told myself it was all going to be worthwhile, imagining something scrumptious like roast beef and Yorkshire pudding at the end of my culinary rainbow. Or perhaps a juicy T-bone with baked potato. Or maybe even—dare I hope?—homemade beef stew!

But, alas, I soon discovered that Lance was cooking a most appallingly healthy meal of poached fish and steamed veggies.

Plus a foul-smelling cauliflower soup, and lo-carb gluten-free dinner rolls.

And Mom thought *she* had it rough with Daddy's popalicious roast chicken.

Finally, I got so disgusted listening to the sound of vegetables chopping, I abandoned my computer and trotted off to the bedroom, making my changes in longhand. I'd just have to transcribe them onto my computer later that night.

I could still hear Lance banging around and cooing sweet nothings to Mamie, but at least it was somewhat muted, and I managed to finish the assignment just in time to hear him announce:

"Dinner is served!"

I had to admit, the dining room looked beautiful.

Lance had cleared my office paraphernalia from my dining room table and set it with some beautiful placemats and napkins from his own apartment.

He'd dimmed the lights, lit some candles, and poured us some chardonnay.

All of which helped deaden the blow of the meal to come.

Nothing like poached fish and cauliflower soup to send your taste buds into a coma.

"Isn't this dee-lish?" Lance asked, spearing one of the many veggies littering our plates.

"Dee-lish," I echoed with a wooden smile.

"Sorry about the fishy cauliflower smell. It should go away in three or four days."

Somehow I managed to plow through the main course, occasionally casting envious glances at Mamie's dog food.

Then came time for dessert.

"Tada!" Lance said, unveiling his surprise finale—a watery, gray rice pudding, with all the allure of Elmer's glue.

"It's got no dairy whatsoever," he boasted. "Made from nonfat soy milk."

By now my taste buds were on their knees, begging for mercy. And that's when he dropped his bombshell on me.

"I've really got to start cooking you dinner more often."

"No!" I blurted out before I could stop myself. "I mean, it's way too much trouble."

"Don't be silly. In fact, why don't I come back tomorrow and cook something else? It's about time you started eating right." His eyes lit up with messianic fervor. "I'm going to put you on a whole new diet regime. Nothing but health foods! By the time I'm through with you, the pounds will be positively melting away!"

At that moment, the only thing I wanted to see melting was some mozzarella on a pizza.

"So," he asked, digging into his rice pudding with gusto, "what do you want to watch on TV tonight?"

Oh, lord. He wanted to stay and watch TV again. It was all I could do not to impale myself on my fork.

And then, just in my darkest hour, a miracle happened. Lance's cell phone rang. A friend, calling to see if he wanted to go to the movies.

"I'd love to, Ben," he said, "but I just promised my neighbor I'd watch TV with her tonight."

"No!" I shrieked. "Go! I insist!"

"But I'd have to leave right now if I want to catch the show. And I wanted to do the dishes."

"That's okay, Lance, I'll do them. I don't mind. Really. You've done enough for one night."

To my enormous relief he told his buddy he'd meet him at the movies and got up to go.

"You really don't mind?" he asked, scooping Mamie into his arms.

"Not at all," I said, practically shoving them out the door.

The minute they were gone, Prozac jumped down from where she'd been hiding behind P. G. Wodehouse.

"Hey, Pro," I said, holding out the fish I'd buried beneath some vegetables on my plate. "Look at the special treat I've got for you!"

One sniff and she recoiled in disgust.

I've upchucked hairballs that smelled better than that.

This from a cat who considers the garbage can a gourmet dining spot.

And without any further ado, she began howling for something else to eat.

Screwing up my courage, I took a deep breath and headed into the disaster area otherwise known as my kitchen. Every drawer was open, every pot dirty. It was *Apocalypse Now* with spatulas.

I couldn't possibly face cleaning it tonight. I'd wait till tomorrow, when I was fresh and perky and had regained the will to live.

Instead I tossed some Chunky Lamb Innards to Prozac and hunkered down at my computer to type in the changes to *You and Your Septic Tank.*

After faxing them to Toiletmasters, I treated myself to a nice long soak in the tub, tossing in an extra handful of strawberry-scented bath salts. Unfortunately, they did not begin to mask the toxic cloud of cauliflower hanging over my apartment. But I didn't care. I was just happy to be in a Lance-free zone. I laid there, letting the hot water soothe my weary muscles, giving thanks to the humanitarian genius who invented the bathtub. And the Double Stuf Oreo, a package of which I'd brought along to keep me company.

Eventually I pried myself from my sudsy paradise and collapsed into bed.

I was in a deep sleep when the phone rang and woke me. In a fog, I picked it up. Too late, I realized it might be Lance. But it wasn't.

"Jaine, my beloved!"

Vladimir's voice came humming across the line.

"I call to beg you to give me one more chance and have dinner with me tomorrow night."

Without missing a beat, I replied, "Sure, Vladimir."

Now don't go packing me off to the loony bin. I hadn't taken leave of my senses. There was a perfectly logical reason why I agreed to go.

True, our last date had been a bit of a disaster. But at least no cauliflower had been involved. I had no idea what cavalcade of vegetables and bad TV Lance had planned for me tomorrow night.

All I knew was that I didn't want to be around to find out.

YOU'VE GOT MAIL!

To: Jausten
From: DaddyO
Subject: Out of Stock!

Tragic news, lambchop! I called the Turbomaster people to order some more Secret Spice, and they're out of stock! And they won't be getting in a new shipment for another month! I've been trying to cook without it, but my food just doesn't taste the same. Especially my *Popalicious Chicken à la Hank*. Without the Secret Spice, it's not nearly as Popalicious. Every time I think of Lydia Pinkus and her evil plot to keep me from winning the cookathon, I see red.

But fear not. Your old daddy's ever-nimble brain has come through again. I've thought of a surefire way to get my Secret Spice back from Old Pruneface.

More later . . .

XOXO,

Chef Hank

(aka Daddy)

To: Jausten
From: Shoptillyoudrop
Subject: Of All the Nerve!

Of all the nerve! Your father actually expects *me* to sneak into Lydia's kitchen during our next bridge game and look for his silly Secret Spice. Well, I absolutely refuse.

He can pout all he wants, but I am not about to take part in any of his ridiculous schemes!

Your thoroughly disgusted,

Mom

To: Jausten
From: DaddyO
Subject: Justice Will Prevail!

All I can say, lambchop, is that I'm very disappointed in your mom. I asked her to do a simple favor and snoop in Old Pruneface's spice rack, and she refused. To think, after all these years of marriage, I can't count on my own wife in my time of need.

It looks like I'm just going to have to take things into my own hands. Somehow, some way, Lydia Pinkus's evil plot to destroy me will be thwarted!

Justice will prevail!

Love 'n' hugs from,

Chef Hank

(aka Daddy)

Chapter 18

"Shhh!" I hissed at Prozac, who was clawing my chest bright and early the next morning, yowling to be fed.

What if Lance heard us stirring and came racing over with some ghastly whole-grain breakfast? That would never do. So I hustled my little noisemaker off to the kitchen to silence her with Hearty Halibut Guts.

My heart stopped when I saw the mess awaiting me.

No miracle had occurred in the night. Every drawer was still open, every pot still out on the counter. Perhaps they'd even multiplied. If only I'd put the dishes in the sink to soak. Now the remains of last night's dinner were practically welded to the plates.

After tossing some halibut guts in a bowl for Prozac, I began the hellish task of cleaning up. I doubted Lance would hear me all the way in the kitchen, but if he did, so be it. There was no way I could live with this mess.

Arming myself for battle, I put on my rubber gloves and dug in. I washed dishes and glasses, pots and pans, and knives I never even knew I owned. Half a bottle of Palmolive, two S.O.S pads, and three broken nails later, I was finally through.

By now I was starving, so I nuked myself some coffee and an ancient cinnamon raisin bagel I uncovered in my freezer. I slathered the bagel with butter and strawberry jam. Heavy on the jam. I deserved it after what I'd just been through.

Carting my breakfast to the living room, I eyed the front door warily. Dared I risk opening it for the newspaper? What if Lance was lying in ambush, waiting to pounce with a pitcher of carrot juice?

Unable to resist the lure of the crossword puzzle, I took a chance and cracked the door open. Thank heavens all I saw was my neighbor's azalea bush. So I snatched up the paper and scurried back inside.

Normally there's nothing I like better than doing a crossword puzzle with my morning coffee. I relish the challenge of coming up with seven-letter answers for obscure vice presidents. But that morning, I jumped every time I heard a noise, certain it was Lance about to barge in.

This was no way to live. If I didn't find the killer soon and get Lance his job back, I'd have to sign up for a witness protection program.

It was time to get my fanny in gear and pay a visit to the next person on my suspect list: Ellen Cooper. I'd gotten a glimpse of the fury lurking beneath her sunny smile and was eager to lob a few questions her way.

I called Owen at Mattress King. He was happy to give me her address and phone number. Well, not exactly happy. But given what I knew about his torrid affair with Bunny, he was in no position to turn down my request.

Ellen was home when I phoned and agreed to see me later that morning.

I whiled away the next half hour or so catching up on my e-mails and trying not to think about Daddy on the hunt for his Secret Spice. Then I got dressed as quietly as possible and poked my head out the front door.

Once again, I breathed a sigh of relief to see a Lance-less horizon.

Slinking past his apartment, I got in my Corolla and set out to question the jilted ex-wife.

Ellen Cooper lived in a condo on the Wilshire Corridor, a strip of astronomically priced high-rises in Westwood—minicities complete with 24-hour valets, tennis courts, and state of the art gyms.

I drove up the circular driveway of Ellen's mammoth art deco building, where a doorman dressed as a five-star general gave my Corolla the once-over. Clearly he was not impressed with what he saw.

"Deliveries around back," he said, motioning with his thumb to the rear of the building.

"I'm not making a delivery," I informed him frostily. "I'm here to see Ellen Cooper."

"Sorry, ma'am," he said, not looking the least bit sorry. "My mistake."

Grudgingly he opened my car door for me. As I walked off I could hear him say to a valet:

"Park this thing where nobody can see it."

Well, he could just kiss *his* fifty cent tip good-bye.

I pushed my way through a set of spotless revolving doors and entered a lobby straight out of a sultan's palace: travertine marble floors, humongous floral arrangements, and chandeliers I wouldn't want to be standing under during an earthquake.

Having scaled the doorman hurdle, I now had to pass muster with a gimlet-eyed concierge who practically demanded my social security number before he let me past his desk.

At last I was on a brass-railed elevator zooming up to Ellen's thirtieth-floor penthouse. I had no trouble finding the place since there were only two condos on the floor.

I rang what looked like a 14-karat gold doorbell, and seconds later Ellen came to the door in a baby blue sweatsuit, a smudge of chocolate on her cheek. She was as out of place in that joint as a Kmart shopper on Rodeo Drive.

"C'mon in, honey," she said, waving me inside.

My feet sinking in the plush carpeting, I followed her past her vestibule and into her living room, where I gazed in awe at her panoramic view of Wilshire Boulevard to the south and—in the distance, but visible nonetheless—the mighty Pacific Ocean to the west.

"What a view!"

"Just one of the many perks of the Waldorf Hysterical. That's what I call this place. A little over the top, don't you think?" she said, gesturing to her football field-sized living room. "You should see the other tenants. Some of these women get a facelift just to pick up their mail. Frankly, I miss my old house in Encino. But after the divorce, I wanted a change of scene. And it is fun being right here in town. Ellen Cooper, Jet Setter, that's me."

She graced me with one of her apple-cheeked grins.

"Say, I was just about to dig into a box of Krispy Kremes. Want one? Oh, of course you do. I know a fellow donut-holic when I see one. Make yourself comfy and I'll be right back."

I sank down into one of two chenille sofas facing each other in front of her massive fireplace. Ellen's furniture, like Ellen herself, looked out of place in the grand expanse of the room. Her stuff had to be at least twenty years old, well-worn, no-nonsense pieces that she probably bought at the beginning of her marriage and never bothered to update. Shabby chic, without the chic.

In no time, Ellen was back with a box of donuts, which she set down on a large pine coffee table between the two sofas.

"Help yourself, hon."

Needless to say, I did.

It was a toss up between jelly and chocolate glazed, but as always, chocolate triumphed.

Ellen grabbed one, too, and plopped down opposite me, tucking her legs beneath her generous tush.

"Sarah tells me that, despite your totally inept appearance, you're some sort of private eye."

Okay, so she didn't say the part about my inept appearance, but I could read between the lines.

I assured her that I was indeed a part-time unlicensed private eye and proceeded to ask her the usual questions about the night of the murder. Unfortunately, I got the usual disappointing answers. She saw no one out on the patio because she was too busy staring at me single-handedly destroying Bunny's guest bathroom.

When I asked her if she could think of anyone angry enough to have wanted to see Bunny dead, she responded with a hearty chuckle.

"Oh, sweetheart," she said, "take a number. Everybody hated her."

At which point we were interrupted by an ear-shattering whining noise.

I looked up, alarmed.

"Don't worry," she said when the noise had stopped. "It's only the plumber. He's snaking the drain in the master bath."

"Ms. Cooper!" A man's voice drifted down the hallway. "Can you come here a minute? I got a problem."

"Why is there *always* a problem?" Ellen sighed, hoisting herself up from her sofa. "I'll be right back."

"Help yourself to another donut!" she called out as she started down the hall.

I did not waste valuable minutes stuffing my face with a donut. Nope, I wasted only seconds scarfing one down. Then, wiping chocolate from my fingers, I started casing the room. With any luck, I'd run into a desk drawer jammed with incriminating evidence.

I scooted around, opening drawers and rooting under seat cushions. But all I found were a colorful collection of cocktail napkins, coasters, and playing cards. Plus fifty-six cents in change under the sofa cushions.

Across the hall I could see what looked like a small den. I was tempted to dash over and check it out. But just as I was screwing up the courage for this daring move, I heard footsteps approaching.

I quickly sat down and assumed a casual pose, leafing through a photo album from the coffee table.

The album I grabbed was white and frilly, the words *Our Wedding* etched in gold on the front. I just assumed the happy couple inside would be Sarah and Owen. Imagine my surprise when I saw that it was filled with pictures of Ellen and Marvin. Or, I should say, what used to be Marvin before his head had been gouged out from each and every photo.

I turned the pages, wide-eyed.

"Crisis averted!" Ellen breezed back into the room. "The guy's such a prima donna. You'd think he'd never snaked through a hairball before."

Then she looked down and saw the album on my lap.

"Ah. You've discovered my wedding album."

I nodded mutely.

"I guess you could say I was a little bitter when Marvin left me."

She wasn't going to get an argument from me there.

"But I'm all over it now," she assured me. "I keep it out for chuckles. It's hilarious, isn't it?"

Au contraire, lady. Laurel and Hardy were hilarious. Decapitated ex-husbands, not so much.

"It's funny how everything worked out for the best. If it hadn't been for the divorce, I would've never met my boyfriend." She flushed with pleasure. "You must've seen him at the party. What a doll, huh?"

"Indeed," I said, remembering her foxy silver-haired date.

"Well, I hate to cut this meeting short," she said, "but I'm meeting my honey for lunch and I've got to start getting ready. Let me show you to the door."

I thanked her for her time and headed out to the elevator, boggled by what I'd just seen.

Not the mutilated Marvins. They were creepy, of course, but not all that surprising. I'd known all along there was a lot of anger lurking beneath that apple-cheeked grin.

No, what knocked me for a loop was what I'd seen when I walked past her vestibule closet on my way out.

The door had been open slightly and I'd glanced inside. There, propped up next to a pair of boots, was a bottle of weed killer.

Now I ask you: What the heck was a woman who lived on the thirtieth floor of a high-rise doing with weed killer?

Just something to think about between chapters.

Chapter 19

Bidding a tipless adieu to the Waldorf Hysterical doorman, I took off down Wilshire Boulevard. Now that I'd questioned all of the Cooper clan, it was time to hit some of the other party guests.

First on my list was Fiona, Bunny's celebrity stylist.

Was it possible that underneath her apparently genial working relationship with Bunny, she'd harbored a secret grudge? Some bitter quarrel over a Versace evening gown, perhaps?

I dug in my purse and fished out the business card she'd given me the day I met her at Bunny's pool party.

"Sure, I'd be happy to answer a coupla questions," she said when I gave her a buzz on my cell phone.

Was it my imagination, or was she slurring her words? Could she possibly be tootled at 11:30 in the morning?

She gave me directions to her apartment in a scuzzy part of town, not far from the panhandlers on Hollywood Boulevard.

Her building, The Royale, was anything but. A dingy five-story stucco affair, festooned with graffiti and security bars, its swellegant days had vanished along with silent movies.

I gazed up at a man's undershirt drying on a window ledge. *This* was where a celebrity stylist lived? No wonder

Fiona always brought her clothes to Bunny; she surely wouldn't want any clients coming here.

I pressed a button on an intercom heavily etched with the F word, and Fiona buzzed me in. Not that she needed to. The lock on the lobby door was missing. I gaped in disbelief at the hole in the wood where the lock had once been. Was it possible someone had actually stolen the dead bolt off the door?

"I'm in 5J," Fiona said, her voice a distant scratch. "And the elevator's busted. You'll have to walk."

Indeed I did, trudging up five endless flights. That explained why Fiona was so thin and wiry. I'd be thin and wiry, too, if I had to face this obstacle course every time I came home.

I made my way up the dank stairwell, stepping over empty wine bottles, grateful there were no accompanying winos. By the first landing, I was gasping for air. I cursed myself for not working out more—or ever, for that matter—and prayed I'd make it to the top without collapsing or getting mugged.

By the time I reached the fifth floor I was ready for an oxygen tent. At last I managed to catch my breath and began trekking down an all too long hallway, dimly lit and grimy with age. Somewhere I heard a baby crying.

When I arrived at apartment 5J, Fiona was standing in the doorway in a faded silk robe, a drink in one hand, and—I was most disconcerted to see—a gun in the other.

"Don't mind the stun gun," she said, waving me inside with the stubby weapon. "I need it for protection in this hellhole."

I followed her into her apartment, a large studio dwarfed by all the furniture jammed inside.

A huge canopy bed was lined up against one wall, dominating the room. Fighting for space were an ornate settee, two matching armchairs, a mahogany dining set, and at least three racks full of clothing.

The furniture looked like quality stuff, but like Fiona, it had seen better days.

"Excuse the mess," she said. "Maid's day off. Haha."

I forced a weak smile.

"Can I get you a scotch?" She took an impressive gulp of hers. "It's Rite Aid's finest."

"No, thanks, but I'd love some water."

"Help yourself. Kitchen's right behind those racks."

She pointed to two clothing racks that screened the kitchen from view.

Squeezing between them, I found myself in a space not much larger than a shower stall.

I turned on the tap, setting off a painful squeal of pipes, and a gush of rusty water spurted from the faucet. I waited till it was running reasonably clean, then poured myself a glassful, hoping it wasn't swimming with carcinogens.

"Check the fridge if you're hungry," Fiona called out.

I was a tad peckish after climbing all those stairs, so I opened her mini-fridge, but all it contained were the same darn martini olives that graced my own abode.

I made a mental note to throw mine out.

Sucking in my gut, I once again squeezed between the two clothing racks and rejoined Fiona, who was now sprawled out on her settee.

"Have a seat," she said, gesturing to one of the two armchairs jammed between the bed and the settee.

I lowered my fanny and felt a spring poking against my tush.

"So whadja wanna know?" she asked, her eyes droopy with booze.

But before I could ask her anything, my eardrums were suddenly assaulted by the godawful crash of wood splintering. Holy Moses! Someone was busting down Fiona's door!

My heart lurched in my chest as an earsplitting gunshot rang in the air.

Oh, Lord, no! Some hoodlum had just broken in! I was going to be shot in broad daylight! I could see the headline now:

FORMER CELEBRITY STYLIST SHOT DOWN IN SENSELESS TRAGEDY
WOMAN IN "CUCKOO FOR COCOA PUFFS" T-SHIRT ALSO FOUND
POLICE SUSPECT DRUG DEAL GONE WRONG

I'd die with everyone thinking I was a druggie!

Instinctively I ducked for cover.

Fiona, however, did not blink an eye. Cool as a cucumber, she just banged on the wall with her fist.

"Turn down your goddamn TV, Thelma!"

She rolled her eyes, disgusted.

"Damn old lady next door is deaf as a doornail. Loves to watch *The Rockford Files*."

Feeling quite foolish, I now heard the strains of *The Rockford Files* theme song filter in from the next apartment. I poked my head out from behind the armchair and checked the front door. No signs of forced entry.

With an idiotic smile on my face, I got up from my cowardly crouch and resumed my seat on the broken spring.

Fiona banged on the wall again, and at last the sound was lowered.

"I can't believe I'm reduced to living in such a dump," she said, staring morosely into her scotch, "but my business is in the toilet. Has been for years."

"But I thought you were a celebrity stylist."

"I *was*, honey. Past tense. Most of those celebs are dead or retired now. The only client I had left was Bunny. Now she's gone, and I can't even afford this hellhole."

She consoled herself with another big gulp of booze.

"Without Bunny," she sighed, "it's all over. Next stop: Working the perfume counter at Neiman's."

"But, Fiona, you've got great taste. Surely there must be plenty of people out there who'd hire you."

"Have you forgotten where you're living, hon? This is L.A. Where it's practically illegal to be over forty. All the hot stylists are tootsies straight out of diapers."

I tsk tsked in sympathy.

"What about you, doll? You sure you couldn't use a stylist?"

Unhappily I informed her that the only thing I could afford on her racks were the hangers.

"Too bad," she sighed, and polished off her drink in a single gulp. "Mind getting me a refill, hon?"

Actually, I did mind. The last thing her liver needed was any more alcohol.

"Are you sure you wouldn't like some water instead?"

"Never have I been surer of anything in my life," she said, holding out her glass. "Scotch is over there. Under the bed." And then she added with a wink, "I've been keeping it handy lately in case I need a little nip in the middle of the night."

I looked under the bed and blinked at the sight of a ginormous jug of scotch. I'm talking huge, the Alkie Special, *Lost Weekend* size.

"Life sucks," I heard Fiona muttering, as I struggled to pull it out. "And to think, that stupid fortune-teller at Bunny's party told me wonderful things were headed my way. What a dufus."

I remembered Fortuna, the gypsy-clad actress stashed away in Bunny's den the night of the party.

"Yes, she did seem pretty crummy at reading the future."

"Read the future? The woman couldn't read the first line on an eye chart. I'm surprised Bunny didn't fire her on the spot. Especially after what she said."

"Really?" My ears perked up. "What did she say?"

"I was standing out in the hallway, waiting for my session, when I heard her call Bunny a sadistic bitch. She said she hoped Bunny'd rot in hell for ruining her life."

Hello. All along I'd assumed Fortuna was just another hired hand, but clearly she had some sort of history with Bunny.

I flashed back to the night of the Dirty Martini Party. Fortuna had begged me not to tell Bunny how she was screwing up. *If I know that bitch,* she'd said, *she'll have me fired.* At the time I thought it was just a figure of speech. But now I realized it was because *she really did know her.* Lord knows what simmering resentment she'd been harboring.

It looked like my clueless fortune-teller had just become a juicy murder suspect.

"Jaine, hon, what's taking you so long?"

Reluctantly I poured Fiona her drink, but you'll be happy to know I did no further damage to her liver. By the time I shoved the vat of scotch back under the bed and returned to the settee, she was passed out cold.

As I watched her lying there, her spiky hair matted and unwashed, one arm dangling limply to the floor, I could not for the life of me picture her as a killer. She had everything to lose from Bunny's death. Of course, there could always be a hidden motive, but I sure couldn't see it.

I let myself out of her apartment and made my way back down the hallway, filled with pity for Fiona, but grateful for the lead she'd given me.

I needed to talk with Fortuna. And pronto.

After a quick but satisfying rendezvous with a Big Mac, I zipped over to Casa Extravaganza, hoping Marvin would be able to put me in touch with Fortuna.

A gardener's truck was parked in the driveway when I showed up, and as I got out of my Corolla I could hear the drone of lawn mowers out back.

I hurried to the front door and rang the bell, setting off a volley of chimes inside. Tapping my feet impatiently, I waited for somebody to answer it, but no one did. Oh, drat. What if nobody was home? Or what if they couldn't hear me over the sound of the lawn mowers?

So I rang it again. And again.

I was just about to give up and leave when the door opened a crack and Marvin poked his head out.

"Marvin! Thank goodness you're home! I'm so sorry to disturb you, but I really need your help."

"What is it?" he asked, making no move to invite me in.

"Do you know how I can reach the fortune-teller Bunny hired for her dirty martini party?"

"No, I'm afraid not."

"Fiona told me she was an acquaintance of Bunny's."

"Really?" he said, still peering at me through the crack in the door. "Bunny told me she hired her from an agency."

"Do you remember the name of the agency?"

"Sorry, no."

And with that, he started to close the door.

"Wait!" I cried. "Maybe she wrote the name down somewhere. Or kept a business card. Would you mind awfully taking a look?"

I did not tell him that if I didn't find the killer soon, I might wind up committing Lance-o-cide, but I guess he sensed the urgency in my voice.

"Well, okay," he relented, and finally opened the door to let me in.

No wonder he didn't want me to see him. He was still in his bathrobe, one of those belted white terry affairs guaranteed to turn a tubby guy like Marvin into the Pillsbury Doughboy. It was all I could do not to give him a poke in the tummy.

The last time I saw him, scarfing down an empanada and poring over his spreadsheets, I'd wondered if his grief over

Bunny's death had been just an act. But if the guy was still in his bathrobe at this time of day, maybe he really was depressed.

"Wait here," he said. "I'll take a look in Bunny's office."

"One more thing," I begged, "if you could find a guest list for the party, that would be great, too."

I put on my most winning smile.

He nodded curtly and rushed off, clutching his robe so it wouldn't flap open in the breeze.

As I waited in the foyer, I couldn't help but think how peaceful the place seemed without Bunny. Instead of the elaborate floral arrangement that used to stand on the foyer table, there was a pitcher of fresh-cut daisies. The air no longer reeked of Bunny's expensive perfume, but the heavenly scent of garlic and onions. Lupe's latest culinary triumph, no doubt.

It took a while, but Marvin finally came puffing back with some papers in his hand.

"I found the name of the agency. And the guest list, too."

He handed me my booty and was just about to open the front door to let me out when a woman's voice called down from the top of the stairs.

"Marvin, darling, what's keeping you so long?"

Marvin blushed furiously, right up to the roots of his few remaining hairs.

So that soulful mourning shtick of his was just an act, after all. He'd already moved on to another bimbette.

But the woman who came down the stairs just then was no bimbette. *Au contraire.* She was a middle-aged gal in a Lanz granny nightgown and pink fleece scuffs.

She was, much to my surprise, Ellen Cooper.

Wait a minute! What happened to their bitter breakup? Hadn't I just that very morning seen Marvin decapitated in her wedding album? What the heck was she doing calling him "darling" in her Lanz nightie?

* * *

"I guess we've got some explaining to do," Marvin said with a sheepish smile.

I was sitting in the living room across from the ex-Mr. and Mrs. Cooper, still staring in disbelief as they sat thigh to thigh on Bunny's designer sectional.

"How long have you two been an item?" I managed to ask.

"Pretty much since I got back from my honeymoon with Bunny," Marvin confessed.

"You had, what, a whole two weeks of wedded bliss?"

"Not even that long. Three days into the honeymoon, Bunny was showing her true colors. Screaming at our hotel maid, making a scene if she didn't like our table at dinner. I soon realized what a fool I'd been to leave Ellen."

He looked over at his ex-wife with such love in his eyes, I expected to hear violins playing in the background.

And I suddenly understood why Marvin never seemed to have had time for Bunny, why he'd always been buried in his work. I thought he was your garden variety workaholic, but in truth, he was just avoiding her.

"At first I was pretty angry," Ellen said, "as you well know from the wedding album. But then I saw how miserable Marvin was with Bunny, and the next thing I knew he was sneaking over to my place for meatloaf and *Seinfeld* reruns."

And a little mattress action, I figured, eyeing her nightie.

"I wanted a divorce," Marvin said, "but I knew how vindictive Bunny could be. She was sure to rake me over the coals."

"You didn't have a pre-nup?"

"Bunny said it took all the romance out of love, and I was dopey enough to go along with her. I could shoot myself for being such an idiot."

"Don't be so hard on yourself, darling." Ellen said, running her fingers where his hair would have been if he'd had any.

"Ellen and I sweated bullets for our money, and we hated the thought of Bunny walking away with a chunk of it. Besides, I soon suspected that Bunny had a lover."

If he only knew it was his own son-in-law.

"We kept hoping that she'd be the one who'd want the divorce," Ellen said. "Which would've made things a whole lot easier. So we kept our affair a secret and pretended to be bitter exes."

"And then," Marvin said, "when Bunny got killed, we realized how bad it would look if people knew we'd been having an affair. I'd be the prime suspect for sure. So we've kept up the pretense."

"What about your boyfriend?" I asked Ellen. "The silver-haired fox?"

"Escort service." She winked. "A hundred bucks an hour. Two hundred after midnight."

"Does anyone else know about all this?"

"Just Lupe. But she's not about to go to the police. She knows we aren't killers."

And indeed, sitting there side by side, holding hands, a pudgy middle-aged couple, they didn't much look like the murdering kind.

But looks can be deceiving. Just ask any vet who's ever looked into Prozac's innocent green eyes and called her a sweet little kittykins.

For all I knew, Marvin and Ellen decided to bypass a messy divorce with a dose of weed killer. Which led me to my next question.

"And the weed killer I saw in your closet?" I asked Ellen.

She had to think about this for a beat before she realized what I was talking about.

"Oh, that. I didn't use it to poison Bunny, if that's what you're thinking. It's for our weekend house in Santa Barbara. Marvin and I have been meeting there when we get the chance."

Sounded plausible. Not necessarily true. But plausible.

After promising that I wouldn't squeal to the cops (not yet, anyway), I told the lovebirds I'd let myself out and left them sitting on the sectional, Marvin still gazing goo-goo eyed at Ellen.

I only hoped some man would look at me that way some day. Preferably without the Pillsbury Doughboy bathrobe.

Chapter 20

Like a jungle cat lying in wait for his prey, Lance pounced on me as I headed up the path to my apartment.

"Hey, Jaine," he cried, bounding out his front door. "About dinner tonight—"

He looked so eager, I felt a sudden stab of guilt about finking out on him.

"I was thinking of making skinless boneless chicken on a bed of steamed veggies."

And presto, my guilt was gone. If God had meant us to eat steamed veggies, she would have never invented hollandaise sauce.

"I'm so sorry, Lance, but I checked my calendar, and it turns out I've already got plans."

Thank goodness I'd accepted that date with Uzbekistan's least eligible bachelor.

"That's okay, Jaine. I was just about to tell you that, after all my recipe planning, I can't make it, either. I'm going to a stress management class."

"Fabulous! I mean, that you found a class."

He did seem a lot perkier, and for that, I was grateful. I wished him good luck with his fellow stressees and trotted off to my apartment, thrilled to be out from under the steamed veggie threat.

I was happy for all of about thirteen seconds before it

dawned on me that I'd accepted a date with Uzbekistan's least eligible bachelor for nothing.

No need to panic, I thought, as I let myself into my apartment. I'd simply call Vladimir and break our date.

Yes, I know. A person of your high moral caliber would never cancel a date at the last minute. But that's because you've never gone out with Uzbekistan's least eligible bachelor. You'd change your tune fast enough if my rhyming Romeo showed up on your doorstep.

I was about to pick up the phone when I realized I didn't know his number. Oh, well. No problem. I'd just look up his number on my caller ID.

I didn't see the name "Trotsky" when I scrolled down my list of recent callers, but I did find an "out of area" number for the time he'd called last night. Eagerly I dialed it, but there was no answer. I must've let that damn phone ring twenty times. For crying out loud, didn't the Trotskys have an answering machine?

With hours to kill before my ordeal, er, date with Vlad, I should've plowed ahead with my search for Fortuna. But the prospect of another date with Vladimir had pretty much drained me of all energy.

So instead, I whiled away the rest of the afternoon with Prozac—and a bag of Corn Doodles—watching Ellen, Tyra and Judge Judy.

(Prozac doesn't much care for Dr. Phil.)

Every so often I'd get up during a commercial and try the Trotskys, but there was never an answer.

After Judge Judy had browbeat her last plaintiff, Prozac began yowling for her dinner. I sloshed some Tasty Tuna Innards in her bowl and gave the Trotskys another try.

This time someone actually picked up.

"Whaddaya want?" a gruff male voice asked. Probably a relative I hadn't yet met.

"Can I speak with Vladimir, please?"

"Vladimir ain't here."

"What about Aunt Minna?"

"She ain't here, either."

"Well, can you give Vladimir a message for me?"

"No, I can't give Vladimir a message, lady. This is a pay phone. There ain't no Vladimir here. Now would you get off the line so I can call my parole officer?"

So much for canceling my date.

Reluctantly, I started getting dressed for my rendezvous with Vladimir, skipping any attempts at beautification. The last thing I wanted was to encourage the guy.

I tossed on some old elastic-waist pants and a pilly acrylic sweater. I didn't even care when I discovered a ketchup stain on the sleeve. Then I pulled my hair back in a scrunchy and slapped on an unflattering shade of lipstick I'd found in the dollar bin at the drugstore.

Needless to say, I didn't bother with perfume.

At precisely seven o'clock the doorbell rang. With heavy heart, I trudged to the door and opened it.

"Jaine, my beloved!"

Vladimir stood on my doorstep, decked out in a red vest and bow tie, his wiry curls freshly lubed for the occasion. I suppose this was what passed for spiffy in Uzbekistan.

"A present for you," he said, handing me a half-empty pack of Juicy Fruit.

"Gum. How very thoughtful."

"And flowers, too!" From behind his back, he whipped out what was clearly a stalk of blooms from my neighbor's azalea bush. First Mrs. Hurlbut's tulips. Now the azaleas. This guy could not seem to keep his hands off my neighbors' flowers.

I hurried to the kitchen and put the azaleas in water, hoping I wouldn't soon be getting a bill for a new azalea bush.

"Ready, my darling," he asked when I came back out to

the living room, "to dine at the finest restaurant in all of Los Angeles?"

"I sure am. But where are you taking me?"

Okay, I didn't really say that. I just forced a halfhearted smile and said, "Sure."

Outside, Vladimir linked his arm through mine and led me down the path to the curb.

"My car is parked down the street."

Good lord. Had he actually managed to bring Boris's rust-mobile back from the dead? No matter, I wasn't about to climb in that thing again. I'd insist we take my Corolla.

"Here we are!" he said, pointing to a shiny late model Mercedes.

I blinked in disbelief. Vladimir—the fellow who gave stolen flowers and used gum as gifts—driving a Mercedes?

"Vladimir, where on earth did you get this car?"

"A friend loaned it to me," he grinned, bursting with pride.

"That's some generous friend."

"Allow me, dear lady." He opened the passenger door with a flourish.

I settled in the luxurious depths of the leather, wondering if perhaps Vladimir was going to take me to a nice restaurant after all.

He turned on the ignition and the engine sprang to life. Minutes later, tooling along on our automotive Comfort Cloud, Vladimir launched into his latest love poem, a mushy rhyme-fest involving tresses, caresses, and wedding dresses.

I tuned him out around about the time he longed to experience the heavenly bliss of my tender kiss.

Instead I focused on the meal to come. The finest restaurant in all of Los Angeles, eh? Maybe he was taking me to a steak joint. I salivated at the thought of a T-bone smothered in onion rings. Talk about heavenly bliss. Of course, he could be taking me to a French place. Or an Italian. In which case, I'd get the lasagna for sure. I was lost in thoughts of a crusty loaf of garlic bread, dripping with butter, when I heard him say:

"We're almost there!"

For the first time I realized we were in a pretty seedy neighborhood.

"Here it is," he said, pointing out the window. "The finest restaurant in all of Los Angeles!"

"The House of Plov?" I said, reading a neon sign flashing above a tiny storefront restaurant.

"None other! You know what plov is, my beloved Jaine?"

"I don't suppose it's Uzbek for T-bone steak?"

"No, it's like rice pilaf. Only better!"

Okay, so it wasn't steak. Or lasagna, for that matter. But I'd always liked pilaf. At the very least, it was an improvement over steamed cauliflower.

How bad could it be?

Stick around and see for yourself.

Vladimir parked the Mercedes in front of the restaurant. No trouble getting a parking spot in this neighborhood. I only hoped the car would be there at the end of the meal.

Once more linking his arm in mine, he ushered me into The House of Plov, a kitschy joint with red checked tablecloths, linoleum floors, and plastic flowers on the tables.

A strolling accordionist wandered among the tables, playing what I assumed were Uzbek folk tunes.

"I got us the best table in the house!" Vladimir grinned.

Clearly, he didn't have to pull too many strings. The place was practically deserted. Just one guy in the corner getting drunk on what looked like vodka shots. And a table of six rather large men in the back. When I say large, think rhinos on steroids.

Now I've never actually met a member of the Russian mafia, but I'd bet my bottom blini that those six guys had tossed a few corpses into the river in their day.

There was no sign of a hostess, so Vladimir led me to a table for two in the center of the room.

"Here's our table!" he said, pointing with pride to a coffee-stained "reserved" sign propped up against the plastic flowers.

"Lucky for us," he said as he held out a chair for me, "Cousin Sofi works here and saved it for us."

"Sofi works here?" I gulped.

"Sure! She's their number one waitress!"

As it turned out she was their only waitress, but her status at The House of Plov was the least of my worries.

If you recall, the last time Cousin Sofi and I had met, she'd threatened me with extreme bodily harm if I so much as smiled at her beloved Vladdie. What the hell would she do if she saw me here on a date with him?

I was about to find out.

For just then she came clomping out from the kitchen, hauling an enormous tray of food for the mafiosi.

One look at me and thunderclouds began gathering over her head.

"Guess what, Vladimir?" I chirped. "I've got this sudden craving for a Big Mac. Whaddaya say we hop on over to Mc-Donald's?"

"McDonald's?" he sneered. "Ptui! House of Plov million times better than McDonald's."

Having finished serving the goons, Sofi now stomped over to our table, shooting me a death ray glare from under her massive unibrow.

"Welcome to House of Plov," she grunted, hurling a menu at me.

I must confess, I was relieved when Vladimir ordered us

drinks. Something told me I would need a little assist from Mr. Alcohol to get me through this evening.

"Bring us two Plov Martinis!" Vladimir instructed his cousin. "And don't be stingy with the vodka."

"Two Plov-Tinis," Sofi snarled.

I just hoped mine didn't come with a dollop of her spit.

Across the table, Vladimir was staring at me with a lovestruck grin. Quickly, I opened the menu to avoid eye contact.

I scanned the list of entrees, not one of which appeared to be vaguely edible. There was goat plov, sheep plov, horse-meat plov, and the special of the night, camel plov.

Good heavens. Had these people never heard of chicken?

I was trying to decide which dish was least likely to give me nightmares when Sofi showed up with our drinks. She banged them down on the table with thinly veiled fury, but Vladimir seemed oblivious to her anger.

"To my darling Jaine," he said, raising his glass in a toast.

To me your smile is like a dream
With teeth as white as sour cream
I wish on all the stars above
For huggy kissy in The House of Plov

Oh, barf. I reached for my Plov-Tini and—praying it wasn't laced with Sofi's saliva—took a healthy gulp. Yikes, it was strong. I'd be lucky if I still had enamel on my sour cream teeth at the end of the evening.

"So whaddaya wanna eat?" Sofi asked, still beaming me death ray glares.

For one of the very few times in my life, I said the words:

"I guess I'll have the house salad."

"That's it?"

"With a side of plain plov."

"Don't be silly!" Vladimir said. "We'll have Camel Plov for two. With extra camel!"

"Really, Vladimir, I don't think I can handle camel meat."

"You'll love it. I promise. It tastes just like horse!"

Sofi grunted and, with a final glare in my direction, stomped back to the kitchen.

At which point, the accordionist sidled up to our table and launched into a hammy rendition of "Strangers in the Night."

"Shall we?" Vladimir asked.

And without waiting for a reply, he pulled me up out of my chair and started leading me in a frenetic fox-trot, whirling, dipping, and spinning me like a top. At one point my fanny brushed against one of the mafiosi, who rewarded me with a sly pinch and a gold-studded grin.

At last the number was over and I escaped back to my seat, where I took a desperate gulp of the paint thinner posing as my cocktail.

At which point Sofi showed up with our entrees, two ginormous plates of food, heaped with pilaf and the remains of some unlucky camel.

"Dig in!" Vladimir grinned.

I picked at my Camel Plov, avoiding the camel as best I could.

What little appetite I had was squashed to smithereens when Vladimir launched into a story of the time his goat, Svetlana, had gas so bad the vet had to perforate her stomach.

Somehow, between gruesome details, he managed to suck up his meal. When he'd cleaned his plate, he looked over at mine and saw how little I'd eaten.

"What's wrong?" His raisin eyes widened in concern. "You don't like?"

"Oh, no! It's delicious! It's just that I had a really late lunch."

"Okay, then. I'll eat."

With that, he took my plate and started inhaling its contents.

When he had consumed enough camel meat to grow his own humps, he finally threw in the towel and belched gently.

"Excuse me, my beloved. I go to the Little Commissar's Room to take pee."

Still numb from the saga of Svetlana's gastroenterological woes, I did not even flinch at the mention of his bodily functions.

And as he trotted off to the Little Commissar's Room, I took advantage of the lull in the action to scarf down an old Lifesaver I found at the bottom of my purse.

I'd just popped it into my mouth when suddenly I felt myself being yanked from my chair.

"We need to talk," Sofi's voice hissed in my ear. And before I knew it, she was dragging me into the kitchen, a steaming hovel that, from the looks of it, had last been cleaned when Catherine the Great was in pigtails.

Under the bored gaze of a toothless chef sweating into a vat of plov, Sofi grabbed me by the neck of my sweater and held my face mere inches from hers.

(I didn't say anything at the time, Sofi, but if you happen to be reading this, you might want to try the occasional breath mint.)

"I told you to leave my Vladdie alone," she growled.

"I swear, Sofi, there's nothing between us. We're just friends!"

"I don't believe!"

She now shoved me perilously close to the open range, and the sight of those flames (not to mention a most unattractive wart on Sofi's nose) put the fear of God in me.

"But it's true," I wailed. "Honestly, after tonight, I'm never going to see Vladimir again!"

"You swear?"

"I swear!"

Reluctantly she let me go.

"If I find out you lie to me, you in big trouble."

My knees trembling, I made my way out of the kitchen. If only I'd brought my Corolla I could make a dash for it and get the heck out of there.

But alas, I was trapped.

Sofi was right behind me as I headed back to my table, where Vladimir was waiting for me. The minute he saw me, he signaled the accordionist, who, much to my horror, began playing the "Wedding March."

The cue for Vladimir to get down on his knees and take another one of his damn poems from his pocket. To the best of my memory, it went something like this:

TO MY BELOVED JAINE

Soon you will be at my side
My very own, my blushing bride
Your skin as soft as ripe banana
Just you and me and my goat Svetlana

Sofi snorted like a bull as Vladimir took a ring from his pocket.

"What are you doing?" she bellowed. "That's my mama's ring!"

"I know, Sofi. I borrow for tonight."

Then he turned back to me.

"As soon as we get to Uzbekistan, my beloved Jaine, I get you the finest cubic zirconia money can buy.

"So how about it, honey bun?" he asked, looking up at me with eager raisin eyes. "Will you marry with me?"

Over at the mob table, the goons broke out in a loud cheer.

"You say yes," the head goon instructed me. "He nice boy."

Oh, lord. If I said no, would they take me out back and break my legs?

On the other hand, if I said yes, Sofi wouldn't even wait to take me out back. She'd mince me into plov meat right here in the restaurant.

Besides, no way on earth was I possibly going to marry this guy.

I was just about to risk the mob's wrath and ring in with a resounding no when the front door burst open, and two cops came charging in, followed by a distinguished-looking bizguy in a designer suit.

"That's the guy!" the man shouted, pointing at Vladimir. "He's the one who stole my Mercedes!"

Vladimir may have been the world's least eligible bachelor, but he was not, you'll be relieved to know, a car thief.

"I do not steal car!" he shouted, jumping up from where he had been kneeling at my feet.

"Of course you did!" the bizguy shouted back.

"It's all her fault!" Sofi said, pointing to me.

"How on earth is this my fault?" I cried, unwilling to be pawned off as some kind of Uzbek Ma Barker.

One of the cops, a wiry Asian guy, held up his hands for silence.

"Everybody calm down. You'll all get a turn to speak. You first."

He pointed to Vladimir.

"I do not steal car!" Vladimir repeated, driving his theme home. "I was standing at bus stop in front of restaurant when this man drive up in nice car and throw me his keys."

"Of course I threw you the keys," Mr. Mercedes said. "I assumed you were the valet."

Indeed, in his red vest and bow tie, Vladimir did bear a striking resemblance to a parking attendant.

"Valet?" Vladimir blinked, puzzled.

Clearly he was unfamiliar with the concept.

"I thought he loan me his nice car. I said to myself, 'Vladimir, what a friendly place America is. The people are so kind, so generous!' "

"You thought I loaned it to you?" Mr. Mercedes shook his head in disbelief.

"I shout out to him, 'I return your car after my date with my beloved Jaine,' but he didn't hear. He was already inside restaurant."

"See?" Sofi piped up. "It's all her fault."

"I had nothing whatsoever to do with this!"

I didn't care if she minced me to plov meat; I was getting darn sick of her accusations.

The mobster who'd pinched my tush now put in his two cents: "He no steal car, he's good boy." His fellow hit men nodded in unison. "He just ask girl with big fanny to marry him."

And yes, he did call me the girl with the big fanny. If I hadn't been so terrified of winding up with my feet in a cement block, I would have given him a good piece of my mind.

"You came here to propose?" Mr. Mercedes asked Vladimir, visibly touched.

"Congrattalashuns!" the drunk in the corner piped up.

"Yes, I come here to propose," Vladimir said. "But I didn't get my answer."

Once more he got down on his knees in front of me.

"My beloved Jaine, will you marry me?"

How awkward was this? Everybody in the restaurant was looking at me: Vladimir. The cops. Mr. Mercedes. The mobsters. The drunk in the corner. And of course Sofi, who was still beaming me her death ray glares.

I hated to turn Vladimir down in front of an audience. But I had to put a stop to this ridiculous marriage proposal, or I'd

wind up walking down some aisle in Uzbekistan with Svetlana as my goat of honor.

"I'm sorry, Vladimir. You're a very sweet guy, but I can't
marry you."

Vladimir gasped in dismay.

Over at their table, the hit men muttered in disgust.

"You not nice girl," my fanny pincher hissed.

Indeed, everyone in the restaurant was giving me the evil
eye as poor Vladimir sat down at our table, crushed, his head
in his hands.

"I told you she no good," Sofi gloated.

The cops turned to Mr. Mercedes. "You still want to press
charges?" one of them asked.

"No, of course not. Anyone can tell this poor guy would
never steal a car."

"In that case, I guess we'll be going."

Having served and protected, L.A.'s finest made their way
out the door. But not without first giving me a dirty look.

"C'mon, buddy," Mr. Mercedes said, putting a comforting
hand on Vladimir's shoulder. "I'll give you a ride home."

"What about me?" I asked.

"After the way you broke his heart?" Icicles dripped from
his voice. "You can get your own ride."

With a final tortured glance in my direction, Vladimir allowed Mr. Mercedes to lead him out the door.

"Women!" I heard Mr. Mercedes saying, his arm draped
around Vladimir's frail shoulder. "Can't live with 'em. Can't
shoot 'em."

"Really?" Vladimir replied. "Not like back home."

Stranded in the middle of nowhere, I sat back down at the
table and phoned for a cab. I wasn't about to bus it in this
neighborhood.

Behind me, I could hear the mob muttering what I was certain were Uzbek curses. I only hoped they weren't busy ordering a cement mixer.

I was sitting there wondering if I could possibly fend them off with a butter knife when Sofi came stomping over to the table.

"It was pleasure to serve you," she snarled, slapping a check down in front of me. "Don't forget tip."

YOU'VE GOT MAIL!

To: Jausten
From: Shoptillyoudrop
Subject: The Nerve of That Man!

Darling, you won't believe what happened during our bridge club lunch at Lydia's today. It was horrible. Simply horrible. Not the lunch, of course. Lydia fixed her Salmon Wellington, which was divine. Honestly, her pastry crust is nothing short of miraculous. How Daddy ever expects to beat her in the cookathon with his Popalicious Chicken is beyond me.

Anyhow, we were sitting there eating Lydia's salmon (which Daddy childishly insists on calling Salmon Smellington!) when the doorbell rang. Lydia went to answer it, and when she came back, guess who came barging into the room with her? Daddy!

"I just stopped by to say hi!" he said. Which was a big fat lie. I knew very well why he stopped by: to snoop in Lydia's kitchen. I swear, I wanted to throttle him!

Lydia, always the perfect hostess, asked if she could get him anything to eat. Daddy said no thanks, that he'd just fixed himself a *BLT à la Hank*, but that he was a little thirsty.

"Don't let me interrupt your lunch," he said to Lydia, practically shoving her back in her chair. "I'll go to the kitchen and get myself a Diet Coke."

Well, Lydia wasn't having any of that! You know how house proud Lydia is. Well, I don't suppose you do, do you?

You've never actually met her. But she'd rather be skinned alive than let someone see her kitchen if it isn't immaculate.

"I can't have you seeing my kitchen in such disarray," she said, popping right back up again. "You stay right here, Hank, and I'll get you your Diet Coke."

"That's okay," I said, glaring at Daddy. "Hank can get his own Diet Coke at home. We've got plenty in our refrigerator."

"Oh, all right," he pouted, and stomped out the door.

We went back to our lunch, and I was just beginning to relax again when I happened to look out the window and got the shock of my life. There was Daddy, shimmying up Lydia's palm tree! Honestly, I thought I'd have a heart attack. Thank heavens I was the only one facing the window. Clearly Daddy was trying to break into Lydia's town house through her upstairs balcony! How on earth he thought he could sneak back downstairs to the kitchen without Lydia noticing, I'll never know. But he never got the chance to try. Because just then we heard a piercing scream coming from upstairs.

It turns out Lydia's Aunt Ida was visiting from Minnesota and was napping in the guest bedroom. Apparently Daddy had let himself in through the sliding glass door on the balcony, and she'd seen him standing in the shadows at the foot of her bed.

"Aunt Ida!" Lydia cried as we all came racing into the guest bedroom. "What on earth happened?"

I held my breath, certain that Aunt Ida was going to unmask Daddy as the intruder he was. But when she finally spoke she said, "I just saw your Uncle Alfred! He was standing right there! At the foot of the bed."

What a relief! She thought she'd been dreaming and that Daddy was the ghost of her dead husband. While everyone was fussing around Aunt Ida, I sneaked out to the balcony, just in time to see Daddy jumping over Lydia's hedge and running down the street. If that palm tree had a coconut hanging from it, I swear I would've thrown it at him! I was that angry!

I can't believe he put himself and our reputation at risk, all for that silly Secret Spice, which I still say is nothing more than paprika!!

Can't write any more, honey. I'm too upset. I'm going to the broom closet for some Oreos.

XXX,

Mom

To: Jausten
From: DaddyO
Subject: Daring Rescue Attempt

Well, lambchop, you'll be disappointed to learn that in spite of a daring rescue attempt, I was unable to retrieve my Secret Spice from the evil clutches of Lydia Pinkus.

For some crazy reason, your mom is upset just because I tried to let myself into Old Pruneface's town house through an upstairs balcony. She can't seem to understand that I was just trying to get back what was rightfully mine.

No way am I going to let that battleaxe keep me from winning first prize at the cookathon.

I may have been foiled today, but somehow, someway, I'm going to get back my Secret Spice!

Your very determined,

Daddy

(aka Chef Hank)

Chapter 21

So worn out was I by my disastrous date with Vladimir that I barely blinked an eye when I checked my e-mails the next morning and read about Daddy's attempted break-in at Lydia Pinkus's town house. Normally my blood pressure would have skyrocketed a few notches, but that day I just sat there, staring numbly at the screen.

Nor did I have the strength to put up a fight when Lance showed up on my doorstep with pomegranate juice and gluten-free wheatberry muffins for breakfast.

Now I've never actually eaten cardboard, but I'm guessing it tastes a lot like gluten-free wheatberry muffins. Which, by the way, were annoyingly devoid of any actual berries.

"I've got good news and bad news," Lance said, cutting his muffin into neat halves. "Which do you want first?"

"Good news." I was long overdue for some.

"Well," he said, his eyes lighting up, "I met the most fabulous guy in my stress management class. Honest, Jaine, I think I'm in love."

"That's nice."

I did not even bother to fake enthusiasm. Partly because it's hard to fake enthusiasm when you've just swallowed a mouthful of cardboard. But mainly because Lance, like Kandi, seems to fall in love with the frequency of a public radio pledge drive.

Oblivious to my lukewarm reaction to his newsflash, Lance began babbling about Peter, his latest crush. I only half listened, not wanting to waste valuable brain cells on a guy who'd probably be gone by his next haircut. I just glommed on to the highlights, which were that Peter was a travel agent coping with the stress of losing his longtime companion, a sexually ambivalent parrot named Mr. Polly.

I sat there, sipping the pink Drano posing as pomegranate juice, nodding my head every once in a while, as Lance blathered on about Peter's (and Mr. Polly's) many sterling qualities.

"So what's the bad news?" I asked when he finally ran out of steam.

"Isn't it obvious? I've finally met the love of my life, and I'm about to go to jail."

"You're not going to jail, Lance."

"Why?" he asked eagerly. "Did you find the killer?"

"Not yet. But I've got a ton of suspects."

"Like who?"

"Remember that fortune-teller at the party?"

"The dodo who told me I'd soon be marrying the woman of my dreams?"

"Apparently she and Bunny already knew each other before the party. Fiona overheard her telling Bunny she was a sadistic bitch who ruined her life."

"Wow. You think she lined up that gig at the party to kill her?"

"Maybe. I'm going to track her down today and see what I can find out."

"That's great! Say, do you suppose you could wrap up the case by next Friday? Peter's got us tickets to Barbados."

"I already told you, Lance. I'm detecting as fast I can."

"And I appreciate everything you're doing, hon," he said, actually licking his finger to snag some stray cardboard crumbs from his plate. "Which is why I feel bad about my other piece of bad news."

Whatever it was, it couldn't possibly be worse than these damn muffins.

"I'm seeing Peter tonight, so I won't be able to cook you dinner like I was planning to."

It was all I could do not to break out in a jig.

"What a shame," I said, trying to keep the glee from my voice.

"And I hate to eat and run, sweetie, but I've got tons of stuff on my To Do list. Gotta keep busy. That's rule number One in stress management class."

Grabbing one last muffin for the road, he hurried off to tackle his To Do list.

Needless to say, the minute he left, I threw on some sweats and headed over to McDonald's for an edible breakfast.

One Sausage & Egg McMuffin later, I was on the phone with *Let's Party!*, the agency Bunny had used to hire Fortuna.

"I'm calling," I said to the snooty Brit who'd answered the phone, "because I need to reach one of your entertainers."

"I'm afraid we never give out contact information for our entertainers. All party plans must be made through us."

Clearly, they didn't want customers calling their people and making deals on the side.

"Actually, I'm a private investigator, and it's a matter of utmost importance."

"I repeat," she said, with all the warmth of a pit bull, "we do not give out personal contact information for our performers."

The next thing I knew, I was talking to a dial tone.

Oh, well. It looked like I was going to have to put on a little performance of my own.

Let's Party! was located in a small, three-story office building in Westwood, where parking spots are about as easy to find as hydrangeas in the Sahara. There were none in sight when I showed up, so I pulled into the miniscule private parking lot in back.

Ignoring the tow-away signs festooned everywhere, I parked alongside a green Jag with the vanity plates *LET'S P!* Unless the Jag belonged to a urologist, I was guessing its owner was a *Let's Party!* person.

Then, gussied up in my Prada pantsuit, my mop of curls blow-dried into submission, I headed into the building, hoping to pass myself off as the kind of society dame who could afford to pay top dollar for a bad fortune teller.

A tiny elevator took me to the third floor, where I made my way to the offices of *Let's Party!* Or, I should say, office. The place consisted of a single room, tastefully furnished with Currier & Ives prints, lush ferns, and cherrywood file cabinets. Through the open louvered windows I could hear the sounds of the traffic on Westwood Boulevard.

Sitting at an antique desk was a stunning black woman whose nameplate read Cynthia Hardwicke.

"Well, hello," Cynthia said, shooting me a dazzling smile. "Welcome to *Let's Party!*"

It was the same Brit I'd talked to on the phone. What a difference from her earlier frigid greeting.

"Have a seat." She gestured to a suede chair facing her desk.

Once I was settled in its comfortable depths, she flashed me another dazzler and asked, "How may I help you?"

Time to play society doyenne.

"I'm throwing a little soiree," I said, trying to sound as A-list as possible, "and I need an entertainer."

"What kind of entertainer? Magician? Celebrity impersonator? We have a fabulous juggling Elvis."

"Actually I was at a party at Bunny Cooper's not long ago, and she had the most divine fortune-teller."

At the mention of Bunny's name, Cynthia's perfectly plucked brows furrowed in sympathy.

"Poor Mrs. Cooper!" she tsked. "What a tragedy that was."

Having allotted a whole two seconds of mourning for Bunny, she returned to the business at hand.

"I can't quite recall who we sent out to that party."

"Her name was Fortuna," I prompted.

"Actually several of our fortune-tellers work under that name."

"Well, I want the one who was at Bunny's party. Do you keep a record of who you sent where?"

"Of course we do. But unfortunately, my computer's down right now."

Oh, crud. Of all days for her computer to be down.

"But you can look through our book of head shots and see if you recognize her picture."

With that, she handed me a thick looseleaf folder, jammed with back-to-back eight-by-ten glossy photos.

I grabbed it eagerly and began poring through the clowns, jugglers, and celebrity impersonators until I finally came to the picture of the pretty brunette who'd been such a dud at Bunny's party.

"Here she is!" I exclaimed, showing Cynthia the photo.

"Oh, yes. Fortuna #4. She's one of our best entertainers."

If she was one of the best, I'd hate to see the juggling Elvis.

"So what date do you need her?"

"Date?"

"For your party? Your little soiree?"

Was it my imagination, or did I detect a hint of skepticism in her voice?

"Oh, right. My party. It's, um, next Saturday night. But I need to speak with Fortuna right away."

"Of course. I'll have her give you a call. As soon as I get your deposit."

"What?"

"Your deposit. Two hundred should cover it."

Two hundred bucks? For a woman who couldn't find the fortune in a fortune cookie? She had to be kidding!

"Silly me," I said, pretending to look in my purse. "I forgot my checkbook. Why don't I just drop the check in the mail the minute I get home?"

"No need for that," she said, her smile stiffening. "We take credit cards."

Forget it. No way was I about to rack up a two hundred–dollar charge. Surely there had to be a way around this.

I was desperately trying to think of one when I heard a car alarm go off outside.

Which gave me an idea.

"Oh, dear," I said, once more rummaging in my purse. "My wallet! I must've left it in the car."

"Oh?" By now, Cynthia was positively oozing disbelief.

"I'll be right back!" I cried as I dashed out the door.

Once in the hallway, I made my way to the elevator. But I did not get on. Instead I waited several minutes and then came hurrying back to Cynthia.

"Here I am," I said, waving my wallet.

She looked up, surprised to see me. Clearly she'd had me pegged as a party-planning deadbeat.

"That's wonderful," she beamed, reaching for her card swiper.

Time to put my plan into high gear.

"By the way," I said, "do you happen to drive a green Jaguar?"

"Yes, why?"

"When I was in the parking lot just now, I saw the tow-away guys hooking it up to their truck."

"What??"

And just like I hoped she would, she jumped up and charged out the door.

The minute she was gone, I pulled out Fortuna #4's photo from the looseleaf binder. Like most actors' head shots, it had her resume printed on the back.

And right there at the top was her real name, Marla Mitchell, along with her contact information, which I quickly jotted down.

Then I slipped into the hallway and hid in the stairwell, peeking out from behind a crack in the door until I finally saw Cynthia Hardwicke stomping back to her office.

I figured under the circumstances it was best that we not bump into each other.

My ancient Corolla was lucky to have a steering wheel, let alone a GPS system, so I made a quick pit stop at my apartment to change out of my Prada togs and google directions to Fortuna's place. After printing them out, I put in a call to make sure she was home.

Thank heavens for out-of-work actors. She picked up on the first ring.

"Sorry, wrong number," I said when I heard her voice. No sense warning her of my impending visit.

Fortuna/Marla lived in North Hollywood, a quasi-hip, formerly dreary part of town referred to as NoHo by realtors desperate to unload foreclosed property. I pulled up in front of her apartment building, one of those spit-and-promise jobs that seem to spring up overnight in L.A. like mushrooms in the rain.

A sign out front said, VALLEY VIEW APARTMENTS. But one of the Vs was missing, so it now read ALLEY VIEW APARTMENTS. Quite fitting, since the lucky residents in front had a scenic view of the bowling alley across the street.

After pressing all the buttons on the security intercom, somebody buzzed me in and I made my way to Marla's first floor apartment. The faint sounds of sitar music drifted from inside.

I rang the bell and heard someone padding to the door.

"Who is it?" a woman I hoped was Marla called out.

"It's Jaine Austen."

"Isn't she dead?"

For the 9,876th time in my life I cursed my parents for not naming me something sensible like Hortense or Esmeralda.

"Not that Jane Austen. We met at Bunny Cooper's party. You told my fortune."

The door opened a crack and Fortuna/Marla peered out.

"Oh, right." She smiled. "I remember you. You were one of the nice ones."

She swung open the door, a skinny thing in yoga pants and a big slouchy T-shirt, her dark hair swept up in a careless ponytail. Out of her gypsy garb and heavy make-up, she seemed a lot less exotic than she had the night of the party.

"How did you ever find my address?"

"Marvin Cooper gave it to me."

I figured it was best to leave my good buddy Cynthia Hardwicke out of this.

"Gee, I didn't know he had it. Usually Cynthia is so strict about giving out our contact info. Well, come on in. I was just meditating."

I followed her into her living room, where a yoga mat was unfurled on the floor. Indeed, the place felt like a mini-ashram, with batik throws on her furniture, a serenity waterfall burbling on an end table, and the heady aroma of patchouli wafting in the air.

"With all the rejections I go through as an actor," Marla said, sitting cross-legged on her yoga mat, "I don't know what I'd do without my meditation. It really helps me get centered."

"I'll bet," I said, centering my tush on her batik-covered sofa.

"Want some birch bark tea?" she offered, ever the polite New Age hostess. "It's a great bowel cleanser."

"No, thanks. I'm good."

"How about a stress ball?" She held up a red rubber ball. "Just squeeze it, and release all your tension."

"That's okay," I said, opting to remain tense as well as un-cleansed.

"Well, I really appreciate your stopping by, Jaine. You won't regret it. I've improved a whole lot since you saw me. I've been channeling my Gypsy Persona in acting class and I'm much more convincing.

"So when is your party?" she asked with an eager smile.

Oh, dear. She thought I was there to offer her a job.

"Actually, Marla, I'm not having a party."

"You want me to read your fortune for real? That good, I'm not."

"No, I wanted to ask you a couple of questions about Bunny Cooper's murder."

"What are you, some kind of private eye?" she asked, giving her stress ball a squeeze.

"I guess you could say that."

"I once played a detective on TV. My character got killed before the first commercial, though."

She sighed at the memory of her aborted television appearance.

"So what did you want to know?"

Looking down at her on the yoga mat, so slim and deli-cate, her veins showing beneath her translucent skin, I was beginning to wonder if she was even capable of murder.

But I pushed aside my doubts and plowed ahead, going straight for the jugular.

"I have a witness who overheard you call Bunny a sadistic bitch who'd ruined your life."

"Who told you that?" she gasped.

"It doesn't matter, Marla. All that matters is that I have a witness."

"I didn't call her a sadistic bitch," she said softly, staring down at her stress ball. "I called her an *evil* bitch."

"So you already knew Bunny before you showed up at the party?"

"We worked together at the same modeling agency. It's no secret that I didn't like her. Nobody did. She was always bad-mouthing the other models, trying to steal our bookings."

"Sounds like Bunny," I conceded. "But how did that ruin your life?"

"Bookings weren't all she tried to steal. Bunny liked to steal men, too," she said, giving her stress ball an anxious squeeze. "One day we were sent out to the same catalog shoot. My car was in the shop, so my boyfriend, Charlie, took me to work. When he came to pick me up, I wasn't quite ready. And Bunny moved in for the kill. The next thing I knew Charlie broke up with me. He told me he couldn't help himself, he'd fallen head over heels for Bunny."

So Marvin hadn't been the first man Bunny had stolen from another woman. And something told me there'd been plenty of others, too.

"Two months later, she dumped Charlie for someone else. She never wanted him in the first place. It was all a game to her. She just wanted to take him away from me. Charlie was so devastated, he got crazy drunk one night and lost control of his car on the coast highway. Drove it straight through a guardrail over a cliff. He was dead before the paramedics even showed up."

She blinked back the tears welling in her eyes.

"I've never loved anybody like I loved Charlie, and she took him away from me. Forever."

Sure sounded like a motive for murder to me. But I still couldn't picture her getting up the gumption to pull it off.

"When I showed up at the party that night, I had no idea it was Bunny's house. I just knew I was going to see a

Mrs. Cooper. I wanted to throw up when I saw her in that palace of hers, strutting around in her designer shoes, bragging about her Maserati and her swimming pool and her stupid Marilyn Monroe glasses. She stuck me in that tiny room, lording it over me like I was some kind of peasant. My god, I wanted to kill her.

"But I didn't, of course," she added hastily.

She looked up at me with wide gray eyes, and for the life of me I couldn't see her as a killer. I figured the worst she was capable of was sending out bad vibes.

But she had an undeniably strong motive to want Bunny dead. I had to play hardball.

"Oh?" I said. "So then what were you doing out on the patio that night?"

"What are you talking about?"

Time for a little fib.

"I have another witness who saw you out on the patio alone with Bunny's drink."

"That's a lie!" she said, jumping up from her yoga mat, her face flushed red.

"I'm sick and tired of being accused of things I didn't do!" she shrieked. "I was nowhere near that patio! I didn't poison Bunny's stupid martini. And I didn't steal that sweater, either. I don't care what the security guard at Bloomingdale's says. I didn't even know it fell into my purse!"

It was then that I glanced down and saw a stream of gel oozing out of her stress ball. My god, she'd squeezed that thing so hard, she'd broken the casing.

Far from being a delicate little flower, Marla Mitchell was one angry lady. And apparently a bit of a kleptomaniac, too.

Maybe she was capable of murder, after all.

After adding Fortuna to my growing list of suspects, I hightailed it to the nearest KFC for a much needed spot of lunch and was now chomping on an Extra Crispy chicken breast, musing on how frustrating this case was turning out to be.

I had suspects coming out of the woodwork, but no proof whatsoever. If only I could dig up a witness who'd seen somebody slip out onto the patio.

But as you well know, all the party guests had been too engrossed watching me make a fool of myself in Bunny's guest bathroom. Once more, I wracked my brain trying to remember if there'd been a face missing from the crowd gawking at me. I shut my eyes to visualize the scene, but all I could see was that water gushing from the broken faucet.

That and the KFC fudge brownie parfait I'd been eyeing for dessert. It looked mighty tasty.

Oh, for crying out loud. What was wrong with me, thinking about dessert at a time like this? I'll bet S. Holmes never sat around thinking about fudge brownie parfaits when he had a murder to solve.

I needed to question the other guests at the party. Maybe one of the Barbies saw or heard something incriminating. Maybe one of them was even the killer.

I made up my mind to scoot home the minute I finished my chicken and get that guest list Marvin had given me. But as luck would have it, the minute I finished my chicken, Kandi called me on my cell.

"You'll never guess what happened!" she shrieked, in high panic mode. "It's a miracle I'm still alive!"

"What's wrong?"

"We just had a bomb scare at the studio."

"No!"

"Maggie the Maggot found an unmarked sealed box in the ladies' room."

Maggie the Maggot, for those of you who've never seen Kandi's show, was one of the many talented thespian insects on *Beanie & the Cockroach*.

"She swears her ex-husband sent it. They went through the divorce from hell, and when Maggie got custody of their dog, her ex vowed to get revenge. . . . Wait a minute—great news!"

"They defused the bomb?"

"No, even better. We get the rest of the day off. Let's meet at Century City and go to the movies."

I couldn't possibly go to the movies. I had to get cracking and question those Barbies.

"Absolutely not, Kandi. I'm way too busy."

"Don't be silly. Meet you at the cineplex in a half hour."

"Make it an hour. I'm out in the valley."

Yes, I know I shouldn't have caved. But the thought of spending the next few hours with someone who neither knew nor loathed Bunny Cooper was really quite appealing.

Polishing off the last of my chicken, I wiped my hands with a moist towelette and headed back over the hill to Century City.

Okay, so I headed back to the counter, where I ordered that fudge brownie parfait.

But right after that, I headed over to Century City.

Chapter 22

The west side of Los Angeles is the rich side of Los Angeles. And nothing says money quite like the parking lot at the Century City mall.

I parked my humble Corolla amid the BMWs, Mercedes, and Lexus SUVs jamming the lot, and took the escalator up to the land of Tiffany key rings and seventy-five dollar T-shirts.

I was trotting along, checking out the shoppers and marveling at the wonders of plastic surgery, when I spotted a petite, dark-haired woman heading my way. Something about her looked familiar, but I couldn't quite place her face.

And then I realized it was Lupe, clacking along in heels, tailored slacks, and a blazer. I hadn't recognized her out of her uniform.

"Lupe!" I waved.

Lost in thought, she looked over at me, startled.

"Oh, hello, Ms. Jaine."

Up close, I could see she was wearing make-up. With her shiny hair set free from its usual bun, and a hint of blush on her cheeks, she was really quite attractive.

"What're you doing here?" I asked. Somehow, I couldn't picture her forking over seventy-five bucks for a T-shirt.

She looked around furtively.

"Can you keep a secret?"

I happen to be extremely reliable at keeping secrets. (If you don't count the fact that I'm blabbing everything that ever happens in my life to you.)

"Absolutely," I assured her.

"I'm here for a job interview."

With that, she broke out in an excited grin.

"I got a call from a friend of Ms. Bunny who said she heard what a good cook I am. And now she wants to meet me. If she hires me, she's going to pay me three times what Mr. Marvin is paying me!"

Which, according to my lightning calculations, would put her in a tax bracket three times greater than mine.

"Not only that, she promised to get me a green card!"

"That's wonderful!"

"Of course, I hate to leave Mr. Marvin," she sighed, a frown furrowing her brow. "He's been so good to me. But I need the extra money. And the green card."

"I'm sure he'll understand."

I doubted it would be too much of a blow to him, not with Ellen back in his life.

"I'd better hurry," she said, checking her watch. "We're supposed to meet at the food court, and if I get the job, we're going supermarket shopping so she can show me what foods she likes."

"Well, good luck!"

After all the crappola she'd put up with from Bunny, she deserved some.

"Thank you, Ms. Jaine. I only hope she likes me."

"Don't worry. I'm sure everything will work out fine."

Which just goes to show how little I knew.

Kandi was waiting for me in the lobby of the cineplex with two tickets to one of those romantic comedies she's so fond of. You know the kind, where a size 0 heroine who in real life could have her pick of any guy in the world sits home alone

Saturday nights in impossibly adorable pajamas, eating ice cream straight from the carton and never gains an ounce. Then she meets Mr. Cutie Pie, and after a few funny misunderstandings the two of them wind up in a liplock with Nat King Cole crooning in the background.

"So how's my little bomb threat survivor?" I asked as we rode the escalator up to our theater.

"Actually, the whole thing was a blessing in disguise. That pompous idiot who plays the cockroach is driving me nuts. The guy spends two weeks playing Hamlet in summer stock and suddenly he thinks he's Sir John Gielgud. If he asks me one more time what his motivation is, I'm going to spritz him with Raid.

"Hey, want anything to eat?" she asked, catching sight of the concession stand. "My treat."

"Oh, no, thanks, honey. I just had lunch."

I was not about to let a single morsel past my lips. Not after the cholesterol festival I'd just packed away. So, while Kandi ordered a vat of buttered popcorn, I settled for an anemic Diet Coke.

"Sure you don't want anything?" Kandi asked, as the kid behind the counter rang up our sale.

"Not a thing," I said, vowing not to touch a single kernel of her popcorn.

We found our theater and climbed the steps to one of the upper rows. Thank heavens Century City has stadium seating. Which, if you ask me, is the best thing to happen to movies since Raisinets. The way the seats are raked, you're practically guaranteed an unobstructed view, even if, as so often happens, an inconsiderately tall lunkhead plops down in front of you at the last minute.

Comfortably ensconced in our seats, with about fifteen minutes till the movie started, we settled in to gab.

"So how's your true love?" I asked.

"What true love?"

"The doctor you met on line at Starbucks. The Scrabble lover. The one you were going to marry."

"Oh, him," she said, dismissing him with an airy wave of her hand. "What a jerk."

The woman is amazing. She can go from Wedding Bells to What a Jerk in the time it takes Dale Earnhardt to start his engine.

"You won't believe what happened."

If it happened to Kandi, I'd believe it.

"He was all set to come to my apartment for dinner the other night. It was his first meal at my place and I worked my fingers to the bone ordering takeout from La Scala Presto. I had the table set, the candles lit, and Brazilian jazz playing in the background when I got a phone call from him."

She paused dramatically. Kandi is fond of milking her stories for all they're worth. Which is one of the reasons why *Beanie & the Cockroach* happens to be one of the highest rated cartoons in its time slot.

"He said he was at Starbucks, buying me some ground espresso for after dinner."

"How sweet."

"That's what I thought. Until he told me he'd fallen madly in love with the gal on line in front of him."

"But that's how he met you!"

"Yes. The man is a Starbucks Stalker."

"Aw, honey," I commiserated, "that's too bad."

"No biggie," she shrugged. "I'm well rid of him. It turns out he's not even a real doctor. He's a chiropractor in a mini-mall. And he probably cheats at Scrabble, too."

She reached into her tub of popcorn and popped a kernel in her mouth. She's got to be the only woman on the planet who eats popcorn one kernel at a time.

"So what's up with you?" she asked, munching on her kernel.

I decided not to tell her about my latest freelance detecting gig. Kandi always raises a stink when she knows I'm involved in a murder, nagging me about things I'd rather not be thinking about, like winding up in the morgue with an ID tag dangling from my big toe.

"Nothing much," I replied, playing it safe.

"What about that guy from Mongolia?"

"Uzbekistan."

"Did you ever go out with him?"

"Did I ever."

Cringing at the memory, I gave her a brief recap of The House of Plov fiasco.

"Men," she grunted. "They're all impossible."

Yeah, right. Until she met her next Mr. Wonderful.

"Why on earth did you go out with him in the first place?"

"Kandi! You were the one who insisted I give him a chance."

"Did I?" She blinked, puzzled.

"Yes! You said he sounded charmingly ethnic."

"I don't remember saying that."

"Well, you did!"

"Shhhh!" someone behind us whispered.

I looked up at the screen and saw the movie was about to start. A healthy smattering of gray-haired ladies and unemployed writers had filled the seats while Kandi and I had been chatting.

Shoving our failed love lives aside, Kandi and I sat back and started watching the trials and tribs of the size 0 actress on the screen. In spite of my cynical self, I actually wound up enjoying it. When the heroine finally ended up in a tender embrace with her sweet-but-sexy studmuffin, I looked down and was amazed to discover Kandi's tub of popcorn in my lap. With just a few unpopped kernels rolling around at the bottom.

"What's this doing here?" I asked Kandi, who was gazing at the credits, glassy-eyed.

"I offered you some at the beginning of the movie, and you never gave it back."

Oh, lord. I'd just polished off a vat of buttered popcorn. Had I no self-control? Next thing I knew I'd be eating in my sleep.

We made our way along our row of seats to the steps leading to the exit.

"Wasn't that just the sweetest movie ever?" Kandi sighed, as we started down.

But I did not get a chance to answer her. Because just then I felt someone shove me in my back. Not a jostle. Not a pat. But a major shove.

Which sent me stumbling down what seemed like an endless chasm of steps. Frantically I reached out for the handrail and managed to grab it. Just in the nick of time. One millisecond later, and I'd have been catapulting headfirst to some pretty serious, if not fatal, injuries.

Kandi hurried to my side.

"My gosh, Jaine, did you trip?"

No, I most definitely did not trip. Somebody had pushed me down those steps on purpose.

And I had a sinking feeling that somebody was Bunny's killer.

I looked around for my assailant, but aside from a few elderly ladies in orthopedic shoes, the theater was pretty much empty.

Whoever'd pushed me was long gone.

"Are you okay?" Kandi asked as I made my way down the rest of the steps.

"I'm fine," I lied.

Taking no chances, I checked behind me before I got on the escalator down to the theater's lobby. I wasn't about to take a tumble on that baby.

"You don't look fine," Kandi said, peering at me through narrowed eyes.

"I don't suppose you noticed anyone standing behind me on those stairs, did you?" I asked, trying to sound as casual as possible.

"Why? You don't think somebody pushed you?"

"No, no. Of course not."

"Yes, you do!"

Darn that Kandi. She can read me like a Chinese take-out menu.

"You're chasing after another killer, aren't you? I can always tell!"

By now we were outside in the hazy afternoon sunshine, and Kandi pulled me over to one of the many wooden benches scattered around the mall.

"C'mon," she said, shoving me down onto the bench. "Tell Kandi everything."

And the next thing I knew I was blabbing all about the murder.

"Jaine, Jaine, Jaine," she sighed when I was through. "How many times do I have to tell you? Tracking down killers is dangerous."

"I know. But it adds a jolt of excitement to my life."

"You want excitement? Try the 15-Hour Sale at Macy's."

She would've gone on reading me the riot act, but fortunately I was saved by her cell phone, which started ringing in her purse.

"Damn!" she said, checking her caller ID. "I've got to take it. It's the office."

The good news was I didn't have to sit through her lecture. The bad news was she had to go back to work. The "bomb" in the ladies' room turned out to be a bunch of old scripts one of the cleaning crew forgot to throw out.

"Sorry, hon. I hate to leave you like this. Are you sure you'll be okay?"

"I'll be fine," I said, faking a confident smile.

But I couldn't help it. I was spooked.

"Promise me you'll stop your investigation this instant, and leave everything to the police."

"I promise," I lied.

"If I find out you're lying and you wind up getting killed, I swear, I'll never speak to you again."

After a farewell hug, we parted ways and I headed down to where I'd parked my car.

As I walked along the dimly lit underground lot, I had the uncomfortable feeling that someone was following me. At first I told myself it was just my imagination, but then I heard the squeak of rubber-soled shoes padding behind me.

Someone was out to get me.

But I wasn't about to go down without a fight. Reaching into my purse, I grabbed my travel-sized can of hair spray. One spritz in the eye, I've found, can discombobulate an attacker almost as well as mace.

Then I whirled around and spritzed my heart out.

"What the hell do you think you're doing?!"

I found myself standing face to face with an irate trophy wife in tennis whites and sneakers, whose perfectly coiffed blond hair had all the hair spray it needed, thank you very much.

"Oh, gosh," I sputtered, "I'm so sorry, I didn't mean to spritz you. I thought you were the killer who pushed me down the stairs in the movies."

She looked at me like I'd just wandered in from the nearest psycho ward and without any further ado, made a mad dash for her Lexus.

Can't say that I blamed her.

The Los Angeles evening rush hour, which starts about ten minutes after the morning rush hour, was in full swing when

I left the mall. By the time I slogged my way home, it was after five.

Prozac greeted me at the door with her patented "Feed Me" yowl.

"How's my little Bunnyface?" I asked, swooping her up in my arms.

Hungry! And don't call me Bunnyface.

"Mommy almost got killed today," I told her as I opened a can of Luscious Lamb Innards in Savory Sauce.

Yeah, right. Whatever. Don't be stingy with that savory sauce.

Once her little pink nose was buried in the stuff, I poured myself a wee glass of chardonnay and ran the water for a nice long soak in the tub.

Leaving my clothes in a heap on the bathroom floor, I sank into the steamy bubbles. As I lay there, waiting for the hot water to work its magic, my mind kept replaying that scene at the movies. That awful sensation as I lost my balance, the frightening sight of those steep steps looming below. I knew that shove was no accident. Someone had purposely pushed me. But who? The first person who sprang to mind was Fortuna. After all, I'd just been to her apartment and practically accused her of the murder. You saw how she went bonkers. It would have been easy for her to slip out of her apartment and follow me to the movies.

Yes, Fortuna seemed like a likely candidate. But it could have been any one of my suspects. For all I knew, Bunny's killer had been tailing me for days and waiting for the opportunity to pounce.

Whoever it was wanted to scare the stuffing out of me.

And I must confess, they'd done a darn good job.

Forty-five minutes later, when the hot water had loosened the Boy Scout knots in my muscles, I emerged from the tub and slipped into my bathrobe. Then, grabbing my clothes from where I'd tossed them, I went to my bedroom to hang them up.

How innocent I was in those few seconds as I walked toward my closet, totally unaware of the shock I was about to receive.

"Omigod!" I shrieked in disbelief when I opened my closet door.

No, there was no dead body gazing glassy-eyed at me from inside a garment bag. But it was almost as bad.

Someone had stolen practically all of my clothes!

Only a black cocktail dress, my Prada suit, and a few stray blouses remained, dangling midst a sea of empty wire hangers.

Then I saw a note, pinned to one of the hangers:

> *Jaine, sweetie—I've been meaning to clean your closet for ages, and today I finally got around to it. I left you with a few basics, and now we can start building a fun new wardrobe from scratch!*
> *Love and kisses,*
> *Lance*
> *PS. I threw out your Oreos, too.*

In a flash I was at his front door.

"Lance, you idiot!" I cried, pounding on the door in my bathrobe. "Open up this minute!"

But there was no answer.

Then I remembered. Tonight was his date with Peter, his stress management buddy.

I was heading up the path to my own apartment when I got the uneasy feeling that somebody was watching me. A chill ran down my still-damp spine. Had the killer followed me home to finish me off for good?

I whirled around but saw no one.

Obviously, my nerves were getting the best of me. I had to stop being such a wuss.

Nonetheless, when I got back to my apartment, I dead-bolted the door and went around my apartment twice, checking to make sure all my windows were locked. Still feeling uneasy, I jammed a chair up against my front door and crept into bed with a cast-iron frying pan on my night table. Just in case.

I laid there staring at the ceiling for what seemed like hours, until Prozac's purring body, tucked under my chin, finally lulled me into a fitful slumber.

Chapter 23

The next day dawned bright and sunny. Outside I could hear the reassuringly normal sounds of birds chirping, dogs barking, and Mrs. Hurlbut hollering at Mr. Hurlbut.

With the sun streaming in my window like a klieg light, last night's jitters seemed just a tad foolish.

Sheepishly, I got out of bed and removed the chair I'd propped up under my front door.

Of course, there was still plenty of trouble in paradise. Aside from a killer on the loose, I had that matter of my empty closet to attend to. So the first thing after breakfast, I stomped over to Lance's apartment to get my clothes back.

"Where the hell are they?" I snarled when he came to the door, his blond curls still tousled from sleep.

"And good morning to you, too."

He actually had the nerve to be smiling.

"What did you do with my clothes?" I said, restraining the impulse to slap him silly.

"I gave them to a thrift shop."

"What?!"

"Now, Jaine," he said, in a maddeningly calm voice. "I realize you're upset. But someday you'll thank me for this."

"What day would that be?" I shrieked. "When hell freezes over?"

"Did anyone ever tell you you're cute when you're apoplectic?"

"Which thrift shop did you give them to?" I asked through gritted teeth.

"Trust me, honey. You don't want your clothes back. Just say no to polyester."

"I swear, Lance," I snarled, "if you don't tell me where my clothes are, I'm going to strangle you with one of your Hugo Boss ties."

"Okay, okay." He eyed the throbbing vein in my temple. "Don't have a cow."

Reluctantly he gave the name of a thrift shop run by a local church.

Wasting no time, I sped over there.

In order to protect the innocent (namely me, from a lawsuit), I'm going to call the place the Our Lady of Monumental Chutzpah Thrift Shop.

"Hello, dear," an angelic gray-haired woman greeted me as I came racing in.

She stood behind a glass counter jammed with kitschy knickknacks, her gray curls permed into a tight nimbus around her head.

"How may I help you?" she chirped.

"I want my clothes back!"

At that, her angelic smile faded.

"You want to take back a contribution you made?"

"That's just the point. I didn't make it! Without my permission, my neighbor raided my closet and kidnapped my clothes!"

"But, my dear, the proceeds of all sales go to a very worthy charity."

"I realize that, and I commend you for the wonderful work you do here at Our Lady of Monumental Chutzpah, but I need my clothes back."

"Well, dear, if it's that important to you, let's go find them."

I shot her a grateful smile.

"When did the donation come in?" she asked.

"Yesterday."

"Oh, we haven't sorted through yesterday's donations yet. "Anna, dear," she called out to a tiny porcelain doll of a woman. "Please watch the counter while I help this young lady."

Then she took me out to a back room crammed with boxes and bags of donated items. Several other Monumental Chutzpah ladies were busy sorting through the sacks.

"Here are the items that came in yesterday," my permed companion said, pointing to some bags lined up near the door.

It didn't take long to find a huge garbage bag stuffed with my clothes.

"Thank heavens," I said, hugging my *Cuckoo for Cocoa Puffs* T-shirt to my chest. "I thought I'd lost you forever."

"Oh, yes," my companion said, eyeing my clothing, "I can see why you'd be so upset with your neighbor for giving your clothes away. You have some lovely things."

"Thank you," I replied, happy to find someone who finally appreciated my discerning taste in fashion.

"I can let you have these beautiful garments back for just one hundred dollars."

"One hundred dollars? But you haven't even unpacked it yet."

"Legally, it belongs to us," she said, still smiling that angelic smile, "and if you want it, you're going to have to cough up a C-note."

Can you believe the gall of that woman, charging me one hundred bucks for my own clothes?

"There's an ATM machine right down the street," she pointed out helpfully.

Five minutes later, I was forking over one hundred of my hard-earned dollars to this septuagenarian extortionist.

I only hoped her next perm fried her hair off.

As I pulled out of the Monumental Chutzpah parking lot onto Olympic Boulevard, I noticed a boxy black car in my rearview mirror.

Several blocks later, the car was still behind me.

And just like that, last night's jitters came rushing back. I was convinced it was the killer following me, just waiting for another chance to strike again.

But then, when I turned down my street, the car continued on down Olympic.

With a sigh of relief, I parked my Corolla and headed up to my duplex. I really had to calm down. Hundreds of drivers took Olympic Boulevard each day; that didn't mean they were tailing me.

Back in my apartment, I hung up my clothes, which were, of course, wrinkled beyond belief. I was sorely tempted to drag Lance over and make him iron every darn one of them. The only reason I didn't was that I was afraid he'd stay and cook me one of his ghastly meals.

When I'd finally put away my last fashion treasure, I grabbed myself a Diet Coke and plopped down on my living room sofa.

"That was exhausting," I sighed.

Prozac looked up at me from where she'd been napping on one of the cushions.

Maybe you'll feel better if you fix me a snack.

"Prozac, don't give me that starving orphan look. There's some leftover mackerel guts in your bowl if you want some."

Ignoring her baleful glare, I picked up the morning paper. I'd been so engrossed in the saga of my missing clothes, I hadn't yet gotten around to reading it.

I almost choked on my Diet Coke when I saw the headline:

MAID'S BODY LEFT FOR DEAD IN DUMPSTER

And there, smiling up at me in a grainy black and white photo, was Lupe.

With my heart in my stomach, I read how a homeless man had found Lupe's body in a Dumpster, her head bashed in and left for dead. She'd been brought to USC County General Hospital, where her chances of survival were listed as "slim."

Clearly the killer had struck again.

Poor Lupe must have seen something incriminating the night of the murder, some clue to the killer's identity. Maybe she even saw who did it.

When I'd run into her at the mall yesterday she said she was going to meet a prospective employer. A friend of Bunny's who was willing to pay her three times what Marvin was paying her. She said they were meeting at the food court, and if she got the job they were going to the supermarket so her new boss could show her what foods she liked.

It hadn't occurred to me at the time, but now I wondered why a prospective employer would meet a job candidate at the mall. Didn't people usually interview cooks in their homes? Wouldn't they want to show them their kitchens? And why go to the supermarket to show Lupe what she liked? Why not just write out a shopping list?

I should've suspected that inflated salary was too good to be true.

Yes, Lupe must've seen something important out on that patio. But, afraid to go to the cops lest they deport her, she kept her mouth shut. Somehow the killer found out and, taking no chances, lured her to the mall with the promise of a high-paying job.

It was possible, of course, that Lupe had been blackmailing the killer for a better job, but I had a hard time picturing timid little Lupe as a blackmailer.

Whatever the scenario, I was willing to bet my bottom

Pop-Tart that the woman Lupe met at Century City was Bunny's killer.

And I had to stop her before I became Victim #3.

Armed with Lupe's newspaper photo, I zipped over to Century City to track down my Mystery Woman.

Was it Fortuna, I wondered, the unstable actress whose true love Bunny had stolen? Or Ellen, the ex-wife hoping to reunite with her husband? Or Sarah, the stepdaughter who'd loathed Bunny from the moment she'd laid eyes on her?

Or maybe it was one of the party Barbies. Any one of them could have been nursing a secret grudge.

For the second day in a row, I pulled into the Century City parking lot. Still a bit rattled about yesterday's movie mishap, I was careful to park in a well-lit space.

I made my way up to the food court and groaned to see the place packed with customers. It was almost lunchtime, and the midday crowds were gathering to be fed.

Well, I wasn't about to wait in any lines.

Switching to Take Charge mode, I headed straight for the nearest concession, a place called California Tater, where two teenage kids were cranking out orders.

"Excuse me," I called out. "I need to ask you guys a question."

One of the kids, a moonfaced girl with a purple streak in her hair, looked up from the Coke machine.

"Sorry," she said. "You gotta wait your turn."

"Yeah, lady," one of her customers echoed. "Get in line, like the rest of us."

I turned to see everyone in line scowling at me. Wilting under their collective glare, I crept meekly to the end of the line.

California Tater was one of those places that served baked potatoes a zillion different ways. And I have to confess their bacon-cheese tater looked mighty tempting. But I could not allow myself to be distracted by baked potatoes when I had a killer to track down.

The line moved slowly, but at last it was my turn.

"What can I get you?" the purple-haired teen asked as I stepped up to the counter.

"Like I said eight customers ago, I need to ask you guys a question."

"You sure you don't want a potato?"

"No, I don't want a potato. I just want to know if either of you saw this woman here yesterday."

I held up Lupe's photo, but all I got were a couple of blank stares.

I repeated this process at a few other food stands, waiting on endless lines, flashing Lupe's photo to more teenagers in paper hats. But aside from one kid who identified her as Jennifer Lopez, nobody remembered seeing her.

Trudging to the end of yet another line, I gazed out onto the food terrace. How I wished I were sitting there in the sun, inhaling a bacon-cheese baked potato. And as I watched the busboys running around clearing tables, it suddenly occurred to me that maybe one of *them* saw Lupe's mystery woman.

So I scooted outside to question them. It wasn't easy chasing after them as they hustled about. And communication was a bit of a hurdle since English seemed to be their distant second language.

But at last I struck gold with a stocky brown-eyed guy with a reasonable command of the English language.

"*Si,*" he said, gazing down at Lupe's picture. "I saw her. *Muy hermosa.* Very pretty."

"Did you notice who she was with?"

"She wasn't with anybody. She sat alone for a long time. Like she was waiting for somebody. Then a man came and she left with him."

"A man?" I blinked in surprise.

"*Si. Un hombre.*"

"What did this man look like?"

"I wasn't looking at the man," he shrugged. "I was look-ing at her. Like I said, she was *muy hermosa.*"

Honestly, men are the most irritating witnesses. All they deposit in their memory banks are sports scores and *Playboy* centerfolds.

"Don't you remember anything about him?" I asked.

He pondered a beat and finally managed to dredge up a smidgeon of a description. But as it turned out, his smidgeon was all I needed.

"He was a tall man," he said. "With a hat."

"A hat? What kind of hat?"

"Like that," he said, pointing to a teenager in a baseball cap.

A baseball cap, huh?

Okay, class. Who's the one person who'd been wearing his Mattress King baseball cap since the day I first laid eyes on him?

A gold star, with extra glitter, to all of you who said Owen Kendall.

Chapter 24

Owen was in the Mattress King parking lot when I drove up, giving last-minute instructions to two delivery men. He barked out orders with drill sergeant precision, alert and confident, a far cry from the sniveling wreck he'd been the last time I'd seen him.

I waited till the delivery guys took off, then got out of my Corolla.

"Hey, Owen," I called out.

"Oh, hi, Jaine."

A veil of sorrow slid over his features as he slipped back into the role of grieving lover.

"Can we talk?" I asked.

"Sure thing. Come with me. I just need to get something from the stockroom."

I followed him into the bunker-like building, where he grabbed a carton from one of the shelves.

"Our new mattress samples finally came in."

Flushing at the memory of my purloined mattress sample, I got down to the business at hand.

"I suppose you heard what happened to Lupe."

"What a tragedy," he tsked. "The streets just aren't safe anymore."

"I don't think it was a random act of violence, Owen."

"You don't?"

"No. I think the person who attacked Lupe was Bunny's killer."

"Oh?"

He grabbed a box cutter from a shelf and began opening the carton.

"I'm guessing Lupe saw something the night of the murder, something she shouldn't have seen. And so the killer had to get rid of her."

"Interesting theory," he said, as casual as can be. But he was gripping that box cutter so hard, the veins in his hand were popping like ropes.

"It just so happens I ran into Lupe at Century City yesterday, right before she was attacked. She told me she was there to meet a woman for a job interview. But I don't think there was any job. I think the killer lured her there and then drove her to a deserted alley and bashed in her head."

"Have any idea who it was?" he asked, still Mr. Casual.

"I sure do. I've got an eyewitness who saw Lupe meeting someone at the food court."

By now he'd pulled the mattress sample out of the carton and was examining it like it was the Rosetta Stone. Anything to avoid eye contact.

"My witness swears it was you."

Okay, so I exaggerated a tad.

"What?!"

At last he turned to face me, a phony smile plastered on his face.

"My witness says he saw the two of you leave the mall together."

"How could it possibly be me? You said Lupe was going to meet a woman. Last I looked, I was still leaving the toilet seat up."

"Oh, come on, Owen. It would have been easy for you to call Lupe and disguise your voice. You figured if she told anyone about the interview, the cops would be looking for a woman."

"Don't be absurd. I was nowhere near Century City yesterday."

"Mind my asking where you were?"

"Home. I took off early. I had a migraine and my head was splitting."

"See anybody? Talk to anybody?"

"Of course not. I took a Zomig and collapsed on my bed."

"Not much of an alibi, is it?"

"That's where I was, Jaine." Another plastic smile. "Why on earth would I want to hurt Lupe?"

"My guess is she saw you out on the patio the night of the murder, adding weed killer to Bunny's dirty martini."

At that, all pretense of bonhomie flew out the stockroom.

"I already told you," he said, steely-eyed, "I couldn't have killed Bunny. I was crazy in love with her. I wanted her to leave Marvin and run away with me."

"I'm sure you did, Owen. But I'm guessing she said no. Bunny was a fickle lady. It was fun at first, sleeping with her son-in-law, but after a while she got tired of you. No way was she about to run off with you and give up Marvin's millions. So you flipped out. You figured if you couldn't have her, no one could."

"That's not true, Jaine. And I wouldn't go around telling that story if I were you."

And then he put down the mattress sample and picked up the box cutter. A sudden jolt of fear ran down my spine. That thing had sliced through thick cardboard like butter. I shuddered to think what it would do to my vital organs.

What an idiotic move this had been. Why the hell had I come here to confront him? I should've gone straight to the cops.

"My best friend knows where I am," I lied, slowly backing

away from him. "So if anything happens to me, the cops will know it's you."

He kept coming toward me, that damn box cutter clutched in his hand.

"My friend knows the whole story!" I began babbling. "How you were crazy in love with Bunny and how you killed her in a fit of passion because she wouldn't leave Marvin and run off with you!"

I took another step backward. It turned out to be my last step. I'd backed myself up against a mattress. I was trapped.

It was then that I heard an explosive "Hah!"

I turned to see Sarah standing in the open entrance of the stockroom, her squat body silhouetted in the sunlight.

Owen's box cutter clattered to the concrete floor.

She sauntered toward us, a bitter smile on her face.

"Owen—crazy about Bunny? That's a laugh! The only person Owen is crazy about is Owen!"

"Sarah, sweetheart," Owen cooed, attempting to put his arm around her.

She swatted him away like a pesky fly.

"And as for killing Bunny in a fit of passion, not bloody likely, not when he was busy boffing his receptionist."

Owen's eyes widened with fake innocence. "Honey, what are you talking about?"

"The next time you take naked pictures of your bimbo," she snapped, "find a more imaginative hiding place than your night table."

With that, she reached into her purse and hurled a bunch of photos at him.

One of them landed at my feet. I picked it up and saw Amy, the mousy receptionist, stretched out seductively on a bare mattress wearing nothing but a smile and a pair of stilettos.

Owen's face drained of color.

"Sarah, sweetheart, I can explain everything."

"Save it for my attorney, Owen," she snapped, heading out the door. "We're getting a divorce."

"Honey, please! Wait!"

He ran out after her, but she was already in her car and zooming out of the lot.

Without missing a beat, he got in his BMW with the *M KING II* license plates, and took off after her.

I stared down at the X-rated photo of Amy. So Owen was her boyfriend, the one who was going to take her on a romantic getaway weekend. And that mattress she was lying on—it was the one in the back of the stockroom. That day when I found Owen sleeping there, it wasn't because he was in mourning over Bunny. It was a post-whoopie nap!

So much for my Owen-killing-Bunny-in-a-crime-of-passion theory.

With a dispirited sigh, I began gathering the rest of the pictures. The last thing Amy needed was for the delivery guys to get a load of these. Although with a slimebucket like Owen, they were probably already whizzing around the Internet.

What an operator. Cheating on his wife with Bunny, and cheating on Bunny with poor little Amy. How wrong I'd been about the guy. All along I'd assumed he was the weak one and Bunny was the cold, calculating one.

But wait a minute. What if it was just the reverse? What if Bunny was the one who'd fallen head over heels in love with Owen? What if she was the one begging Owen to leave Sarah? What if she threatened to tell Sarah about their affair and cut him off from the Cooper zillions?

Surely that was a motive for murder!

If only I had proof.

And without wasting another minute, I marched into the Mattress King office to find some.

I found Amy at her desk, tears streaming down her cheeks as she tossed her possessions into a cardboard box. In her prim white blouse and low-heeled pumps, it was hard to believe this was the same gal who'd been stretched out in sex kitten mode in those mattress photos.

Lenny was hovering over her as she packed, patting her shoulder and making sympathetic clucking noises.

"Marvin just called and fired her," he explained to me in a hushed whisper.

"I guess Sarah must have told him about you and Owen," I said, handing her the pictures.

She took one look at them and broke out in a fresh volley of tears.

"I never meant to hurt Sarah," she sobbed. "Owen swore they had an open marriage and that she'd agreed to a divorce."

"What a bastard," Lenny tsked. "Taking advantage of the poor kid like that."

"Owen's more than just your garden variety SOB. I'm pretty sure he's also Bunny's killer."

"Owen?" Amy blinked in disbelief.

"You're kidding!" Lenny gasped, openmouthed.

"Afraid not. I need to search his office. Which one is it?"

Lenny pointed to a door behind Amy's desk.

"Wait!" Amy called out as I started to hurry off.

I thought she was going to try to stop me, to tell me that no matter how big a rat Owen was, he couldn't possibly be capable of murder.

But, no. Blushing ever so modestly, all she said was, "If you find a pair of leopard skin thongs, they're mine."

Owen's office was little more than a glorified cubicle: desk, file cabinet, and no-frills metal visitor's chair.

Hoping against hope I'd find something that would nail him to the mat, I began going through his papers and files, rifling through old work orders, invoices, phone bills, and car service receipts.

Heaven knows what I expected to find. A diary confession? A receipt for weed killer?

Needless to say I found neither of the above. Although I did find Amy's leopard skin thong in his file cabinet, jammed in back of one of the drawers, along with a bottle of scotch and a tube of something called "Stim-U-Lady Love Cream."

I checked the messages on his answering machine, but there were none from Bunny.

If only I could check his e-mail, too.

I sat down at his computer, hoping he might have left his account open, but no such luck. How on earth could I gain access to his e-mail without his password?

Frantically, I started guessing. I tried Owen1. Owen2. Owen3.

This was ridiculous. There had to be thousands of Owens with e-mail accounts. I could be here forever.

"Amy," I called out the open door, "do you know Owen's birthday?"

Lots of people use their birthday as their password; maybe Owen did, too.

"July twenty-first," she sniffled. "That's when we were supposed to get married. He said he wanted the two most special events of his life to happen on the same date."

Oh, barf. What a bucket of bilge.

"What year?" I asked.

"1982."

I tried Owen721, Owen82, and Owen72182. Nada. So I started the whole process over with his last name.

After typing in enough combinations to induce carpal tunnel syndrome, I had to admit defeat.

Elbows propped on Owen's desk, my head in my hands, I glanced down idly at one of the receipts in his in-box. From Santa Monica BMW, for a recent tune-up.

And that's when I saw it. The name on his vanity plates: M KING II.

What the heck? It was worth a shot. I typed it in, and bingo! His e-mails popped up on the screen.

Eagerly, I opened his "old mail" file. In addition to the messages guaranteeing to keep Owen active in the sack for hours on end, there were a bunch of letters from "Bunny-Love."

I scanned the subject lines:

"Missing you." "Have you told her yet?" "Why haven't I heard from you?"

My eyes riveted on the one that said, *FINAL WARNING!!!*

With trembling hands, I clicked it open. It was short and not-so-sweet:

Either you tell Sarah about us, or I will.

So I was right. He'd killed her to shut her up.

At last. I had that shred of evidence I'd been praying for.

My first instinct was to go to the cops. But I couldn't. Not unless I wanted to be accused of computer hacking.

So I called Marvin and told him the whole story. Thank heavens he was able to access the e-mails from Bunny's computer. He put in a call to the cops, and the next day they carted Owen downtown for questioning.

Of course, he denied everything and lined up a hotshot attorney to defend him.

But things weren't looking good. One of the Barbies came forward and told the cops she remembered hearing Bunny and Owen arguing the night of the murder. I told them about running into Lupe at Century City the day of her attack, and how she'd been heading off to meet a prospective employer. Now the cops were bringing in the busboy from the food court to see if he could identify Owen from a lineup. Criminal charges were definitely hovering over Owen's head. Especially if Lupe regained consciousness.

Yes, everything was looking quite rosy. Here on this side of the country, anyway.

YOU'VE GOT MAIL!

EXPLODING CHICKEN ROCKS LOCAL COOKATHON

The annual Tampa Vistas Cookathon was brought to an abrupt halt today when a Turbomaster 3000 convection oven shattered and sent glass flying everywhere.
Early reports are sketchy, but according to the police, the cause of the mishap was an exploding chicken.
No injuries were reported.

To: Jausten
From: Shoptillyoudrop
Subject: Gruesome Details

Dearest Jaine—

Thanks to your father, I can never show my face in public again. I may as well hang my picture in the Most Wanted section at the post office and be done with it.

As you can see from the item in the *Tampa Tribune*, Daddy's chicken exploded and ruined the whole cookathon. The *Tribune* didn't go into all the gruesome details (thank heavens!), but I don't see why I should be the only one who has to be haunted by them for the rest of my life. So I'm sharing them with you, sweetheart.

Here's what happened: Right after breakfast (*Cheerios à la Hank*), Daddy snuck over to Lydia Pinkus's town house to search for his Secret Spice (which I *still* say is nothing more than paprika). He hid in the bushes until he saw Lydia and her Aunt Ida leave for the cookathon. Then he shimmied up her palm tree and let himself in through the sliding glass balcony door, which Lydia hadn't bothered to lock. I shudder to think what would have happened if she had locked it. I wouldn't put it past that crazy father of yours to have busted the glass.

Once he was inside he searched Lydia's town house high and low for the Secret Spice, which of course he couldn't find, because, as anyone with a grain of sense could have figured out, it wasn't there! In fact, right after he left for Lydia's, I found the dratted bottle where Daddy had dropped it behind the oven.

Anyhow, what with all the time he wasted at Lydia's, he was almost two hours late for the cookathon. With only twenty minutes left before the final bell, he stuffed his chicken without popping the popcorn first. He just tossed handfuls of unpopped corn into the bird and doused it with that Secret Spice. Then he threw it into the Turbomaster and ramped up the temperature to inferno proportions.

Needless to say, in the intense heat of the Turbomaster, the popcorn started popping like crazy, and the poor bird just couldn't contain it. The Turbomaster began rattling and making a godawful racket. I told Daddy to shut the darn thing off, but would he listen? Of course not! When does that man ever listen to reason?

The next thing you know the Turbomaster was exploding like a rocket. Glass shattered everywhere. All I can say is it's a good thing nobody was injured, except for Daddy, who got a tiny cut on his arm.

It serves him right.

Your furious,

Mom

PS. I may never speak to him again!

To: Jausten
From: DaddyO
Subject: In the Doghouse

I suppose Mom wrote you about my little mishap at the cookathon. I'm afraid she's in a bit of a tiff.

And apparently she found my Secret Spice behind the oven. She claims I dropped it there, but we both know better, don't we? That's obviously where Old Pruneface hid it to sabotage my chances at the cookathon. I tell you, lambchop, the woman is the devil in support hose.

But I'm keeping mum about my sabotage theory. I'm in the doghouse with your mom, and I can't risk getting her even angrier than she already is.

I'm hoping to get back in her good graces with a dozen roses, and dinner reservations at Le Chateaubriand, Tampa Vistas' finest steak house.

Keep your fingers crossed, lambchop, that she forgives me.

XOXO,

Daddy

To: Jausten
From: Shoptillyoudrop
Subject: Daddy's Peace Offering

If Daddy thinks he can win me over with a couple of roses and a steak dinner, all I can say is . . . he may be right. After all those popalicious chickens, I could go for a nice juicy steak.

Besides, I can tell he feels terrible about what happened. And he's agreed to never again go anywhere near the kitchen except for a glass of water.

Well, must run and get ready for our dinner date. I'm going to wear a fabulous new Georgie O. Armany beaded top I got from the shopping channel, only $49.95, plus shipping and handling!

Love and kisses,

Mom

PS. Now that I think about it, maybe it's a good thing Daddy's chicken exploded. I mean, thanks to this whole cookathon disaster, I'll never have to look at that dratted Turbomaster again!

To: Jausten
From: DaddyO
Subject: Good News, Lambchop!

Good news, lambchop! I'm back in your mom's good graces! She's upstairs right now getting all gussied up for our dinner at Le Chateaubriand.

She's a very wise woman, your mom. She said from the get-go the Turbomaster 3000 was nothing but a piece of junk. And I have to confess, she was right. It *was* very shoddily built.

So I've ordered the new improved Turbomaster 5000! I paid extra for overnight delivery. It's coming tomorrow!

Love 'n' hugs,

Daddy

PS. I'm not allowed in the kitchen anymore, so I'll set it up in the garage. Mom'll never even know it's there.

Chapter 25

Now that he was no longer the cops' number one suspect, Lance was in seventh heaven. Brimming over with gratitude and affection for yours truly, he insisted on taking me out to dinner to celebrate his freedom.

"It's not going to be a health food restaurant, is it?" I asked as we tooled out to Santa Monica in his Mini Cooper.

"No, it's not a health food place. There'll be plenty of high-cholesterol goodies to clog your arteries."

It was one of those rare nights in Los Angeles—balmy and fog free. The perfect night for a drive to the beach. I, however, was not paying much attention to the passing scenery. All I could think about was Daddy and his exploding chicken! Honestly, one of these days I just know he's going to get his own chapter in *Ripley's Believe It or Not*.

The restaurant turned out to be a swellegant converted cottage with beamed ceilings and rustic hardwood floors. A stunning would-be actress ushered us to a table out on a patio dotted with twinkly fairy lights and trendy people picking at their food. The only thing more breathtaking than the setting, I was about to discover, were the prices.

I ordered the Caesar salad and pork chop, which—fasten your seat belts—was thirty-two dollars. For one measly pork chop! And that was one of the cheaper items on the menu. I intended to eat every last sliver of the thing. And possibly have the bone bronzed.

"Fabulous news, Jaine," Lance said, as I slathered a marvelously crusty dinner roll with artisan herb butter. "Neiman's called and I'm getting my job back."

"That's wonderful!" I replied, feeling a lot less guilty about ordering that pork chop.

"Not only that, the cops said I was free to leave town. So Barbados, here I come!"

He was so happy, he barely touched the tiny sliver of arugula on his plate masquerading as an appetizer.

I, on the other hand, dug into my Caesar salad with gusto.

"I can't get over how terrific everything worked out," he gushed.

"Mmmf," I said, reaching for a sesame-studded cracker from the breadbasket.

"Just last week, I was an unemployed murder suspect, and now I'm dating the man of my dreams. Isn't life fabulous?"

"Yeah. And these crackers aren't bad, either. You should give them a try."

"And I owe it all to you! Not meeting Peter, of course. I suppose I should thank the cops for that. But if it weren't for you, I'd still be their number one suspect. How can I ever thank you, Jaine?"

"You can never go wrong with chocolate."

"No, seriously."

"I was being serious."

"How *else* can I ever thank you?"

"By never cooking me a diet dinner ever again."

"Oh, all right," he conceded with a sigh. "No more diets. But I've got to come up with a better gift than that."

"Surprise me. And in the meanwhile, if you're not going to eat your croutons, fork 'em over."

* * *

I smell pork!

I'd just walked in the door, and Prozac was sniffing at me with all the intensity of a bloodhound on a convict hunt.

Where the heck are my leftovers?

"I'm sorry, Pro, but there aren't any leftovers."

Her big green eyes widened with indignation.

Surely you jest!

"There was one measly pork chop. It was barely bigger than an Oreo."

After several more sniffs failed to uncover any pork, she looked up at me again.

Let me get this straight. You're saying there are no leftovers?

"I swear, the only thing left over from that meal was my napkin."

And just like that, she switched into Drama Queen mode, channeling Sarah Bernhardt in one of her hammier roles, tail thumping, green eyes luminous with grief.

If you really loved me, you would've saved me something!

Then she leaped up on the sofa and curled into a furry ball of hostility.

"C'mon, Pro," I said sitting down next to her. "How about a nice long back scratch, with extra scratching behind the ears?"

She swatted me away with her paw.

Not tonight. I've got a headache.

Something told me I'd be sleeping solo that night.

I left her to sulk and was heading for the bedroom to get undressed when the phone rang. My caller ID said "Kendall," and for a frightening instant I thought it was Owen. So I let the machine get it.

I breathed a sigh of relief when I heard Sarah's voice, and picked up the phone.

"Hey, Sarah. How's it going?"

"If you mean, how does it feel to be rid of a lying, cheating slimebag of a husband, the answer is: quite liberating. In fact, as we speak I am eating cookies in bed, dropping all the crumbs I darn well please."

A girl after my own heart.

"Anyhow, I hope I'm not calling too late, but Dad wanted me to invite you and Lance to Bunny's memorial service."

"Marvin wants *me* there? I mean, Bunny wasn't exactly fond of me."

"But Dad is. He's very grateful for all you've done. And so am I. Do you think you can make it? It's the day after tomorrow."

"Of course. Where's it going to be?"

"The rooftop at Neiman Marcus."

"You're having a memorial service at a department store?"

"Bunny always said when she died she wanted her ashes scattered over Neiman Marcus. It was in her will. And Dad is honoring her request."

Which was pretty darn nice of him, I thought, after the way Bunny had treated him and his family.

"Actually, it should be a lot of fun," Sarah said. "There's going to be a full bar, strolling mariachis, and fireworks at the end."

"Was that in Bunny's will, too?"

"No. That was my idea. And considering the occasion, it was worth every penny."

Chapter 26

No expense had been spared for Bunny's farewell bash. Neiman's rooftop had been transformed into a tropical paradise, with potted palm trees, lush gardenias, and flaming tiki torches lighting up the starry night. And, as promised, a trio of mariachis serenaded the guests.

But the most festive sight of all, as far as I was concerned, were a bunch of waiters trotting around with heaping platters of hors d'oeuvres.

Sarah greeted us when Lance and I showed up, a lei around her neck and a wide grin on her face.

Never had I seen her look so happy.

"Hey, you guys!" she beamed. "Great to see you."

Lance had the good grace to blush. As well he should have, after his abominable behavior that day in Sarah's lab.

"Please accept my apologies, Sarah," he said. "I guess I was a tad out of line accusing you of Bunny's murder."

"No biggie." She shrugged magnanimously. "All's well that ends well, that's what I always say."

And for Sarah, Bunny's death had clearly been the happiest of all possible endings.

"Quite a crowd," I said, surveying the scene.

Indeed, the joint was jumping. Marvin and Ellen, in matching Hawaiian shirts, were arm in arm, chatting with Lenny, who glowed with pleasure, happy to have his old buddy back. Statuesque Fiona, dressed to the nines in a startling Marlene Dietrich tuxedo outfit, was working the room, passing out her business cards to the Barbies. Everywhere I looked, happy partygoers were chatting and laughing as they slugged down their cocktails and hors d'oeuvres.

Some of the Barbies were actually eating.

"Well, grab yourself a drink at the bar and enjoy!"

As Sarah flitted off to chat with other guests, Lance and I made our way to the bar. Unlike the one at Bunny's Dirty Martini party, it was stocked to the gills with all kinds of alcohol.

Lance ordered a mai tai, while I opted for a frosty margarita.

"To Bunny," Lance said, raising his glass in a toast.

"For her sake, I hope they sell Manolo Blahniks in hell."

"Oh, Jaine," Lance gushed, gazing up at the stars. "Isn't life marvelous? To be young and tan and free to go to Barbados whenever you want!"

Still on cloud nine over having received his Get Out of Jail card, he'd been waxing euphoric like this for days.

"We're going to have so much fun at this party," he said, hooking his arm in mine. "Just you and me, the two musketeers, best buddies through thick and thin—

"Oh, Marci! Yoo hoo!"

He waved to a Botoxed blonde.

"One of my best customers," he explained. "I'll just go say a quick hi, and be back in a flash."

Yeah, right. That was the last I spoke to my best bud and fellow musketeer all night.

Without wasting another precious second, I tackled a passing waiter and snagged myself a rumaki. (Okay, two rumakis.) I'd just finished scarfing them down and was about to reach for a mini chicken kabob when Fiona came gliding up to me, radiant in her tuxedo outfit. Only a statuesque woman like Fiona could carry off that look so well.

"Jaine, sweetheart!" she cried, giving me an air kiss. "So lovely to see you."

"You, too. You're looking wonderful."

"Quite a difference from the last time we met," she winked.

I'll say. Gone were her bloodshot eyes, her sleep-matted hair. Today she was bright-eyed and b-tailed, her make-up impeccable, her spiky hair moussed to perfection.

"I'm simply mortified over the way I behaved when you showed up at my apartment that day. As you may have noticed, I was a bit under the influence."

A bit? Her breath had been strong enough to start a bonfire.

"When Bunny died, I guess I went a little nuts. So I hit the bottle. But I finally came to my senses. After all, life goes on and all that. I'm working the perfume counter at Saks now.

"It's not so bad." She shrugged. "I get an employee discount and all the shopping bags I can carry. And with any luck, I can build up my business again. Which reminds me, sweetie," she said, handing me a bunch of her business cards, "if you know anyone who needs a stylist, spread the word!"

Then, plastering an upbeat smile on her face, she headed off to work the room.

Which left me free to track down that waiter with the mini chicken kabobs. I spotted him in the crowd and hurried to his side, and as I did I bumped into Lenny.

"Hey, Jaine!" He grinned.

Phooey! He'd just nabbed the last kabob.

I guess he could see the look of disappointment in my eyes. Or maybe I was drooling. It's hard to remember. Whatever the reason, he took pity on me.

"You take it," he said, handing me the kabob.

"Oh, no, I couldn't," I said, whipping it from his hand before he could change his mind.

"What a turnout, huh?" he said, looking around.

"Mmmph," I nodded, my mouth full.

"Give the people what they want, and they'll come out in droves."

Oh, man. Wasn't anybody going to even pretend to be in mourning mode?

"I heard you were the one who fingered Owen. Nice job. Funny, though. I would've never figured him for the killer. Guess that's why I'm a mattress salesman and not a cop. And speaking of mattresses, remember—the next time you're in the market for a Comfort Cloud, you know who to call!"

Leaving me with a jaunty wave, he started for the bar.

With Lenny gone, I'd run out of people to talk to. Feeling a tad awkward standing there alone, I looked around for Lance. But he was still yakking with Ms. Botox.

I spent the next half hour doing a very poor imitation of someone having fun. I wandered around sniffing the gardenias and grabbing the occasional hors d'oeuvre or three, the waitstaff's leading contender for Guest Most Likely to Get Heartburn. I drifted over to the isolated table where Bunny's urn was on display, thinking how she would have hated not being the center of attention. Then, curious, I peeked behind the row of potted palms lined up in the center of the roof and saw they were screening off the party area from the store's unsightly air-conditioning units. I considered hiding out there for a while, but I didn't want to give up the hors d'oeuvres.

At one point, the mariachis stopped to serenade me, and I had to stand there, smiling stiffly through the endless lyrics of "Besame Mucho."

Finally, when I had circumnavigated the party at least five times, Marvin and Ellen rescued me from my wallflower status.

"Jaine!" they cried, still firmly welded together arm in arm, radiating happy vibes.

"We're so glad you could make it!" Ellen's apple cheeks

glowed in the light from the tiki torches. "I can't tell you how much we appreciate all you did to bring Owen to justice."

"We're both very grateful," Marvin chimed in.

"Grateful enough to give me a job?"

Of course I didn't say that, but you can bet your bottom tiki torch I was thinking it. I'd dropped off my mattress slogans at the showroom days ago but had not heard a peep from Marvin.

My employment was the last thing on the lovebirds' minds, however, as they launched into a detailed description of a cruise they were about to take to the Fiji Islands.

When they finally wound down and abandoned me to circulate, I gave up all pretense of being a party person. I did the unthinkable and sat down alone at a table for six near the potted palms. Someone had left what looked like a martini and a chicken kabob behind.

I picked up the chicken and examined it for bite marks. There didn't seem to be any so I started chomping it down.

Oh, don't go all Emily Post on me. I had to do something to while away the time.

Once more I surveyed the room, taking in the happy partygoers, still laughing and chatting and slugging down the booze.

Yes, everyone was in excellent spirits. Except me. And it wasn't just because I was sitting alone at a table for six.

Actually, I was still worried about the murder. I know I should have been happy the cops had set their sights on Owen. But something was bothering me, a nagging question lingering in the back of my mind like a pesky piece of corn stuck between my teeth. If Owen had really killed Bunny, why would he have left such an incriminating e-mail on his computer? Wouldn't he have at least deleted it, or sent it to his recycle bin? Why leave it there for a snoop such as myself to discover with just a click of the mouse? It didn't make sense.

Was it possible Owen *wasn't* the killer? It may have been my imagination, but I could have sworn I'd seen that boxy black car following me the past few days. Surely it couldn't have been Owen. He drove a BMW. Besides, if anything happened to me, he'd be the first person the cops would suspect.

"Gather round, everybody!" Marvin called out from a microphone near Bunny's urn. "It's time for the scattering of the ashes."

Eager for this dramatic climax of the evening to begin, the guests quickly scooted over to where Marvin was standing.

Absentmindedly I reached for my glass and took a final slug of my margarita before joining them.

Wait a minute! What was an olive doing in my mouth? This wasn't my margarita. I looked down and realized I was holding my predecessor's abandoned martini. I'd picked up the wrong drink.

And just like that, it came to me—a whole new way of looking at the case.

What if Bunny drank the wrong drink the night of the murder? There were two glasses out on the patio that night. Lance's and Bunny's. What if someone poisoned Lance's drink, and Bunny drank it by mistake?

Over at the other end of the roof, Marvin was inventing nice things to say about Bunny as he tossed her ashes to the wind. But his words were a distant buzz as I thought back to the night of the murder.

A scenario began to take shape in my mind. Lupe was a clumsy creature, always dropping things when she was nervous. What if, in her haste to bring Bunny her dirty martini, she'd spilled it? And then, terrified of Bunny's angry reaction, she'd hastily poured Lance's drink into the Marilyn Monroe glass.

Omigosh. That would mean that all along, *Lance* was the intended victim—not Bunny!

But who on earth would want Lance dead?

The answer came to me in a flash: *Fiona!*

Bunny was Fiona's last remaining client, the one person in the world keeping her afloat financially. But then Bunny met Lance and *he* became her fashion advisor. Hadn't Bunny raved about what a fashion genius he was? Hadn't they gone on all those shopping excursions together?

I remembered how dismissive Bunny had been that first day at the pool when Fiona stopped off with some clothes for her to try on. She'd waved them aside and gone right back to chatting with Lance. Lance was rapidly becoming her "pet du jour," cutting off Fiona's financial lifeline. So Fiona had to get rid of him. She dosed his dirty martini with weed killer, only to have Bunny drink it by mistake!

I thought back to what Fiona had said the night of the murder, as Bunny lay writhing on the carpet:

This can't be happening. Not to Bunny!

That's because it was *supposed* to have been happening to *Lance*.

"Oh, wow!" I gasped, as a few of Bunny's ashes floated my way. "It was Fiona all along!"

"So you figured it out, huh?"

I whirled around as Fiona stepped out from behind the potted palms. In her hand she held the same stun gun she'd been toting that day in her apartment.

I got up to make a break for it, but I wasn't fast enough. I cringed as a painful jolt of electricity shot up my arm.

Dammit. I'd been zapped.

Suddenly I felt my muscles turn to Jell-O and my knees buckle beneath me.

Before I hit the ground, Fiona grabbed me by my underarms and began dragging me past the screen of palm trees to the far side of the roof.

I screamed for help, but no one could hear me over those damn mariachis. Not to mention the fireworks, which had just begun to explode in the sky.

"Why the hell can't anything ever go my way?" Fiona muttered as she lugged me past the massive air-conditioning unit. "First that idiot Lupe gives Bunny the wrong drink. Then she doesn't die when I bash her head in with a tire iron. And now you have to go butting in."

It wasn't easy dragging my inert body, and she struggled with the load. For once I was glad to be toting around a few extra pounds.

"I've had nothing but bad luck ever since your buddy Lance waltzed into Bunny's life," she continued ranting. "The minute he showed up, I was toast. Everything he liked was gold; everything I chose was crap. That two-bit shoe salesman was stealing my only source of income."

"So you decided to get rid of him with a dose of weed killer."

"It all would have worked out so beautifully, but then Lupe had to go and give Bunny Lance's drink. Can you believe my rotten luck?"

Somehow I was unable to dredge up any sympathy for her plight.

"I figured out what had happened right away," she boasted, proud of her mental prowess. "I convinced Lupe that if she told the cops what really happened, they'd deport her. That scared the stuffing out of her. So she kept her mouth shut. But I couldn't let her live. She knew too much. Just like you know too much."

Ouch. I didn't like the sound of that.

By now some sensation was returning to my limbs. Not enough to fight her off, but at least I could feel something. I had to keep her talking till I got my strength back.

"So you lured Lupe to the mall," I prompted. "And—just in case anyone saw the two of you together—you came to meet her disguised as a man."

With Fiona's short, spiky hair and lanky, androgynous

build, I could easily see why the busboy mistook her for a guy.

"Pretty clever, if I do say so myself," she preened. "I called her, pretending to be an A-list bimbo offering her a job. Needless to say, her future employer never showed up for their appointment. But I did, and after faking surprise at running into her, I very kindly offered her a ride home. I explained my jeans and baseball cap by telling her I'd just come from a softball game. The sap bought it. Then, once she got in my car, I shot her with my stun gun and drove her to an alley in Skid Row."

"Where you bashed her head in with a tire iron," I said, stealing her punch line.

"Bingo, Sherlock. Now it's your turn."

By now we'd reached the edge of the roof.

"In case you didn't realize it, you're about to fall to a very tragic death."

"No one's going to believe I killed myself, Fiona."

"I'll take my chances. Now buckle up." She smiled grimly. "It's gonna be one heck of a crash landing."

That's what she thought. The strength had returned to my limbs and I wasn't about to check out without a fight. As she leaned down to get a grip on me, I punched her in the groin with every ounce of strength I possessed.

Which, alas, turned out to be not much.

I guess I'd overestimated my recovery. I barely grazed her trousers.

I continued to flail at her, but I was no match for the sinewy Fiona. The woman had clearly been working out between trips to the liquor store. She knocked me to the ground with a quick sock to the jaw.

A wave of terror swept over me as she whipped out her stun gun and zapped me again.

Before I knew it she was hoisting my limp body over the parapet.

I looked down—way down—at the deserted alley below. Not a soul in sight.

Was it all going to end like this? Splattered to death behind Neiman Marcus, the ultimate fashion disaster?

"Okay, sweetie. Prepare for takeoff."

Just when I was convinced I was headed for that great Ice Cream Parlor in the Sky, I heard three of the most welcome words in the English language:

"Jaine, my beloved!"

Omigosh! It was Vladimir.

"Have no fear!" my Uzbek Romeo cried, his squinchy black eyes aglow with heroic fervor. "Vladimir will save you!"

Reluctantly, Fiona loosened her grip on me, and I slid back down onto the roof as Vladimir came rushing at us.

But skinny little Vladimir was no match for Fiona, who zapped him with her stun gun before he could say Holy Plov.

"Oh, for crying out loud," Fiona clucked at us in irritation as we lay limply on the roof. "Now I'm going to have to kill the two of you."

Correction. Make that three of us. Because just then someone else came charging on the scene. A thundering mass of fury named Sofi.

That's right. It was Cousin Sofi, in the flesh, all three hundred pounds of her.

"You leave my Vladdie alone!" she cried, as she stomped across the roof.

Unfortunately, the sight of a human locomotive barreling toward her didn't seem to faze Fiona a bit. Before Sofi could even land her first blow, Fiona whapped her with her stun gun.

I fully expected Sofi to crumple to the ground alongside Vladimir and me.

But then a miracle happened.

Sofi barely flinched. Maybe Fiona's stun gun had run out

of juice. Or maybe the electricity couldn't make it past all that padding.

All I know is Sofi hauled off and decked Fiona with a single blow. Now it was Fiona's turn to lie limp on the black tar.

Vladimir looked up at Sofi, stunned.

"Sofi! What are you doing here?"

"I've been following you for days, while you've been following this skinny minnie."

"You were the one tailing me?" I gasped.

"Yes." Vladimir nodded proudly. "I borrow Boris's brand new used car to follow my beloved Jaine."

"What you wasting your time for on her?" Sofi sniffed. "She nothing but a bag of bones. Don't you see, Vladdie?"

"See what?" He blinked, puzzled.

"I love you!"

With that, she took him in her ham-hock arms and laid a giant liplock on him.

"I've always loved you," she said when they finally came up for air. "With all my heart and soul!"

"It's true, Vladimir," I chimed in. "And it's time you gave up this crazy notion of marrying me. Sofi is so much better for you than I am."

"She sure is!" he agreed, just a little too enthusiastically for my ego. "What a terrific kisser!"

He gazed at her with the same lovesick expression that had been beamed in my direction not two minutes ago.

"Lay another one on me, hot stuff!" he crooned.

I sat there, trying to ignore the most nauseating slurpy sounds as the two of them played kissy-face. Good heavens. This was almost as bad as the stun gun.

By now, the other party guests had become aware of the commotion at our end of the roof and had gathered around us in an astonished huddle.

"What on earth happened?" Marvin asked, eyes popping, as he took in the scene.

Sofi and Vladimir were kind enough to stop slurping each other as I offered a brief summary of recent events.

The cops were quickly summoned and, after hearing my tale, wasted no time carting Fiona off to the criminal wing of USC General Hospital.

Watching her still-comatose body being wheeled away, the Barbies buzzed with excitement.

What a night it had been. Mariachis. Fireworks. Attempted triple murder. And best of all—a full bar!

Yes, in years to come everyone would agree:

It was Bunny's best party ever.

Epilogue

Good news, fashion fans! You'll be happy to know that Fiona Williams has been voted best-dressed inmate at her maximum security prison in sunny Chowchilla, California, where she is now doing twenty-five to life.

Lupe, thank heavens, survived her bout with Fiona's tire iron, and—with the help of generous financing from Marvin—has started her own catering biz. Her first job? Marvin and Ellen's wedding. Yep, the ex–Mr. and Mrs. Cooper retied the knot and are now happily ensconced in a Comfort Cloud love nest out in Encino, where Lenny is a regular and most welcome guest.

And Marvin and Ellen aren't the only ones who've made a love connection. Ever since Bunny's death, cupid has been working overtime:

Sarah, rebounding quite nicely from her divorce from Owen, is engaged to Zubin, her lab assistant at UCLA.

Kandi is dating a guy she met at a "Why I Keep Dating the Wrong Partner" seminar.

And mousy little Amy, unable to cancel the rooms she'd booked for her romantic getaway with Owen, checked into the Romeo & Juliet Suite by herself, where she told her tale of woe to a most sympathetic innkeeper. One thing led to another, and by the end of the weekend, they were making sweet love amid the heart-shaped throw pillows. Last I heard, she was working there full-time as his receptionist, and his wife.

On the sadder side of the romantic coin, Lance and Peter went off on their tropical getaway to Barbados, where Peter promptly proceeded to fall in love with their scuba instructor.

Cupid's arrow has also failed to make an appearance at my apartment, which is fine with me. I'm thrilled to be footloose and Vladimir-free.

Speaking of Vladimir, I'm happy to report that he and Sofi exchanged wedding vows and sloppy kisses back in Uzbekistan. They sent me pictures from the wedding. I must say, it's the first time I've ever seen the Maid of Honor eating a tin can.

As for Owen, rumor has it he's working the night shift at a Dairy Queen out in Pacoima.

And you'll never guess what I got in the mail not long ago. A letter from Fortuna. Just as I'd suspected, she was the one who pushed me that day at the movies. She followed me from her apartment, terrified I'd bad-mouth her to the cops. She begged my forgiveness and assured me she had her anger under control, thanks to daily affirmations and enough Paxil to choke a buffalo.

Should you need to reach her, you can find her at 1-800-Call-A-Psychic.

Saving the best news for last, I'm thrilled to tell you that Marvin gave me the Mattress King account! Yes, I am now the official Mattress King copywriter. The winning slogan, FYI, was: *If you can find a cheaper mattress anywhere, I'll eat my crown.*

Okay, so it's not Shakespeare, but it's a paycheck. Yes, thanks to dear sweet Marvin, my checkbook balance is no longer in the Emergency Resuscitate zone. First thing I did with my mattress loot was paint my walls a heavenly shade of inoffensive off-white. Then I treated myself to a new cashmere sweater. I never did join that Fudge of the Month Club.

It was way too decadent, even for moi. Instead, I took the sensible route, and am now a proud member of the Cookie of the Month Club. Next month is Double Dutch Chocolate Chip. I can't wait.

Well, that's it for now. Gotta run. Her royal highness wants her back scratched.

Catch you next time.

PS. I thought you might be interested in the following item from the *Wall Street Journal:*

TURBOMASTER SUED BY CONSUMER PROTECTION AGENCY

The Consumer Protection agency has filed a $3.5 million lawsuit against Turbomaster, Ltd., manufacturers of the Turbomaster convection oven and Turbomaster Secret Spice. According to the consumer watchdog group, Turbomaster ovens are prone to explosions, and their Secret Spice, which Turbomaster claims to be made from fifteen exotic spices, is in reality nothing more than paprika.